KIMBERLY SULLIVAN

Drink Wine and Be Beautiful

SHORT STORIES

First paperback edition May 2023

Book design by Maxtudio

ISBN 979-8-9868844-0-0 (paperback)
ISBN 979-8-9868844-1-7 Digital Edition (ePub)

www.kimberlysullivanauthor.com

*To my Mom, who taught me my love of reading.
Decades later, thanks for having become such an enthusiastic
reader of my stories.*

ALSO BY KIMBERLY SULLIVAN

Three Coins
Dark Blue Waves
In The Shadow of The Apennines

They travelled for thirteen hours down-hill, whilst the streams broadened and the mountains shrank, and the vegetation changed, and the people ceased being ugly and drinking beer, and began instead to drink wine and be beautiful.

E.M. Forster, Where Angels Fear to Tread

Contents

AMICA DEL CUORE
Rome

WHEN PEOPLE ASK how we met, we look at one another with a sly smile. Then Giulia and I would roll our eyes and laugh before one of us would explain. "We became best friends when we both fell for the same guy."

That was twenty years ago, when I first arrived in Rome, fresh off the boat in more ways than one.

Growing up, my family's idea of an exotic vacation was an annual pilgrimage to their Mecca, the Poconos. An impossibly glamorous holiday in their youth, my parents clung to the mistaken notion that it still was. Each summer they dragged my brother and me to the same faded lodge to sit with geriatric crowds playing bingo.

Wednesdays were Italian Nights, complete with an open-mike stage show of Frank Sinatra and Tony Bennett wannabes. My brother and I spent those nights kicking one another's shins under the long tables with their checkered red-and-white tablecloths. We bent our heads low over our overcooked spaghetti drowned in tomato sauce, topped with rubbery meatballs and Kraft parmesan cheese, trying unsuccessfully to block out the nursing home talent show.

Yet it was during one of those dismal Italian Nights, back when I was eleven, that I decided to live in Rome.

When the stage show mercifully ended, the screen on stage was lowered and I watched in fascination as Gregory Peck and Audrey Hepburn raced around Rome on their Vespa scooter. It wasn't cool to like old black-and-white films that were for my parents' generation, but I couldn't help myself. My eyes grew wide as they placed their hands in the *Bocca della verità,* and I longed to be beside them as they passed the Colosseum and the Roman Forum. Rome, I convinced myself, was where my life would begin. My Roman Holiday.

I never swayed from that certainty. It carried me through my unhappy childhood and my awkward teenage years. Money from waitressing stints and babysitting was all squirreled away for my Roman life.

I was the first in my family to attend college, commuting by bus into Pittsburgh each day from my parents' rural home. Living in the dorms was never an option. My university years were spent on the fringes. Since I was never around for the late-night chats, I didn't form close friendships. The few dates I went on were disastrous, but I repeated to myself, *It's better this way.* The perfect guy would only keep me in Pittsburgh.

After graduation, my mother cried when I turned down an offer with the local electric company and announced to my parents I was headed to Rome. I showed them where it was on the dusty globe in our house.

The days before my departure were strained, but my heart soared as I clutched my virgin passport close and boarded the plane to my new life, to the fantasy I'd constructed in my mind.

Soon enough, the fantasy faded, but I couldn't declare defeat. My parents were simply waiting for me to return. So I stubbornly stuck it out, alone and friendless in a chaotic city.

I had no job, no friends, I didn't speak the language, and my savings were dwindling fast. I dressed like a girl from rural Pennsylvania, making me an alien in my new city. I smiled too much and was too eager to please, ripe for the picking. Roberto knew an easy target when he saw one.

MY ROUNDS AT THE LANGUAGE SCHOOLS finally proved successful. I spent my first workday shuttling from lesson to lesson, ignoring the bemused looks of fashionable Italian business professionals as their eyes slid over my slouchy college clothes, my sneakers, and the poodle-curls of my permed hair. I deflected their scorn with forced enthusiasm, eager to improve their English, desperate to demonstrate how important I was to them.

With some money in my pocket, but my spirits unusually low after my first day of work, I sat at an outdoor table at the *Campo dei fiori* and ordered a glass of *Novello*, the cheapest celebratory drink on the menu. I toasted my success, but my smile, as I surveyed all the young people mingling on the piazza, was forced.

A shadow fell over the table and I looked up to see a tall man in dark sunglasses. He wore Levi's, a blue shirt stretched tight across his broad shoulders, and a pair of shoes that probably cost what I'd earn in four months.

"*Americana, vero?*" he said as he sat down across from me, unhindered by the absence of an invitation.

That's the best he can do? I might as well have had the Stars and Stripes tattooed across my forehead for how obvious my nationality was. But sarcasm never crossed my lips; my rural upbringing and naïve politeness towards strangers kicked in. I smiled and said yes, even apologized for not speaking Italian.

He took off his sunglasses. Tall, dark *and* handsome. I loved his accented, lilting English. I loved how he spoke with his hands, his rapidfire Italian when he ordered us more wine. Finally, a Roman was acknowledging *me*, Jamie Bodanski. Someone in Rome even knew I existed.

AFTER THAT DAY, I was hopelessly in love with Roberto: available at a moment's notice when he wanted me, leaving him his space when he didn't. My transformation from blushing virgin to willing partner was rapid. Roberto filled my thoughts when he was away, but even my obsessed brain admitted that his visits were increasingly rare.

One lonely evening I broke his rule—I called him.

"*Pronto*," said a nasally, slightly whiny voice that some Italian women perfect. So, there was someone else. This was something I'd always suspected, but simply pretended wasn't true. I should have hung up, but instead I asked for Roberto in my horrendous Italian.

"Oh, for goodness' sake," said the voice in English. "You must be that *americana*. We need to talk. Meet me at the *enoteca* on Via Panisperna at seven tomorrow. *Ciao*."

I stared at the phone in disbelief. The Other Woman had summoned me, but I'd never meet her.

My resolve dissolved quickly. The Monti wine bar was filled with rows of bottles. The wooden tables were cozy, the clientele fashionable. I scanned the room. How would I find her?

My gaze fell on a stunning woman sitting alone. She sipped her water, her face slightly turned from me. I took advantage to observe her silky blouse, revealing just enough cleavage to be seductive, not desperate. Her tailored pants draped beautifully over long legs, falling to the perfect point on expensive shoes. I sighed as I looked down at my own haphazard wardrobe choices, ready to leave before she noticed me. Too late. She acknowledged me with a nod, waved me over.

I approached her, attempting to look more confident than I felt. My ears burned as she looked me up and down, Italian-style, dismissing the competition. She stood as I reached the table, showing her enviable figure off to perfection. I wasn't the only one to notice.

"I see the eighties are alive and well in Pittsburgh. Nice to meet you, Jamie. I'm Giulia."

We sat. The waiter sprinted over the moment Giulia acknowledged him. He appeared eager to serve her, as I imagined most men were. I may as well have been invisible.

"White or red?" she asked me.

"Red."

She ordered Barolo without consulting me, and I wondered how I'd afford my half of the bill. We sat in awkward silence for a few moments before she spoke.

"So, Roberto." She dug a cigarette out of her purse, lighting it up and taking a drag, a dead ringer for a 1950s Hollywood diva.

"Yes, Roberto...*my boyfriend*," I said, with far more conviction than I felt.

Her laugh was throaty, sexy. "Poor Jamie. I needed to see you for myself. It's exactly as I suspected. You need to be warned away from someone like Roberto."

My eyes narrowed. "I suppose I do. You want him all to yourself, better to have the competition out of the way."

She observed me closely, sizing me up. "*Sei ridicola*, Jamie." She smoked her cigarette again before continuing in an authoritative voice. "Roberto is *not* boyfriend material. And you're clearly not in it for fun. You're setting yourself up to have your heart trampled by an expert."

My face tensed in anger as I observed this vision of perfection, with her elegant hair and makeup, her stylish clothes, her long slim fingers stroking the stem of her glass. She was laughing at me, the stupid farm girl who dreamed of remaking herself in Rome. A tear slipped from my eye, then another.

She reached across the table to hand me a handkerchief, the old-fashioned fabric type. I dabbed at my eyes.

"Jamie," she said gently, reaching across the table to pat my hand, "you'll be eaten alive by the men here unless I take you under my wing. Forget Roberto. He's a *cretino*. You'll find the right man for you, believe me."

That's how our friendship began. Roberto was a cretin, but he's how I met my *amica del cuore*. My friend of the heart. My best friend.

Giulia did take me under her wing. She taught me about Rome and its bewildering cultural differences. She introduced me to her friends—the impenetrable cliques in Italy who've known one another their entire lives. She brought me to her hairstylist, who rid me of my poodle curls. She took me shopping during the sales, and slowly I built a grown-up wardrobe. She taught me to smile less and be less eager to please. Giulia gave me direction.

I took out a loan and enrolled in LUISS University, earning my MBA and finding work as a consultant.

Giulia needed me, too. I comforted her when her father died, when she cried over frequent heartbreaks.

We vacationed together at her uncle's villa on the Tremiti Islands. It was there I met my husband, Teodoro. Giulia saw him first.

"Look at the blond who keeps glancing over. *Un ragazzo per bene.* He's got 'Jamie' stamped all over him. Go talk to him."

Teodoro and I spoke on that beach, overlooking the crystal blue waters and the imposing, medieval San Nicola abbey-fortress on the island just beyond.

Teodoro and I married two years later. Giulia was our witness and the godmother to our first child, Lorenzo. Her son, Andrea, was just six months younger, but her relationship with his father didn't last.

NOW, YEARS LATER, I look down on this face I know as well as my own. I see how it's been ravaged by the chemo, by periods of hope during remission that are dashed by test results. We're at the end now. I know it and Giulia knows it.

Giulia's in tremendous pain, but she's asked the nurse to hold off on the morphine. She needs to talk to me, and to ten-year-old Andrea. Giulia's mother will raise Andrea, but Giulia's asking me to be present in his life, to tell him about his mother.

"Mamma will make me into a saint. No boy wants to remember a saint. Be sure to tell him everything…the good, the bad, the ugly."

She tries to smile, but I can see it causes her pain.

I kiss her forehead and stroke her cheek. "I'll tell him everything. Thank you for being my *amica del cuore*, Giulia. I'm lucky to have you."

I fight to stop the tears. Andrea needs to see me strong. I kiss my friend and see the peace in her face as our eyes meet for the last time. My friend of the heart.

HOLIDAY BLISS

Provence

LUCIANA STEPPED OUT of the car and felt an immediate sense of relief in her legs. The dull chirping of crickets filled the air as she stood motionless in the bright sunlight. The Mediterranean sunlight caressed her body, and she delighted in the warmth on her shoulders and hair.

She knew the bright rays would set off her hair's golden highlights, while masking the strands of grey she'd noticed weaving their way into her locks these past months. She stared at them obsessively in the bathroom mirror each morning, those unwelcome intruders, a daily reminder of her fading youth.

Just beyond her sandaled feet stood the stone border of an herb garden. She bent down to inhale the pungent sage and rosemary. She sensed the sweetness hanging in the air before she observed its source. There, along the edge of the herb garden, were the familiar purple sprays of lavender. For hadn't they timed their visit to coincide with the arrival of those perfumed blossoms?

No matter where Luciana was, the whiff of lavender could stop her in her tracks and immediately transport her mind back to times past in the Luberon. The heady impressions of a young girl. She breathed in deeply. Now she was truly here.

"*Che viaggione*," said Danilo in his booming voice.

She continued observing the garden as he climbed out of the driver's side and locked the door. "Finally! I thought we'd never arrive."

He crossed in front of the car and stood beside her, sliding his arm around her waist before resting his hand on her hip. Luciana fought the urge to flinch.

"Yes," she said, struggling to keep the testiness from her voice. "Here we are. Perhaps we should check in."

Danilo reached for her hand. Once again, Luciana resisted the desire to break free. She allowed her husband to lead her across the lush lawn and past the *mas provençal* dotting the stretch of grass, their stones bathed in golden sunlight, their sky-blue shutters and doors bright points of color against the imposing stones.

She lingered a moment to observe a vine-shaded patio, the dappled light falling across the patio floor while a butterfly flitted through the chiaroscuro patterns.

But her husband had no time for such distractions. Always more practical than poetic, he was eager to check in and get their bags unpacked.

Their apartment was charming, just as the web images had promised. Luciana delighted in their well-appointed kitchen and the simple but tasteful furniture. The vine-hung patio was the highlight of the property. She already envisioned reading her novels in that idyllic spot, a coffee or a glass of wine, depending on the time of day, ready at her side.

As she hung her clothes in the wardrobe, she felt a hand on her shoulder and warm breath against her neck, causing her to flinch.

"Luciana, *amore*," he whispered in her ear. "Let's take advantage of all this solitude before we go shop for dinner."

Danilo was sliding his hand along her bare shoulder, and she wished she could pull away from him. But what would Doctor Franceschini say? Would her alleged frigidity be the focus of their next marriage counseling session? Better to just give in and not risk censure at the appointment that would inevitably follow their return.

After all, this trip was devised by the unimaginative couples' counselor to bring Danilo and Luciana closer together. Wasn't a romantic holiday the ultimate cliché?

Surely, Luciana could concentrate on some point on the bedroom wall, or run through a list of the hill towns she'd want to visit this week, until it was over. It's not as if she hadn't already done so countless times before.

DANILO AND LUCIANA walked around the Goult town square, examining the produce and local specialties on display and selecting their purchases for dinner that evening.

Danilo was in a good mood following their afternoon intimacy, and Luciana was relieved that those moments were over and would not require an encore for at least the next few days. If she were lucky.

For conjugal intimacy had long ago ceased to be pleasurable for Luciana. She doubted that one week of therapist-mandated closeness would do much to change that, whether it was in a picturesque mas on the rolling hills of the Luberon, or at home on the familiar street of grey, soulless Torino.

When you stripped a marriage down to its essentials, you were always left with only two people. If the combination was flawed, all the suggestive scenery and all the heady scent of lavender in the world could do nothing to narrow the rift that grew daily between the ill-fated couple.

But Luciana knew the therapist would be placated by certain signals, and Luciana was adept in feeding the shrink the information he wished to hear.

She turned her attention back to the stall and selected ripe tomatoes for that evening's salad. She forgot her misery as she spoke in her long-forgotten French to the saleswoman.

So I haven't lost everything over the years, she thought. *Although often it may feel that way.*

LUCIANA AND DANILO SAT OUT on the terrace and toasted the summer solstice with their glasses of chilled rosé, purchased in Goult that very afternoon.

Luciana sipped her wine and gazed across the stunning hilltop skyline of picturesque Gordes. Despite the late hour, daylight still hung in the air. She could identify the spires of the hilltop church and just make out the castle tower on the edge of the town square. *How well I remember that square,* thought Luciana with a sigh.

She turned her attention back to the table to see Danilo observing her, and she forced a smile. "How do you think your mother's holding up with the kids?" She noticed the disappointment in his eyes.

"Luciana, you know we're not supposed to turn all conversation back to the kids. What would Doctor Franceschini say?" He tilted his head in a way that had always annoyed her.

Who gave a damn what Doctor Franceschini said? Who invited him into their lives in the first place? Doctor Franceschini himself, Luciana knew from Torino gossip, was divorced after a brief, failed marriage. Why were she and Danilo shelling out obscene amounts of money for therapy from a man who couldn't even salvage his own marriage? *Our flawed savior,* Luciana thought with a grin.

But Danilo was an engineer. He'd toiled away for years at Fiat, ensuring that the cars met all safety standards. He oversaw crash tests, then returned to the drawing board, mapping out intricate flow charts to find out which flaws needed to be addressed. Everything could be improved with the right engineering. He truly believed that.

And it wasn't just cars. In Danilo's mind, flow charts could be applied to any of life's flaws in order to reengineer them.

His son's cries for attention simply demanded more discipline. Alberto was enrolled in the Scouts and in soccer, a sport he loathed. Danilo bought intricate car models for him, and father and son spent entire afternoons together constructing them in Danilo's home office. When he was younger, Alberto craved attention from his father, even if it meant partaking in activities he detested. But Alberto's teenage disdain was palpable now. He purposefully ruined the models and made it clear to his father that he had no intention of attending Politecnico to become a "geeky engineer."

Danilo simply returned to his flow charts, devising longer hours for soccer practice, enrolling Alberto in a mechanical engineering class sponsored by Fiat for high school students. He ignored the seething hatred his son developed toward his father as he attempted to mold his boy into something he was not.

Danilo never had much use for his solitary, artistic daughter. Paola never delighted in the construction sets Danilo insisted on buying her for each birthday and Christmas. Paola passed her days writing poetry and drawing. She observed the world around her, yet seemed to participate only sporadically.

Her teachers praised her intelligence in Italian and foreign languages and her creativity in writing, but they worried about how shy and withdrawn she was. Danilo could never get over her average grades in math and science, and slowly, he gave up on flow charts for his daughter. Danilo and Paola lived as two strangers under the same roof, exchanging niceties then escaping from one another's company as quickly as they could.

"Luciana, Luciana!"

Luciana turned away from the fading light over Gordes and fixed her gaze on her husband's impatient face.

"If we want to make this work," he said, "I think we have to stick to Doctor Franceschini's ground rules."

She observed him tapping his fingers together impatiently, as she'd seen him do several times while instructing his team of engineers, the sycophantic young hires who relied on her husband to obtain the Holy Grail: *il contratto a tempo indeterminato*—the long-term job contract. A job for life.

"Number one," Danilo continued, "if we're going to make this work, we have to listen to one another. This isn't a time for daydreaming."

"No, Danilo. We're on holiday in Provence," she said dryly. "We certainly wouldn't want any of that." She took a sip of her wine, hoping to hide the rigid set of her mouth.

"Sarcastic comments don't help, Luciana," he continued. "Good communication is the cornerstone to all strong marriages. Remember what Doctor Franceschini always says."

"And he should know," said Luciana, but Danilo chose to ignore her remark.

"And number two: This vacation is about us. You can't spend the entire time bringing up the kids. That will only drive a wedge between us." He smiled at her. "Now, I'll wash up tonight so you can relax out here a while longer."

After he gathered their plates and went into the kitchen, Luciana tucked her legs under her and gazed out across the lawn, to the illuminated pool the guests in the mas apartments shared.

She sipped her wine as she gazed up at the vines hanging over her head. *No, Danilo. You're wrong. The kids aren't driving a wedge between us. They're the only thing keeping us together.*

LUCIANA WALKED BESIDE HER HUSBAND, through the streets lined with Rousillon's distinctive ochre-colored houses. They had eaten well at a restaurant one of Danilo's work colleagues recommended and now they made their way to visit the old ochre quarries.

"Look here, Danilo," she said. "It says there are seventeen different tints of ochre and that they started mining here in prehistoric times." She turned to her husband, but he was eyeing his cellphone.

"*Amore*, I'm sorry, but I see work has been trying to reach me. I know it's against Doctor Franceschini's rules, but I'll have to take this one." His eyes pleaded with her.

"Well," she sighed. "You know how fond I am of following Doctor Franceschini's rules precisely, but I'm willing to overlook it. Just this once, mind you."

"*Grazie, amore.*" He smiled. "You go ahead on the path. I'll catch up with you."

Luciana descended down into the ochre quarry, wondering at the myriad shades of reds and burnished oranges, so bright against the lush green pine needles. The fine ochre sand covered the toes peeking out from her sandals.

She smiled at the strong colors all around her. How long had it been since she'd last been here, back when she was studying art history in Aix? How exciting her life had seemed back then, during her year abroad.

She was a small-town girl from Umbria. The leap from Perugia to Paris seemed too large for the hesitant girl she had been, and so she settled on a program in little Aix-en-

Provence. Perhaps it had been a wiser choice for that timid girl of long ago. She quickly made friends and cautiously climbed out of her shell.

Luciana had loved her art history classes and her fellow students. She loved speaking in French each day and the impassioned student discussions that went late into the night, often while sitting out on one of the many fountains dotting the ancient town.

Luc had simply been part of the local color, part of what she loved about Aix in those days. He'd been all wrong for her, of course. Irresistible, that was clear. She hadn't stood a chance when the handsome rake all the girls were in love with turned his sights on the pretty but timid Italian exchange student. But Luc was moody and passionate, when she required constancy.

Their love story was exciting, for a while. But soon the fights set in. She always had cash around the apartment from payment she received tutoring students in Italian; he stole money from her. She knew this, but always chose to ignore it. Then a treasured ring that used to belong to her grandmother went missing from her apartment, and Luc was the only one to have a key. Of course, he swore he'd never betray her trust. She'd known that wasn't true, but chose to ignore the signs until the day she walked into her apartment to find him in *her* bed with another woman, and she couldn't ignore it anymore.

Luciana was devastated. Jeanne, a university friend, came to her rescue and whisked Luciana away for a holiday week back at her family home in Gordes.

Luciana did her best to put Luc out of her mind on the visit to that beautiful perched hill town. She walked around the winding, medieval streets and sat with a novel on the terrace of her friend's home, with its sweeping views over the Luberon valley.

One evening, following a visit to Roussillon, she and Jeanne had a drink out on Gordes' town square, and they began chatting with a group of young French and Italian mechanical engineering students. The students had just been visiting Renault and Citroën headquarters in France and were in Gordes for a short holiday before continuing on to Fiat in Torino.

A young Italian engineering student from Torino took the seat beside Luciana's, and they spoke the entire evening in their shared, native language. They didn't actually share many interests, but Luciana was still impressed with Danilo. He was handsome. He seemed so steady and serious, the complete opposite of unreliable Luc, who had shattered her young and inexperienced heart.

Luciana and Danilo spent entire days together that week, exploring Gordes and renting a tiny Renault to visit the Dentelles, the Isle-sur-la-Sorgue and Fontaine-de-Vaucluse.

Luciana soon forgot her heartache. She convinced herself that she needed to be with someone steady. Maybe she understood her countrymen better. A French boyfriend would simply trample on her heart yet again. That couldn't happen another time.

On that last evening in Gordes, Danilo asked her to come visit him in Torino during her return to Perugia, for the end of her year abroad was rapidly approaching. She agreed.

"Honey, what are you thinking about?"

Luciana jumped at the voice beside her and the hand on her shoulder. "Oh, my goodness," she said, her heart pounding as she stood before Danilo. "You startled me!"

"You were off in your own little world. What were you thinking about?"

She leaned against the wooden railing and looked out over the ochre formations below. "About being here with Jeanne, all those years ago. You remember Jeanne, don't you?"

"God, that seems like ages ago. You lost touch with her, didn't you?"

"I lost touch with a lot of people," she said softly. Then she forced a smile and turned to her husband. "Ready to walk down?"

LUCIANA PROPELLED HERSELF through the water, stroke-stroke-breath, stroke-stroke-breath. She executed a tight flip turn and thrust through the water, delighting in the power and purpose she felt when navigating across the pool. If only she could feel the same confidence when navigating through her life.

She was just about to tuck her chin and execute another flip turn when she heard her name called above water. She stopped and treaded water, pulling up her goggles.

Danilo stood at the edge of the pool. He wore khaki pants and a polo shirt, his hair wet from the shower that followed yet another afternoon of love-making. "Doctor Franceschini's orders," he'd said with a smile.

The following day was their last full day in paradise, and Luciana already looked forward to a return to the rhythms of real life, where she would not be forced to undergo all this prescribed marital closeness, twenty-four hours a day. Danilo would return to the office, and she would occupy herself with the kids and the household and the myriad of tiny details that filled each and every day. It would be bearable.

"Honey," he was saying, waving to get her attention, "there you are, off in la-la land again." There was no affection in those words, just the tinge of frustration she'd grown accustomed to over the years. "I don't want to feel guilty. It's work again. Emergency on a project. I need a minute—and then we can head off to Lacoste. Okay, hun?"

"Fine, Danilo. I'll just finish off here."

As soon as he stepped into the apartment, she lost the desire for further laps. She lay on her back, arms outstretched, feeling each weightless finger buoyed by the water. The sun warmed her face and she closed her eyes to welcome the balmy rays that caressed her.

She opened her eyes briefly and glanced at her floating form. *Not bad for forty*, she thought. She took pride in her athletic build, her slim waist. Not much reminded Luciana of her youthful self, but she was pleased that her figure had not changed drastically from that of the young girl who arrived in Provence all those years ago.

Danilo was drawn away by work. He always was. If only she could be, too. When she'd come to France all those years ago, she'd been an ambitious young woman. She'd wanted to earn her doctorate, perhaps teach at the university or work in a museum. She'd envisioned a life steeped in culture, far away from her charming but sleepy hometown. France seemed so exotic back then.

She started chipping away at those dreams the moment she set foot on Italian soil. She finished her degree in Perugia, then went up to Torino to join Danilo. They'd been happy at first. He was studying for his doctorate, and she managed to start hers at the university in that grey city, so far removed from the sun-drenched squares of Aix.

But two students couldn't make ends meet for long. Her part-time hours rapidly grew longer to earn more. Soon she spent more time working for wages than completing her dissertation.

When she discovered she was pregnant, she gave up on her doctorate completely. They married and she stayed home while Danilo finished his degree. Back then, she still thought about finishing her doctorate, about starting her career eventually. But Danilo got the job offer at Fiat, and Paola followed Alberto. Time passed. Slowly, almost imperceptibly, Luciana stopped thinking about picking up where she had left off.

She supported Danilo on his rise through Fiat and made sure everything ran smoothly at home. During those first years, when the kids were small, the days flew by so quickly that Luciana didn't have time to stop and think. The kids needed her, constantly. Danilo needed her, too, and it seemed that every moment of the day was necessary to meet those demands.

But the kids grew, and Danilo eventually had a small staff working under him in his managerial role. Then she faced long days yawning before her. Some mornings she dreaded rising from bed—scared to confront her empty day, wondering how she would fill the years stretching endlessly into her future.

LUCIANA AND DANILO SPENT THE LAST DAY of their blissful holidays on Gordes' main square, having a drink at the same outdoor table where they met nineteen years earlier.

"To us," said Danilo, as he clinked his wine glass against hers.

She tried to remember that evening clearly. Her wounded heart, her rebound state-of-mind that managed to make Danilo appear the perfect man for her.

When Danilo excused himself to go to the men's room, Luciana sat at their table alone, the golden rays of the evening sun warming her as she sipped her wine and looked out over the square. The scent of lavender wafted through the air, and she turned to see a shop beside the café, its proprietor busy setting out sachets of dried lavender to be bought by tourists hoping to bring back a memory from their holidays, to be inserted into their routine days.

When she returned her gaze to the square, she caught her breath. *Could it be?*

A man sat on a bench, reading a paperback. The sun shone in his hair, picking up coppery highlights. His face was set in determination, concentrating on the words before him. Just like that evening nineteen years ago.

Back then, Luciana sat on the same bench, trying to read, but barely able to concentrate. She'd just met Danilo, but something nagged at her. Was she racing in too quickly simply because he was the opposite of Luc? A young man sat down beside her, opening the same book. When he turned and saw her cover, his gaze met hers and they both laughed.

"It seems great minds think alike," he said.

"Seems so." She smiled.

"You're Italian, aren't you? Your French is perfect, but I hear that lilt in your voice. I love Italian. And Italians." He smiled. "You know the famous Jean Cocteau line: 'French people are Italian people in a bad mood.'"

She laughed. "No, I didn't know that one, but I'll use it. And yes, I'm Italian. I'm studying at Aix, but my year is coming to a close and I'm returning to Umbria."

"What a shame. I met you too late. I should have come down from Paris to visit my grandmother earlier." He smiled and his face lit up. He was perfect. "I'm Marc."

"Luciana."

"A beautiful name for a beautiful woman."

Something deep inside her screamed out, *"Luc! Remember Luc!"* But she was able to hold caution at bay. They spoke about books, about art, about travelling and their dreams for the future. They chatted for over an hour. Luciana felt a familiar tugging at her heart, and it scared her.

"Would you like to have dinner with me, Luciana?" Marc asked.

She paused for a long time, examining his handsome face and gathering the courage to say yes. But a gnawing feeling in the pit of her stomach reminded her that Luc had been sweet and charming, too. Better for a man to be safe and reliable, not too foreign for her to comprehend.

"I'm sorry. I'm meeting a date later this evening. An Italian I just met."

"*Tant pis,*" he said, a faint smile on his lips. "Seems I'm too late." He stood up and looked down at her. "But you never know. We may meet again."

She smiled up at him, but her smile wavered as his figure grew smaller in the distance.

Luciana was jolted to the present by Danilo's cell phone. She was ready to let the call go directly to voicemail. She changed her mind when she saw his secretary's name and hastily picked it up without saying "*Pronto.*"

"Hey, Danilo, *amore mio.* It's impossible to reach you on this little let's-patch-up-our-crummy-marriage trip. I've been lonely all week. My bed's cold. Can you get away from the witch on Sunday? You know I'll make it worth your while ..."

Luciana remained immobile, certain her heart had stopped.

"Danilo ... what? Is the Ice Queen there? Can't speak now?"

"*Buona sera,* Jessica. It's the Ice Queen in person." Her voice was calm. "Danilo can't come to the phone right now, but I'm certain you'll have lots to catch up on later. Let me just be the first to say that you really deserve one another." She paused. "By the way, I owe you one for the favor."

Luciana snapped the phone shut and released it into Danilo's full glass of wine.

She stood and walked across the square, skirt swaying, her tanned, muscular legs more alive with each step. She broke out in a smile as her nostrils filled with the familiar scent of lavender. The sun shone down on the golden highlights of her hair, masking the greys.

The man on the bench looked up from his book as she passed.

ABANDONED TOWERS
Santo Stefano di Sessanio

I EMERGED FROM THE TUNNEL and, despite myself, felt the knot tighten in my stomach. The bright light and the sudden view of the mountains took me by surprise. I struggled to breathe normally.

After putting on my sunglasses, I tightened my hands on the steering wheel.

To my left, the medieval tower of Torano loomed in the distance. The castle had long ago crumbled. But I'd always loved that lone, abandoned tower. Dwarfed by the mountains, it had stood tall and proud in that spot since the Middle Ages. On journeys, the tower always signaled that I wasn't far from home.

Home. Even if I'd been preparing myself mentally for this return, I'd underestimated the difficulty. Here, confronted with the mountains of my childhood, the memories assaulted me. All the emotions I thought I'd buried long ago came rushing back, and I was helpless to stop them.

My breathing was labored. Observing a sign for a rest stop, I released a sigh of relief. An espresso would help clear my mind and steady the tremor in my hand. The craggy mountains stretched out endlessly on the horizon, causing my heart to race once again.

Would I have the strength to follow through? How I longed to turn around and trace my route back to Rome, to drop my rental off at the Fiumicino airport and board the long flight back to Virginia. To safety. I wished to relegate this rugged world to distant memories that emerged only in rare, unguarded moments.

But this time I had no choice.

Two hundred meters to the rest stop. As soon as I pulled into the parking lot, a police officer in a patrol car waved me over.

"Buongiorno, Signora. I documenti, per favore."

"Buongiorno. Ecco il passaporto e la patente."

He examined them. In my adoptive country, the idea of random police checks instigated impassioned debate. How had I forgotten that random checks were not an invasive infringement on personal liberties, just a fact of life in Italy?

"You're American, *Signora*?"

"I am now, but I was born here in Abruzzo." The silence embarrassed me, and I felt the inexplicable need to explain myself. "It's odd to be back after almost twenty years away, especially after all that's happened."

He offered me a weak smile. *"Bentornata."* Welcome home. He looked to the distant mountains. "You may find it changed after the earthquake, but people are starting to return home."

I felt panic. My hands began to sweat. I thanked him, then parked the car.

Fifteen minutes later, calmer with caffeine coursing through my veins, I ascended the mountains for a voyage back to my past.

I COULD HAVE MADE GOOD TIME to Santo Stefano di Sessanio, but I dawdled, eschewing the highway for the meandering state road. It led me higher up, to the Altopiano delle Rocche, the high, fertile plains.

My weakness scared me; I hadn't expected it to emerge so soon. I parked my car in Rocca di Mezzo and walked around town. I stopped at a restaurant, despite the knot in my stomach. The hearty mountain foods of my childhood held no joy for me now. I chewed mechanically, too agitated to enjoy the rich tastes forgotten from my past.

The waitress was chatty. I tried to hold up my end of the conversation, even if I was in no mood.

"We haven't had tourists here in a long time. Soon the summer season'll be upon us, and we have no idea if they'll come or not," she said, hands on her hips. "Of course, it doesn't help that the aftershocks continue. Every time that happens, the whole town is out in the streets. My neighbors are sleeping in tents or in their cars because they're too scared to be in their own houses."

"It's terrible," I agreed, my voice soft. "It must leave everyone feeling so vulnerable."

"It sure does, every time we feel a tremor. Where did you say you're headed? Not L'Aquila, I hope. It's all been leveled."

Did she see me flinch? When I spoke, it was slow and measured. My voice betrayed nothing. "No, not L'Aquila, but nearby. Santo Stefano di Sessanio."

She was silent for a moment. "Oh, yeah. The town that was all saved except for the tower. They kept showing photos on the news." She shook her head. "I remember that. Most of the houses had been renovated before the quake. Funny how that works, isn't it? One town destroyed and the one just next to it emerges without a scratch. I hope your family is okay."

I gave a distracted nod, praying she wouldn't press. To my relief, she hustled off to the kitchen with the dirty dishes. Gazing up at the town clock tower up on the hill, I willed myself not to cry.

Later, I tried to digest my *gnocchi* and sausages with a walk around town. The streets were deserted. The waitress was right. The second homes owned by Romans were all abandoned, their owners too scared to visit this region where the earth had not yet ceased to tremble.

Many homes displayed enormous crevices running down their façades. The ancient stone may have held up under the quake, but the buildings would require extensive work before their occupants could once again inhabit them. Yet Rocca di Mezzo had been one of the lucky communities. The structural damage was much less evident than just down the road in L'Aquila.

I walked through twisting, cobblestoned streets, climbed the steps up to the church and its bell tower. The bell tolled, its chimes reverberated off the surrounding mountains and filled the empty streets of the medieval town. I cast my gaze on the plains below and the tent villages hosting the homeless from L'Aquila, all those waiting for new homes to be built so that they could sleep under a roof once again. Those makeshift villages dotted the landscapes of the high plains. All those lives on hold.

I remembered coming here back in high school for the Narcissus Festival held each May, picking hundreds of the fragrant Narcissus flowers alongside my classmates, and decorating our float with those blooms for the competition. In our junior year, we'd taken third place. How happy our little group from Santo Stefano was when they announced that ours was the winning float. On stage to claim our prize, tears of happiness ran down Claudia's cheeks; Beatrice jumped up and down with joy.

Then, of course, there was Luca. He threw his arms around me and planted a kiss on my cheek, his stubble scratching my face, the scent of his familiar soap sending a tingle of excitement up my spine. Just looking at Luca always caused the breath to catch in my throat.

I hadn't thought of him in years, yet being in this familiar landscape brought back the long-forgotten contours of his face, the feel of his rough hands in mine. My surroundings played tricks on my aging brain. They made me long for the pressure of his lips against mine, despite all the years that had passed.

I thought running away had helped, but being back brought all those long-repressed memories flooding back.

BY THE TIME I ARRIVED in Santo Stefano, it was late. As I'd planned. I needed a night to sleep and prepare myself mentally for what lay ahead. Although I'd sworn never to return, Renata's letter forced me online to buy the next available ticket back.

And here I was, parking on the edge of town and shouldering my small duffle bag on exhausted shoulders. Treading over the uneven cobblestones, I was pleased to have remembered my rugged trekking shoes. Dainty shoes were useless on Santo Stefano's slippery cobblestones.

The familiar smells of fireplaces in use and lamb skewers grilled over the flame filled the air. The smells of home.

Later, in my room, I unpacked my few belongings. To my relief, the guesthouse owner was a new arrival to Abruzzo. She did not know me or my deceased parents. For in these little towns, even after years away, there was no escaping local busybodies.

Dinner wasn't until eight, but my legs were restless. The mountain evening was cool, and I wrapped a shawl around my shoulders as I emerged into the crisp air. The narrow streets were silent, everyone inside preparing dinner.

It all seemed so familiar, yet different at the same time. Stone homes had been reconstructed since my youth. The town looked more prosperous than I remembered it. Freshly painted signs for new guesthouses and restaurants now hung on centuries-old grey stone walls. I wandered through narrow passageways and under ancient arches. I peeked into stone courtyards, filled with flower boxes. Flashes of color animated the cool stone staircases leading up to the homes. Would tourists return after the recent quake, or would fear keep them from spending their summer here?

The town was so peaceful, so untouched by the devastation that shattered lives just a few kilometers down the road in L'Aquila. The waitress had been right: one town destroyed and its neighbor spared. The injustice. I thought of the images I'd seen of the L'Aquila University dormitory leveled by the quake. I thought of the young lives extinguished during that night of terror. The tremors that stopped me from ever putting things right.

I brushed a tear from my cheek, filled my lungs with crisp mountain air, and continued walking.

WHEN I ROUNDED THE FAMILIAR CORNER, I wasn't prepared for what I saw. I blinked twice.

The tower was gone. A pile of rubble cordoned off by yellow police tape occupied its place. The tower that had loomed over Santo Stefano since the Middle Ages was reduced to a pile of broken, impotent stones.

My legs felt weak as I gazed at that heap of grey stone. To think the whole town was spared, save the tower. I knew it was a blessing. No one had perished. Yet that empty space still caused an ache in my heart.

How often had Luca and I climbed those steps together, carefully checking that no one observed us before we used his father's key and ducked through the door?

Our love story blossomed quickly, that attraction of polar opposites that only seems probable to young lovers. I was the star student eager to shed her small-town roots, a Francophile headed off to Paris to study literature. Luca barely scraped by. If his father weren't the mayor, he would have been shown the school exit long ago. All Luca cared about was his motorcycle—and me. At least at first.

Our afternoons making love on the tower's top floor, overlooking the town and the mountains beyond, thrilled me. I understood he was all wrong for me, but I didn't care. I felt so fortunate he'd singled me out, terrified only of losing him.

I needn't have worried that my studies abroad would drive a wedge between us. My unplanned pregnancy managed that long before I ever booked my ticket abroad. He offered to pay to take care of it. I refused. The model student suddenly wasn't looking so brilliant.

But mamma came to my rescue. We invented a story about me taking part in an intensive French class in a small French town before starting my university studies in Paris. Instead, I was stashed away with relatives in Cremona until my baby girl was born. The following autumn, I began classes in Paris. Much later, I would move to America for my doctorate and stay to teach literature at a Virginia university.

Luca's love for his motorcycle lasted much longer than his affection for me. Until one stormy evening, when he took one of the hairpin mountain curves at the terrifying speed he always loved best, and plunged over the edge of one treacherous bend. His father buried him in the town graveyard that overlooked our tower.

Mamma told me that my little girl was adopted to a family in Sardinia. When they took my baby away from me, I cried so desperately I needed to be sedated. Still, I believed what she told me, that my baby would be better off with a welcoming and well-off family ready to care for her. I always imagined her growing up in a large home along the beach, light years away from the rugged mountains of my childhood.

When I couldn't have any more children, when my marriage to a fellow professor fell apart, it was always her laughing face I saw, bobbing in the waves of the warm Mediterranean Sea.

Little did I know, my baby was here all along.

For mamma had lied. She'd given my baby to a local woman who couldn't have children of her own. This allowed mamma to follow her granddaughter's life. In exchange, Renata promised to safeguard my secret, even after mamma died.

Only the unthinkable could cause Renata to break her promise.

BACK IN MY ROOM, I removed the letters from their well-worn envelope. Gingerly, I placed Renata's on the dresser and smoothed Luisa's on my lap.

I knew the words by heart, but I never tired of gazing at that lovely, confident writing.

Cara Serena,

I don't know if I will ever send this to you. I don't want to hurt mamma. A neighbor told me the rumors that you are my real mother. I haven't confronted mamma yet, but I looked you up on the internet. We look so much alike.

I'm studying literature at L'Aquila University. I've read your articles and wish I could speak to you in person about them. I am certain you would have much to teach me.

Maybe one day I will have the courage to send this letter. Until then ...

Yours,
Luisa

My heart soared the day I received the letter, then plunged into darkness when I read Renata's accompanying words. The very words that drew me back.

ABANDONED TOWERS, abandoned daughters.

I thought I'd be able to escape my past, to distance myself from my birthplace in order to be free. But I never was. Not in my dreams, not in my daily life. These mountains, these ruins kept calling me back. And I always thought there would be time to make things right.

But as I gazed on the rubble of the tower in the distance, I knew I'd lost that chance.

"Serena."

I heard Renata's voice speaking softly behind me. She knelt beside me and lay her hand gently on my shoulder.

I felt her fingers twitch. Nerves, just like me. We were both in unchartered waters.

"Come home with me. I've organized Luisa's photos and writing notebooks. She would have wanted you to see them."

The compassion in Renata's voice—a compassion I didn't deserve—made my heart ache. This was the woman who raised my baby, who kissed away her tears, who loved her and cared for her when I chose not to, when I listened to others who told me I shouldn't ruin my life so young. When I was willing to hand over a young, innocent creature to an unknown fate. When I was so convinced my meaningful life was elsewhere.

"You can stay as long as you want. We have so much space—too much space ..."

I heard her voice catch in her throat. How had she coped when Luisa's lifeless body was extracted from the rubble of the university dormitory?

"... too much space for just us. Come stay for a while."

I placed my hand over hers and breathed in deeply through my nostrils, in a useless attempt to stave off the tears I felt welling up in my eyes. I knelt forward and kissed the cold gravestone. The kiss I never gave to my beautiful daughter during her short life.

I took one last look at my daughter's grave, with the tower ruins and the rocky mountains beyond. In that moment, I knew I would stay. I wouldn't run anymore. It was time to return to my daughter.

It was time to return where I belonged.

LOVE AND HONOR

Vicenza

SOMETIMES, WHEN IT'S QUIET, I can remember what my life was like before moving to Buffalo Plains.

The kids are older now. They no longer need me as the once did. The way they used to seek me out at the end of the school day, their eyes shining with sheer joy as they raced into my warm embrace, is only a distant memory now. I miss those days when they were eager to tell me about classes, and friends, and soccer goals. I never wanted to be a source of embarrassment to my children, but sometimes I see a look in my son's eye that expresses all his frustration at what I'm not.

If I'm honest with myself, it was only a matter of time.

I keep busy pouring my energies into my volunteer work with my church, with its widows' support group, or the hours I spend with Meals-on-Wheels, visiting elderly neighbors who are so heartbreakingly eager to have someone sitting across from them in their lonely houses. The musty smell of their living rooms fills my nostrils as I listen to the same stories told over and over again. I smile or nod at the appropriate places. The spark in their eyes helps me to understand how these visits keep them going. That same spark helps me feel a sense of worth I often lack.

Cooking, cleaning, and gardening fill up the unscheduled hours of my days. Those moments scare me. When I am still, my thoughts flow unfiltered. Only ceaseless activity manages to banish painful memories.

Yet, when all is quiet, the moon is full, and a gentle breeze wafts through my bedroom window, carrying with it the smell of honeysuckle, my mind refuses to obey. My memories shift back to my life before moving to my peaceful, Midwestern town. My life before Buffalo Plains.

THE SCENT OF HONEYSUCKLE hung in the air as I emerged from the car. Pure adrenaline fueled me after the trans-Atlantic flight and the drive from Milan to the Veneto.

My friends had all been envious about my move to Italy. Like me, they longed to visit new, exotic places.

The army wives were more jaded. They'd seen it all, explained to me the ins and outs of life in Vicenza: where to live on or off base, where to shop, all about the schools. They agreed it was light years away from Oklahoma, especially if I could talk Brad into taking me on holidays around Italy.

"Or maybe," they winked knowingly, "you'd prefer to travel alone. The Italian men are irresistible."

My cheeks would burn, and I'd glance behind me for my husband's tall form. If Brad ever heard such joking, he'd be livid.

But standing in front of the home we rented on the outskirts of Vicenza, on that balmy spring day, my husband was in a good mood. He was as excited as I about the new posting. For him, this wasn't only the chance to work abroad, it was a promotion. He'd just been made Captain, and he was eager for the increased responsibilities awaiting him at his new base.

His mood improved in the months leading up to our move, and I was happy to have the old Brad back, the one I'd fallen in love with so many years earlier. I knew the stress at our old base slowly wore away at him. He was always unhappy, drinking too heavily. The children's crying or misplaced toys could set him off in a rage.

Jeff and Alice were so young back then. Still, they knew enough to shrink from their father when he slipped into one of his black moods. Nothing I did could coax him out of it. In fact, everything I did when he got in that state seemed to enrage him more. But it was better that way. I preferred that he turn his rage on me, not the children.

Happiness enveloped me as we stood in front of our new home, with its shaded lawn and neat garden plot, with the bicycle path that bordered our property and continued on to Vicenza. Everything would be different. Brad would be appreciated in his new position. He'd finally be content. I would be a better wife to him, and have more time to dedicate to the children and to making our home a haven for him.

My heart swelled as I gazed at their sleeping forms in the backseat. The long flight had wiped them out. Bleary-eyed by the time we landed in Milan, their energy held out until the car rental agency. Jeff snored gently and Alice sucked her thumb, indifferent to their first drive through the Italian countryside. Spring bloomed all around us and the Italian landscape rolled past our windows, but the children stubbornly slumbered on.

"It's beautiful, isn't it?" Brad slipped his arm around my waist.

"It is," I agreed.

A light breeze ruffled my hair. The scent of honeysuckle filled my nostrils. A sense of peace enveloped me. *We'll be happy here. Everything will be different.*

ARMY BASES ARE ODD PLACES. An American enclave abroad, the whole complex is designed to trick everyone who steps onto its soil into thinking they'd never left home. There's no need to learn the host country's language, no need to shop in the town markets if one doesn't wish to, nor to learn about the local culture. Peanut butter and Doritos are always just an errand away.

Sunday afternoons saw the Italian families in our neighborhood eating leisurely lunches with family and friends, and then going for the ritual *passeggiata* in Vicenza, their Sunday best so much more impressive than anything I owned. Certainly, more fashionable than the shorts and flip-flops that were the norm on Sunday afternoons on base.

Living off base, surrounded by Italian families, I often chatted with the Italian mothers at the local playground. They'd invited me to countless Sunday lunches, but I always had to refuse.

Our Sundays were religiously dedicated to barbeques in a revolving series of backyards on base housing. Sitting on lawn chairs, drinking Budweiser and eating hot dogs, hamburgers, and coleslaw as the children ran through sprinklers, I always felt we could have been back on base in Oklahoma.

I listened to the soldiers and their wives complain about local customs and lazy Italians. They griped about plumbers who didn't speak fluent English, and the horrors of having to venture out of the base post office to take care of business in the unbridled chaos of what was the *Posta italiana*. I smiled at the repetitive stories, watching the husbands consume beer after beer, and I thought of the fashionable mothers of my neighborhood, wondering what it would be like to sit at their tables instead, with their homemade pastas, rich meats, and seasonal vegetables, accompanied by the full-bodied local wines.

That Sunday in July, Brad and I said our goodbyes to our hosts and the other army families. We made our way to the car, the exhausted kids limp as rag dolls in our arms as we tried to snap them into their car seats without waking them.

"Why don't you let me drive, Brad, and you can relax? You have to be up so early tomorrow."

He fixed his gaze on me. I could see it was an effort. I'd had three or four polite sips of the awful beer, but I'd seen my husband consume five bottles, at least. And, despite having kept a steady eye on him, I was certain there were others that had slipped my notice.

Brad never wanted to be embarrassed in front of his colleagues, didn't want "a controlling bitch of a wife," but sometimes he could be coaxed into resting while I took over at the wheel. On those occasions, a tremendous sense of relief washed over me as my husband snored in the seat beside me and my beautiful children slept safe and sound in the backseat.

But Brad was not in a cooperative mood that evening.

"I'm fine. Get in."

My heart beat wildly in my chest. I dug my fingernails into my clenched palms. Weakling that I was, I slid into the passenger seat and hoped for the best. Yet again.

"Not very social today, were you? Trying to show me you're pissed off about not going over to that Italian bitch Livia's house, huh? As if I'd endure an entire lunch with a woman who has a permanent pole shoved up her ass. Plus, that bore of a hotshot lawyer husband, with his fake English accent."

I waited a moment before responding, observing how his eyes did not seem fully focused on the road, watching the kilometers tick perilously upward.

"I was being social." My voice was meek. "I'm going to help the wives organize the annual August picnic. I'll be at Morgan's tomorrow afternoon for a planning meeting."

"'Bout time you got involved. This is a big deal for me. I need you to spend more time helping out on base. Can't keep having an absent wife. Doesn't make me look good."

"Settling in took longer than I expected." His swerving was making me nervous, and I saw too many Sunday cyclists on the edge of the road for things to end well. Brad came dangerously close to them as he passed by well over the speed limit. "But I'm ready to be more active now. I've spoken to the wives. They understood."

His face grew red and his voice was the familiar yet dangerous timbre I'd heard too often over the years.

"That's what they'll say to your face, but it's not what they say when they're alone talking to their husbands." He clenched the steering wheel tighter. "A wife can make or break her husband's career. What the hell, Lorrie? I thought you knew that was part of the deal."

"I did ... I do," I stammered. "Please slow down." My voice sounded pathetically weak to my own ears.

Each morning, I observed my reflection in the mirror and marveled at the spineless creature who stared back at me. Now my children slept soundly in the backseat as my husband risked all of our lives, and all I did was ask him to please slow down, in a groveling voice.

"Stupid bitch!"

His punch was so quick that it caught me by surprise. Usually, my reflexes were quicker.

"I'll go as goddamned fast as I want, you dumb cunt."

Through my throbbing eye, I watched the speedometer tick up. *God, if I'm going to die, please save my children.* I could hear Jeff stirring in his car seat.

"Mommy?" came a hesitant voice from behind me. My baby needed my assurances, once again.

"It's okay, darling," I said, in as calm a voice as I could muster. "Just close your eyes." I turned back to my husband, fixing my good eye on him and hissing, "Brad, slow down."

"Screw you and your constant nagging. I'll do whatever the hell I want."

The road was too narrow for the speeds we were travelling. I caught my breath at each curve.

The sound of screeching tires was amplified by the silence of the countryside and the chirping of the crickets. The crash occurred in mere seconds, yet in that time, my mind raced through how I would free the kids and sprint with them far away from the ensuing explosion. *Get the kids to safety*, I repeated to myself like a mantra.

I suppose we were lucky the grassy embankment slowed us down before we smashed into the tree. Otherwise, we all would have died along that small, peaceful road in the Veneto. Springing into action, I released the children, dragging them far away from the twisted car. My husband stood beside the driver's side, unsteady on his feet, concerned exclusively for his own welfare.

I ignored him as I tried to soothe my children's cries. Their hearts raced like those of frightened animals. Their tiny bodies trembled. Kissing them and pressing them to my breast, I struggled to keep my voice soothing. "It's okay, darlings. Just an accident. We're safe."

Their wails cut through the sound of the leaves rustling in the soft summer breeze. Cyclists reached the side of the road and hollered down to us. "*State bene?*"

One pulled out his cell phone as he came towards us. He'd be calling the police. He'd certainly witnessed my husband's reckless driving before the crash.

Brad came closer, panic evident in his eyes. His voice was low, his back turned to the approaching cyclist.

"Little bitch, this is all your fault. How can anyone drive with your constant nagging? When the cops come, tell 'em *you* were driving."

BRAD WAS AWAY FOR TWO WEEKS, on exercises in Germany. The house was silent. A gentle breeze caressed my shoulders as I washed dishes at the sink. The smell of honeysuckle filled the air. When I told my neighbor, Livia, how much I associated that smell with Vicenza, she laughed and told me not to expect it much longer. Temperatures were rising and the honeysuckle would soon dry up, and I'd have to wait another year to enjoy the fragrance once again.

After the accident, I'd tried to hide from Livia, but the children kept begging to go to the local playground where my neighbor took her children. Jeff and Alice raced over to play with their young Italian friends. Despite the cosmetics masking the worst of it, Livia blanched when she saw my swollen cheek.

"It was the accident. Nothing broken." I tried to laugh off her concern.

"Lorrie," her voice was soft, "if you ever need anything, my husband's a lawyer. He could help you."

She looked me squarely in the eyes. I knew she could detect every lie I'd told to everyone over the years, see through every layer of makeup I'd ever applied as artfully as a professional makeup artist to cover the marks of my shame.

"We've had lots of army families passing through," she continued, as if that explained everything. "My offer stands, whenever you're ready."

A breeze fluttered a lock of hair before my eyes as I recalled her look of concern. Hands soapy with detergent, I wiped the strands away with my forearm. I heard Jeff and Alice playing behind me at the new kitchen set Alice recently received for her fifth birthday.

"I'm hungry! Where's dinner?" yelled Jeff.

I smiled when Jeff trilled the 'r' with an Italian accent, like his neighborhood friends. It annoyed Brad, but thrilled me to know my son could do things I would never be able to match.

"Dumb bish!"

My blood turned cold in my veins as I heard my son's cry. So familiar, so terrifying.

"You burn everything to hell! Get me another beer, you stupid cunt."

I turned to see Jeff flailing at his sister. Dropping to my knees, I restrained him. Pulling him tight to me, I fought against the lump forming in my throat. "What are you doing? Why would you hurt your sister?"

As if I didn't know.

He cried out in pain from the pressure on his shoulder. I pulled back to see his face, but I didn't loosen my grip.

"We're playing house, Mommy. We're pretending to be you and Daddy."

Innocent brown eyes observed me with fear and confusion as the tears cascaded down my cheeks.

THE CHRISTMAS TREE LIGHTS twinkled optimistically, casting a cheery glow over the room.

Putting Jeff and Alice to bed, I hadn't heard the front door and I startled to see my husband sitting in the dark room, a beer in hand, the cheery, blinking Christmas lights contrasting with the scowl on his face.

"So, cunt, complaining to the neighbors again?"

The hair on the back of my neck rose, an animal confronted by her predator. I could tell by his slurred words that he'd been out drinking. I changed topics.

"The kids are excited about the Christmas pageant. We were rehearsing their lines."

"Didn't you hear me, bitch?" He sneered and his whole face looked ugly. "What the hell did you whine about with our neighbors? Why is cunt Livia's husband coming up to me to suggest the name of a local anger-management counselor?"

I sensed the danger and backed away, trembling. "I didn't say *anything*, Brad. I swear!"

"Goddamned lies! You no-good, whiny whore! Don't you remember your vows? You promised to love and honor your husband."

He closed the distance between us, and I heard the whoosh as his arm gathered speed. He hit me, and I lost my balance. He jumped on top of me. He pummeled my face, my chest, my stomach.

My ears began ringing. Brad grabbed me by the hair and smashed my head to the hardwood floors, once, twice, three times. I soon lost count. The pain was excruciating. If I passed out, surely, he'd stop.

"Mommy?"

Jeff stood on the staircase, looking so small in his Superman pajamas, holding Alice's tiny hand in his own. The look of terror in his eyes forced me to react. I tried to smile, battling the metallic taste of blood in my mouth as Brad pounded on my ribs. He'd succeeded in breaking three that night. In his rage, he didn't even notice the children behind him.

"Go over to Livia's, babies. Don't come back until I come for you," I whispered.

For a moment, I feared Jeff would disobey me, try to defend me and be beaten once again. He hesitated a split second before he signaled his sister to be silent and padded down the steps, silently unlatching the front door, as I'd taught him.

When the Carabinieri arrived soon after, I was slipping in and out of consciousness. Brad still straddled above me, pummeling me, screaming, "Love and honor!" at the top of his lungs. When two burly officers pulled my husband off of me, he waved a clump of my hair in his fist like a war trophy.

That's the last image I remember.

YES, OF COURSE I DROPPED ALL CHARGES, for that's what abused wives do.

I even let him slink back, spineless coward that I was. I ignored the hurt and disappointment in Jeff's eyes, and took comfort in believing Alice was too young to understand. As if a child couldn't comprehend that her mother married a monster. But it was better for a while.

A little over a year later, everything came crashing down. Those are the memories that flood back in quiet moments.

Brad was drunk following a lakeside party. We had stayed after the gathering broke up. The kids were sleeping on a blanket. He continued drinking on the dock at the edge of the lake, until he became enraged at some perceived slight and began throwing unbalanced punches at me. When I dodged one blow, he lost his balance, plunging into the depths of the chilly water.

Brad never learned to swim, while I'd been captain of my swim team back in high school. Funny to think I'd once been so strong and competitive, someone my rivals feared.

"Lorrie! Help me!"

The fear and desperation in his voice almost made me pity him.

Almost.

I looked around me. We were utterly alone. I knelt down and brought my face closer to his. He flailed his arms, as drowning victims always do. If only he'd put the same panicked effort into kicking his legs, he'd stay afloat. Why did drowners never realize that tiny key to survival?

Despite the darkness descending, I detected the terrified glint in his eyes as I leaned closer.

"Thank God." His relief was palpable. Using his last strength, he extended a hand to me.

I observed that hand in silence. His panicked breathing enveloped me. Slowly, I reached for him, but not for his hand. Clutching his short hair, I tilted his face toward me. His glistening eyes pleaded silently with mine, holding out the promise that things would be different.

I knew that look of contrition. It was always there when he'd gone too far. When he'd convinced me to drop the charges with the Carabinieri. When he'd broken Jeff's arm. When he'd given tiny Alice a black eye, then swore to the emergency room doctor she'd fallen from a swing. I remembered the tears flowing from my little daughter's swollen eye as she silently learned not telling lies didn't apply to the adults in her life.

I'd fallen for that look more times than I could count, but now I met it with a gaze containing years of pent-up rage.

Gently but firmly, I pushed his head under the surface, watching the bubbles explode on the smooth surface of the water.

Until they stopped.

THE CARIBINIERI RULED IT AN ACCIDENT. Elevated blood alcohol levels. No signs of foul play. Livia's husband handled everything, represented me free of charge.

With my widow's pension, I moved to the Midwest, settling in Buffalo Plains. We were strangers in town, free to start again.

Two years ago, when he was fourteen, Jeff asked me if I'd been responsible for Brad's death. I could see from those eyes that he wanted the truth, wanted to know I'd stood up for us, even if it meant killing his own father.

But those wasted years of his childhood were my fault alone. As much as his youthful righteousness believed he could respect me for what I'd done, how could he cope with the knowledge that his mother ended his father's life? I couldn't make him party to my crime, even if he longed to detect a glimmer of strength in me. I vehemently denied it.

But I can't deny it to myself in those quiet moments in the middle of the night. While Buffalo Plains slumbers, I lie awake. Brad's eyes plead with me on sleepless nights.

Those eyes will surely haunt me on my day of reckoning. That's why I struggle to keep them at bay, why I try so desperately to forget the life I lived before moving to Buffalo Plains.

STARI MOST

Mostar

"YOU'D BETTER START LEARNING better customer service, or your shiny, new lobby will be empty in just a few months! Have you ever thought about that?"

Victoria's neck snapped up from up her spreadsheets to observe the source of the hollering. From the safety of the one-way glass, she was free to examine the obnoxious man at the front desk. Big, dressed in an ill-fitting T-shirt and patterned shorts that made his bulky frame look even larger, he stood like a bear in the center of the tasteful lobby. His combover managed to deflect some attention from his beefy face, red from the brutal Balkan sun and his exertions in yelling at hapless, young Mirko. His shapeless wife stood beside him, looking wilted as she dabbed uselessly at the beads of perspiration that formed anew after each swipe of the handkerchief.

Victoria gazed down at the guest list and tapped a well-manicured fingernail under the names: Herbert and Martha Prince.

Just as she suspected. Cruise ship refugees who had unwisely opted for a longer shore excursion. She shook her head. They were continually more trouble than they were worth. Why were they always so adamant?

Perhaps it was the chance to feel smug as they recounted to their neighbors back in Cincinnati about their brush with adventure. Yet it was so clear to Victoria, and to anyone who looked at them, really, that their comfort zone did not venture far from the plush cruise deck lounge chairs, the safe perch from which they could observe the exotic ports, drinks firmly in hand. If the doctor ordered adventure, surely a guided day excursion could meet their needs, with the added benefit of returning in time for the evening stage shows and the just-enough-to-seem-exciting-but-not-*too*-exotic food.

But no, sighed Victoria, that was never good enough. And so, here were Herbert and Martha Prince in her hotel, taking their frustrations and vague fears of foreignness out on poor Mirko.

Victoria stood slowly, smoothing her elegant sheath dress, and tugging at the sleeves of her perfectly tailored jacket. Her shoulders were squared, and her exquisite heels click-clicked across the marble floor as she approached the slumping, perspiring couple. She knew her fair hair piled up artfully made her long, lithe frame appear even taller, and she watched as three heads swiveled as she approached, all eyes expectant.

She turned slowly to the flustered young man. "Mirko, it's time for your break. Why don't you go ahead? I can take over here."

She noted the fear in Mirko's dark eyes and offered him a reassuring smile. As he hurried away, she turned her smile to the Ohio couple.

"Mr. and Mrs. Prince," she said. "What a pleasure to finally meet you. I'm Victoria Whitman, the manager during the hotel launch."

She observed the couple soften as they noted her elegant demeanor, heard her unaccented English, the absence of foreignness her presence conveyed. Their fear dissipated before her eyes.

"Now, Mr. and Mrs. Prince, perhaps you can tell me how I can be of assistance." She heard the collective sigh of relief. Americans were so bloody predictable.

"Oh, Ms. Whitman," said Herbert, his fleshy face awash with relief. "Finally, another American! My wife and I can't listen to any more of this Croatian. I was just telling that Mirko-fellow that the maid didn't even understand us when we asked about our pillow selection."

Herbert's frustration was evident as the words flowed through him. Everything seemed to disturb them—the strong Mediterranean sun, the maids who chatted in Croatian in the hall and greeted them with an unfamiliar *Dobar dan*, the fact that Mrs. Prince's fish was served *with the head still on*.

Victoria did her best to suppress a smile while nodding along sympathetically. If only the Princes had not ventured so far from their cruise ship chaise lounges. No such luck. There never was. She feigned interest in the hapless couple's travails and offered up another of her insincere smiles, the one that seemed to inspire the most confidence in couples such as the Princes.

"Yes, Mr. and Mrs. Prince, things are different here from back home." She tilted her head slightly, and fixed her kind gaze upon them. "We can't expect all the same comforts you enjoy in Cincinnati, after all."

She observed the couple and noted the predictable, wide smiles of comprehension spread across their sun-blotched faces.

"Now," she said in the firm voice she perfected over the years when speaking with difficult clients. "I will send the head of housekeeping to your room for your pillow selection and," she extended her hand to Herbert, offering her card, "if you have any questions or concerns, feel free to contact me at the extension here." She paused before delivering the words that would allay all their fears. "Any time, of course."

Herbert fell over himself thanking her before he and his wife made their way to their room, forgoing the ancient, defensive walls of Dubrovnik in favor of selecting the perfect pillows. Victoria shook her head as she watched two pairs of white sneakers retreat across the elegant lobby to the sleek elevators.

"Snežana," Victoria said to the young woman who passed by. "Could you come and cover the front desk until Mirko returns?"

Victoria made her way to the break room, where Mirko slumped over the table, smoking sullenly. He snapped up as Victoria slipped into the seat beside him.

"Mirko," she said, "don't let this get you down. There are lots of Herberts and Marthas out there. The first encounters with them are always the most traumatic. You'll get better at identifying them and avoiding problems in the future."

She saw the relief wash over the handsome lines of his face and she smiled. "*Dobro*, Mirko?"

"*Dobro*, Victoria. *Hvala*."

"Now get out there, Mirko, and face the Yankee barbarians." She gave him a playful jab in the arm. "They won't be the last if you want a career in the hotel industry. The trick is to learn to see through them."

BALKAN MUSIC BLARED from the ancient speakers, its frenetic strains oddly soothing. The bus bumped and shuddered along the road, brakes screeching wildly—and worryingly—as they drove down each hill.

Victoria gazed out the window at the Neretva River and the snow-capped mountains beyond. The abundance of water in this tiny country never failed to surprise her. The bus drive from Sarajevo had been a good idea. It gave her the chance to observe the beautiful nature all around her, without requiring her to maneuver those roads alone or worry about directions.

She longed to lose herself in the stunning landscapes surrounding her, but her mind was weighed down by the visit that preceded her flight to Sarajevo.

Seeing Daniele again had been harder than she'd imagined it would be. It was easy to banish him from her mind with an ocean between them, harder when they were just on opposite sides of town—and even worse in a town like Bologna that contained so many memories of happier times.

Back in Bologna, Victoria took a deep breath before ringing the buzzer on the familiar entryway. She instructed her feet to stay in place when the husky, familiar voice said *"Pronto"* over the intercom. She swallowed hard before her voice could greet him without betraying her fear.

She trudged up the familiar stairs with as much enthusiasm as a condemned prisoner being led to the executioner. *You can do this, Victoria*, she repeated with each step. By the time she reached the landing, she almost believed it.

Then the door opened and she saw his broad shoulders filling the doorframe, the soft sweater and jeans that clung perfectly to his toned body, the square jaw with just a hint of stubble, those expressive, dark eyes that had come as closely as anyone ever had to cracking her open and exposing her vulnerabilities.

She took a deep breath, inhaling the familiar scent of his cologne. Even today, on the streets of Chicago, her knees grew weak when a man passed by wearing the scent she always associated with Daniele.

"Ciao, Daniele. Ti trovo bene." She stood on her toes to kiss him on both cheeks. She attempted to remain rigid when he rested a hand on her shoulder, when all she longed for was to

melt into his embrace. "Obviously, life without me has treated you well." She leaned back and looked into those eyes, forcing her smile.

He was observing her, like she used to catch him doing when they were at home alone together. Sizing her up, she used to think.

"I could say the same about you," he said, before leading her inside.

She sat on the Minotti couch they purchased together all those years ago, back when they were young and hopeful. And happy. She remembered christening the couch with Daniele long ago, and the memory caused her to blush. *Get a hold of yourself,* she chided herself as Daniele handed her a glass of wine and took the seat across from her. It felt familiar. How often had they done the same, after a long day at work, or simply unwinding with friends? It seemed ages ago.

"*Salute,* Victoria," he said, clinking her glass. "I can't tell you how happy I am to see you sitting there again."

She suppressed a smile. It felt comfortable for her, too. This was why she contacted Daniele so rarely. Seeing him was too painful. It made her forget why she'd felt the need to leave in the first place.

She forced a tight smile. "How are your parents? How's the factory?"

Daniele's family owned a successful pasta manufacturing company, and Daniele was being groomed to take over the family firm when his father retired. He'd grown up with the business. It was in his blood. Daniele understood his business like she understood hotels.

When they were married, they often let off steam talking about work problems together. She'd valued Daniele's insights. He'd helped her to grow in her position, and she had been sorry to lose that friendship when she decided she wasn't cut out for marriage. Somehow, she hadn't prepared herself for the loss of her best friend alongside the loss of a husband.

"We're doing well, thanks," said Daniele, swirling his wine glass in his hand. "Demand is strong from foreign markets."

"I'm so pleased. You deserve it."

Daniele fixed her with that intense gaze that could still make her heart flutter. How had she forgotten that?

"And you, Victoria? How's the new hotel?"

"It's a beauty," she said. Talk about work carried her far away from uncomfortable footing. "What a stunning location, just along Dubrovnik's walls. Ancient exterior, the interior all modern, done by an up-and-coming Croatian interior designer. Filled with cruise ship tourists, unfortunately. They're always afraid to venture outside into the big, scary Croatian world."

She watched Daniele's eyes crinkle up when he laughed. She'd always found that so sexy, and she fought the urge to lean across the distance separating them to press her lips against his, to feel the heat of his body flush against hers. *Control, Victoria.*

"The staff is strong and the manager I'm training seems confident," she continued. "Time to step away and let them spread their wings. Mother bird needs to leave the nest and let them take flight on their own."

The mood in the room shifted. She could sense it. She saw the tightness in Daniele's jaw and bit the inside of her cheek. *Oh damn, the mother bird reference.*

Everything had fallen apart when Daniele started talking about having children. Her career was taking off and, even if she had convinced Chicago headquarters to base her in Bologna to be with Daniele, she needed the freedom to take off to Saigon or Berlin or Cartagena with little advance notice whenever a new hotel opened. She was a pro at hotel startups:

whipping the staff into shape, setting schedules and work patterns, coddling clients—then retreating as quickly as she had arrived. How would a child fit into that schedule?

And what right did she, of all people, have to bring a helpless human being into this world, a being who would rely primarily on her for his or her survival? Surely, no baby deserved such punishment.

But she could never completely explain her feelings to Daniele. Their marriage didn't implode immediately, but it was the start of a slow decline. The love, the happiness that had fueled their relationship until that point began to die a slow, painful death. By the time she took the headquarters offer and prepared her move to Chicago, the split seemed inevitable.

That was three years ago: in the snail's pace of Italian divorce laws, just enough time to see a divorce through to fruition. The papers would be finalized in two weeks' time, and Victoria would pass through Bologna again to sign alongside her husband of six years, unofficial ex of three.

This visit was meant to soften the blow before they met before a judge in some sterile office to scratch their pens decisively across an official document, dissolving the ties that bound their lives together. This visit was to prove that they were modern adults about this arrangement, still friends, even if Victoria knew that was far from the truth.

The wine and attempts to lighten the mood weren't helping. The discomfort in a room that had once held such promise for the young couple was palpable.

"And where are you going during your temporary exile from Dubrovnik?" Daniele asked.

He remembered how company policy worked. Victoria had to go far enough away to allow the new staff a trial run, but close enough to return quickly, if needed.

"Bosnia," said Victoria, forcing a smile.

"Bosnia?" said Daniele, tilting his head to examine her better and running a hand though his thick, tousled hair. She'd forgotten how that endearing habit of his always made him appear like a distracted schoolboy.

"I've got to hand it to you, Victoria. You run those five-star hotels like no one I know, but you're a backpacker at heart. I miss those old trips of ours."

Victoria saw him turn to the window. The golden sunlight highlighted his strong cheekbones, played in the strands of his hair. How many times had she passed him as he pensively gazed out that window onto the porticoed sidewalks of Bologna? She'd taken it all for granted, assumed she could catch him in those quiet moments of reflection whenever she wanted.

Sitting across from him, Victoria realized how much she missed them. Missed him. How much emptier her life had seemed since the day she made the decision to walk out their front door and return to Chicago.

Slowly, he turned away from the window, his gaze fixed firmly on her own.

"It's too bad work is so busy just now. Otherwise, I'd love to join you."

Victoria's heart skipped a beat before she smiled at his comment. Not the confident, dealing-with-the-Cincinnati-Princes smile she perfected at the hotel, but a weak smile that allowed her skepticism to seep through. They both knew what Daniele said wasn't true.

"*Molim*," said the young soldier sitting beside her, pulling Victoria back to the present. He smiled broadly at her, offering her a piece of gum.

Victoria observed the young soldier, registering his blond, close-cut hair and handsome face. He was dressed in camouflage, a crisp insignia on his shoulder—blue and yellow, with the white stars of the Bosnian national flag rising diagonally.

She smiled politely and gently shook her head as she met his light brown eyes. "*Ne, hvala.*"

He continued to gaze at her. He was a soldier, after all.

Victoria felt uncharacteristically embarrassed, needing to fill the silence. "*Ja sam amerikanka.*"

His smile widened and they sat quietly. She had exhausted her Bosnian language knowledge, and he clearly didn't speak any English.

She couldn't help examining him every time he looked out the window on the opposite side of the bus, and wondering how old he was. How old had he been during the war? A child, she imagined.

Had his parents struggled to keep the child version of this muscular soldier locked up safely in their home or cellar as their town was shelled? Had he longed to go out and risk the shrapnel—risk death—in exchange for a day of sledding or playing in the park? How she longed to know more about that generation of children who'd been robbed of their childhood.

She'd wandered the hills of Sarajevo—the same hills that had sheltered snipers not so many years earlier. Her heart clenched as she observed the endless rows of graves that now covered those rolling, verdant hills. All were carved with deceased dates between 1992 and 1995, the years of the siege. She shuddered involuntarily.

Yes, the handsome young soldier smiling flirtatiously beside her must certainly have been a child during those years. Could he still remember the daily terror of his childhood, or had he blocked out those painful memories?

They bumped along the curving road skirting the river, and Victoria was even more aware of the buildings they passed that still displayed the bullet holes and shrapnel damage inflicted during the war.

The soldier seemed to press flush against her shoulder at each curve, and she doubted it was accidental. When they pulled into the town of Konjic, she saw, from the corner of her eye, his camouflaged form stand beside her, as he reached for his duffle bag in the overhead bin. She felt strangely disappointed.

She turned when he addressed her.

"*Do viđenja,*" he said.

"*Do viđenja,*" Victoria responded, offering him a smile.

"*Sretan put,*" the soldier said with another wide smile. He hesitated a moment before touching Victoria lightly on the shoulder and squeezing gently with his strong fingers. She looked up, meeting his gaze. There was something so familiar about the look in those hazel eyes. An understanding passed between them in that precise moment. Then the spell was broken and he released his grip, turned, and stepped down from the bus. Victoria felt a slight tingling at the spot where his fingers had rested, and a vague sense of unease as his blond head and camouflaged form grew smaller in the distance.

Victoria released the breath she had been holding and gazed out the window. Her young staff in Dubrovnik had taught her the local expression for *bon voyage*. Victoria loved the lyrical imagery the words conveyed—heartfelt trail.

Yes, it is turning out to be just that, she thought, as the driver turned on the groaning engine and the bus pulled away from Konjic on its voyage to Mostar.

VICTORIA WOKE WITH A START. The images were still fresh in her mind. The feeling of helplessness and terror. The sound of the wind swaying the branches of the trees, the crashing sound of water. The moonlight illuminating grey stones. A look—but whose?—that caused her heart to freeze.

It was always the same. She hadn't experienced the dream in a long time. At least, not since she began her frenzied pace of work in Dubrovnik four months ago. The dream often disappeared, but experience had shown that it returned eventually. It always did.

She shook her head and allowed the last remnants to disappear. Looking out the window, she saw the sign welcoming them to Mostar. The bus pulled into a drab bus station and Victoria lifted her backpack from the overhead bin and joined the line of travelers descending from the bus.

LATER THAT AFTERNOON, Victoria deposited her backpack in the guest house where she was staying. She made her way down the stairs, greeted the owner, and stepped out into the bright May sunshine. The guesthouse was simple, but clean and pleasant. It was light years away from the pretentious hotels she managed around the world, including the hotel she had just left behind in Dubrovnik.

Daniele was right. She had a knack for managing five-star hotels, for ensuring that their grand openings occurred without a glitch, that their staff was well-trained, and their schedules calibrated with the precision and dependability of a Swiss watch. She knew how to ensure the clients felt sufficiently coddled. But she had no affinity for those places herself, or the unimaginative clientele they attracted.

On her own, Victoria preferred simple guesthouses like the one she just checked into. Those were places where a traveler could feel at home. No pillow selections, no tuck-downs, no complicated, space-command-sized control panels to be found in the room, no cloying, ever-present customer service. Just a bed, a chair, and a shared bathroom. For one was not expected to spend all of one's time in the room, not when there was a world to explore just beyond the guesthouse walls.

Victoria walked down Brače Fejiča, the sun warming her face. The smell of sweet honeysuckle filled her nostrils as she admired the minarets in the distance. She always associated that comforting scent with her grandmother's garden. Despite the warming sun and the sweet scent of the breeze, Victoria felt exhaustion seeping through her body, settling deep in her bones. She hadn't wanted to nap at the guesthouse, but as she neared a pretty mosque, she noted the outdoor tables and decided to stop for a Bosnian coffee. Just the thing to provide her with needed energy before she explored the town.

Victoria ordered, then watched the people passing by on the street and the young people chatting at the surrounding tables. She sat quietly under the umbrella, stretching her long limbs and observing the world around her.

The waiter approached and placed before her the tray with the copper *džezva*, the coffeepot, with its twice-boiled coffee. She had learned from the young Bosnians on her staff about coffee traditions. She knew to let the hot coffee sit for a short while before grasping the long handle and tipping the *džezva*. She poured the thick, sludgy coffee into her tiny cup. Just as her young charges had taught her, Victoria picked up the sugar cube and dipped it into the rich mixture. She brought the coffee-drenched sugar cube to her mouth and took a delicate bite before placing it down and sipping the strong coffee, careful not to sip too close to the murky grinds settled at the bottom of the cup.

Victoria repeated the ritual, feeling the energy course through her with each sip. She gazed up at the minaret above her, allowing the caffeine to revive her exhausted body.

Victoria let the strong coffee work its way through her veins, wakening her deadened senses.

Not for the first time, she found herself wondering what was wrong with her. So strong and pulled together on the outside, such a mess within. Why was she incapable of revealing her feelings to Daniele? She'd never managed to open up with boyfriends—or even with her soon-to-be ex-husband. Would it have killed her to try back in Bologna? She'd let the moment pass and done what she'd always done before—slink off to some new destination with entirely new people, safe in the knowledge that no one would know about her failures and disappointments.

Relationships had never been her strong suit. Victoria was too wedded to her independence to make a relationship work. Yet she possessed that deadly combination of beauty, intelligence and self-sufficiency that was a veritable aphrodisiac to eligible men. If only she'd attracted the rogues, she could have satisfied her short-term needs and watched in relief as they edged away, never waiting for her to break things off.

Yet, despite her unsuitability, Victoria always attracted the smart, handsome, sensitive men most women lamented were an endangered species. They were drawn to Victoria, who efficiently broke their hearts when they demanded too much intimacy. She kept hoping they would run off with some woman more worthy of their decency, but they never did. They stuck it out to the bitter end, trying to change her. And in return for their efforts, she fled.

Victoria had long stopped frequenting men too close to home. It was far too complicated. She favored brief relationships with men she met in the far-flung locales in which she worked. At least she knew those love stories had a clear "expire by" date, and it soothed her conscience to know that she would not be viewed as a mercenary heartbreaker when it was time to say goodbye.

But it hadn't worked out according to plan with Daniele.

At the time, Victoria had been an assistant fixer. She flanked more senior managers when they swooped in on a new, troubled hotel opening. She learned the trade from the best in the business, and she had a knack for pinpointing troublesome areas and ironing out management problems in new properties.

The resort on the Tuscan coast had been her first opportunity to fly solo. Even if Victoria often seemed to resolve the most thorny problems singlehandedly and effortlessly, she'd always been operating under the management of a more seasoned colleague. The Tuscany property simply had to work. It was her first opportunity to shine on her own.

And shine she was determined to do. The property was breathtaking, the marketing campaign targeted at the jet-setters. Everything appeared perfect. That is, until the hotel manager she was training took off, leaving a trail of shady business dealings in his wake, and the star chef she'd nabbed from Milan, unwilling to take orders from a fresh-faced young American, followed closely behind.

Victoria had no wiggle room. Defeat was not an option. She needed the victory to impress headquarters.

At first, the handsome young pasta vendor was a mere gadfly. Yet, he also supplied them with other food items and represented a friend's Tuscan vineyards, stocking their ample cellar with fine Tuscan and Piedmont wines. Victoria, steeped in her desperation, refused to give the earnest, young man from Bologna the time of day, let alone listen to his suggestions of what was to be done.

But one day, Daniele caught her in a moment of weakness as she sat alone in the kitchen, a bottle of expensive Barbera open before her, attempting to drown her sorrows.

"Victoria," said the young man who slipped into the seat before her, placing his hand over hers and tracing gentle circles on her palm with his thumb. It felt strangely soothing.

"You have to let me help you," he said, his dark, soulful eyes seemingly looking right through her. "A Tuscan five-star hotel with an AWOL chef can never succeed. Let me help. My family has lots of contacts in Bologna and Milan. Let's get a rising talent here temporarily, someone who wants a shot at running the show. And let's take another look at your supply orders."

He dried the tears that slipped from her eyes; she shivered at the touch of his fingers against her face. He leaned in closer, his lips brushing against her ear as he spoke. "Victoria, you're new to Italy. You don't know how things work yet, and you're not ready to go it alone. I want to help you. Let me."

Daniele did help her. He secured a chef and helped her interview new hotel managers, he helped her to oversee the first successful summer season, to understand what her Italian clients wanted, and to anticipate their needs. Daniele shared his industry knowledge, and he shared her bed. He commuted regularly between Bologna and the Tuscan coast to spend more time with her.

Victoria sensed the danger. She felt herself growing too close to Daniele, breaking from her habit of keeping men at an arm's distance, far from her heart.

She knew she'd mishandled Daniele, allowed herself to become too dependent, but as the hotel flourished and the manager began taking charge, Victoria longed for the next posting in Asia, or Latin America, or even Alaska, somewhere far away from the eager young Italian, with his open, trusting face and the power he held over her when they were alone together. Distance could cure this ache in her heart, she was certain.

But Chicago was impressed with her first solo assignment. Following her Tuscan triumph, they offered her a new property in Modena, just a stone's throw away from Bologna. Her heart sank in direct proportion to Daniele's enthusiasm. Her flawed exit strategy.

Victoria tried to maintain distance, but hotel operations ran smoothly, and Daniele was constantly stopping by or bringing her down to stay at his apartment in Bologna. When it was time for her period of exile, allowing the hotel to run without her, she retreated to Daniele's apartment for two weeks. Playing house was more appealing than she'd imagined. She was helpless to fight him, and so she gave up trying.

Looking back, those were the happiest days of her life. Victoria allowed herself to truly fall in love with Daniele. It wasn't like her earlier experiences falling in love, when, even when you were happy, one eye was always aware of the door and subconsciously devising ways for an eventual exit.

With Daniele, she let down her guard. She grew close to his friends; they became hers. She developed a relationship with his family. She didn't try to steer conversation elsewhere when he discussed their future.

After the Modena project came an assignment in the Veneto and then in Austria. Daniele convinced her to make her base in Bologna, in his apartment. To her surprise, her company agreed.

And that was when things grew complicated. Daniele and Victoria grew closer. Victoria thrived in her job as a hotel startup fix-it woman, but she was equally pleased to wrap things up, turn the hotel over to the new hotel manager so that she could return home to Bologna, Daniele, and their life together.

Daniele sensed this change in Victoria, this small but widening chink in her armor, and he pressed it to his advantage. He started to speak about marriage and, for the first time, Victoria did not feel the urge to flee. They married in Bologna, and Victoria felt things were ideal those first years, until the fights emerged over the decision about when to start a family.

Victoria sipped too far down into her Bosnian coffee, spluttering as the sludgy grinds slid down her throat. She hastily set down the tiny, copper cup and reached for her glass of water. From the minarets around town, the call to prayer filled the air, and she looked up at the leaves swaying gently in the breeze. Victoria breathed in deeply, hoping to inhale the sense of peace.

She stood and continued on her walk, stopping before a cemetery and noting the gravestones. Just like in Sarajevo, she saw that they were all erected for the war victims, mostly 1993, Mostar's worst year. She felt the knot in her stomach as she observed that many of the graves were for young people who should have been out enjoying their town on this bright spring day as young adults, strolling with wives and husbands and new babies in shiny strollers.

Victoria made her way to the Koski mosque, paid her entrance fee and picked up a head scarf provided for female visitors. She gave only a cursory glance at the small mosque before making her way to the steps of the minaret, the steep narrow steps that seemed to go on forever in the narrow stairwell that allowed only cracks of light to filter through. She was relieved to eventually see the golden light filtering into the stairwell, indicating she had finally reached the top.

As Victoria stepped into the bright sunlight, she caught her breath. It was so overwhelmingly perfect. The rugged cliffs to her right. The smooth, glassy surface of aquamarine water of the Neretva River, the lushness of the green trees framing the cool, grey stone of the buildings on either side of the river.

And there, at the center of it all, *Stari most*, the Old Bridge. The ancient Ottoman Bridge was destroyed in the shelling of 1993 and painstakingly rebuilt, stone by original stone. Man had created such beauty, destroyed it, and erected it once again. She admired its high, elegant arch suspended gracefully between two bulky watchtowers, spanning the green-blue waters of the Neretva and casting its shadow below.

A perfect first view, thought Victoria, soaking it all in. Victoria treasured these moments of beauty when she travelled. She stood in absolute silence, willing the image to fix itself in her mind. She felt the warmth of the sun and the light breeze that lifted her hair. She breathed deeply. Surely life should always be filled with perfect moments like these.

LATER IN THE DAY, Victoria sat at an outdoor terrace with a view over the Kriva cuprija, the Crooked Bridge. This smaller Ottoman Bridge spanned a tiny creek, with quick-moving, translucent water flowing beneath the arch and over the grey and golden stones of the creek bed. From her perch on the sun-drenched terrace, Victoria could admire the grey stone bridge and the minaret towering above it. She closed her eyes, tilting her face upward, feeling the sun's rays tanning her cheeks.

The waiter returned with ćevapčići, šopska salad and a bottle of ice-cold Sarajevsko pivo, which he poured into her glass. "Živjeli!"

"Živjeli—to life, it is," Victoria said, holding up her glass. "Thanks, Zoran."

He left her with her meal. She lifted the glass to her lips and sipped the cold beer. Victoria had been glad to drop her pidgin Bosnian when Zoran revealed he'd lived in the States for years and studied at Ohio State. He'd only just recently returned to Mostar to help his family out with their restaurant and tour business.

Placing her glass down on the table, Victoria cut into her ćevapčići, the spicy sausages that became addictive the longer she remained in the Balkans. She'd asked the chef at the Dubrovnik hotel for the recipe, so that she could continue eating these back in Chicago.

After each of her postings abroad, she always needed to take a piece of her new destination back home with her. Victoria could never decide if this was a positive personality trait, indicating how open she was to new cultures and cuisines, or if it simply managed to highlight how unformed her own personality was to feel the intense need to always adopt rituals from other countries.

She took bites of her šopska salad, enjoying the cool textures of the tomatoes and cucumbers alongside the salty shredded cheese. As if on cue, a gypsy band set up at the edge of the Crooked Bridge, playing Balkan music for the tourists passing by and holding out their hats to gather tips.

The frantic music, the rush of the brook, and the taste of the food and beer all blended together into one harmonious feeling of happiness as she ate her meal under the hot Balkan sun.

The gypsy band moved away as Victoria finished the last bites of her sausages and cleared the last forkfuls of salad from her bowl. Beer glass in hand, she gazed again on the elegant lines of the tiny Crooked Bridge, the dainty cousin to the more famous Mostar bridge.

A young man walked up to the bridge's edge, his blond hair shining in the bright sunlight. He leaned over too far, and Victoria felt her heart flutter wildly. Her hand trembled and she dropped her glass, the remains of beer splashing onto her table. Heads all around her turned to stare. Zoran, the young waiter, came quickly to the table.

He brought his face close to hers as he spoke quietly. "Victoria, are you alright?"

She looked into his eyes, not comprehending. Those hazel eyes looked too familiar. She felt a tremor in her hand again and she dropped it into her lap, immobilizing its wrist with her free hand. She took a deep breath and turned towards the blond man, who had been joking for his friend's camera, and was now walking away.

She looked directly into Zoran's eyes. They no longer terrorized her. "I'm fine, thank you. I was silly to get nervous when that man leaned so far over the bridge." She raised her voice for the benefit of her fellow diners. "I was afraid he might fall."

Heads swiveled back to their tables, and Zoran smiled understandingly.

"Maybe I could use a Bosnian coffee," Victoria said. "Calm my nerves and all."

Zoran left and Victoria kept one hand over the other. Her hand could tremble in her lap below the table, where no one else could see. She sat quietly, gazing out at the bridge and the mosque, with its sharp minaret piercing the sky. She concentrated on her breathing, willing the breaths to become slower and shallower. She felt a release of her clenched heart. Normalcy, or its semblance.

Zoran returned some minutes later with the twice-boiled coffee, and she anticipated its soothing effect. He placed the copper tray down, with its beautiful, intricately designed *džezva* that contained the steaming, strong coffee. She saw the familiar sugar cube and a small tray filled with calorie-laden Turkish delight.

Victoria forced a smile. "*Hvala*, Zoran."

"*Molim*, Victoria." He turned toward another diner signaling him.

The trembling had diminished, but it was still present as Victoria grasped the *džezva*'s long handle and poured the rich coffee into the tiny copper cup. She picked up the sugar cube and dipped it in, watching with the fascination of a young child as the coffee worked its way upward, staining the virgin white grains of sugar.

She placed the cube in her mouth, taking a tiny bite and allowing the familiar taste of coffee-tainted sugar to soothe her and diminish her anxiety. She took another bite, and then lifted the coffee cup to her lips, sipping the rich Balkan brew and feeling it course through her body. Her breathing slowed and she gazed on the brook and the Crooked Bridge with the same sense of peace she experienced earlier.

THE SUN WAS STILL HIGH in the afternoon sky as Victoria walked down the stone staircase, past the throbbing music of the terrace bars preparing for their evening clientele, past the souvenir stands selling copperware, kitsch reproductions of the bridge, and shell cartridges gathered from the millions that had rained down on Mostar during the war. Now they sat on display, polished and beautifully carved with images of the Old Bridge, to be taken home with tourists as a macabre reminder of their holiday.

She continued down to the steps until she reached the pebble beach where a group of middle school students were gathered. They threw stones into the Neretva River as their teachers stood together chatting in a group, ignoring their charges.

Victoria found a place to perch on a boulder, far enough from the rock-wielding students for comfort, and looked up, twenty-one meters above her head, to the delicate arch of the *Stari most*. She ignored the shouts of the students and concentrated fully on the dramatic lines of the bridge, so impressive from far below.

The teachers herded up their unruly students and led them back to the stairs. A few minutes later, Victoria had the entire riverbank to herself. She leaned back on her elbows and watched the tourists crossing the bridge, the late afternoon sun setting off their hair. She heard the rush of water dripping down from the tiny waterfall and, for the second time that day, a sense of utter peace enveloped her. She breathed in deeply, feeling the clean air fill her lungs. The past, the mistakes she made back then, were relegated to those distant times, where they belonged. Today, there was only peace, and beauty, and rebuilding destroyed dreams, stone by stone, if necessary.

Victoria did not know how long she stayed still in that position along the riverbank. Ten minutes? A half an hour? Hours?

All she knew was that the low-hanging sun warmed her body, the elegant arch of the Ottoman bridge spanning across the sturdy towers appealed to her aesthetic sensibilities, and she felt eager for the days before her, before she would head back to Dubrovnik, for final closure before the official hand-off. Then it would be a quick detour for another final closure— signing divorce papers before returning home to Chicago. Bologna already seemed far away. She could handle it.

The sense of well-being was so complete that Victoria's eyes were half-closed when she observed the movement at the bridge's highest point. She snapped to attention.

She saw it clearly, the gleam of a little blond head leaning too far over the bridge's edge. Where was his mother? Terror coursed through Victoria's body, every muscle tense with dreadful anticipation. She felt the throbbing in her head, the clutching of her heart. Victoria opened her mouth to yell a warning cry to the distracted mother high above her, but her throat was dry. No sound emerged.

The throbbing in her head grew bolder. It matched the pumping of blood through her veins. She could hear it all, alongside the manic beating of her heart. She feared it would explode. She resisted her terror and allowed her eyes to roam back to the tousled head at the top of the bridge.

Victoria sucked in a deep sigh of relief when she saw a mother's hands at the top of the bridge, clutching the child back from the jaws of death, scolding him for his naughtiness. Victoria caught her breath, felt her heartbeat subside.

"Thank God," she muttered, her voice returning to her. It felt important to Victoria to have command over one bodily function after fear terrorized her.

The bridge, she thought. Blond hair. Hazel eyes. A grip on her shoulder. A smile that made promises. The smashed, lifeless body of a son a mother had been unable to save.

Her heart raced yet again, but this time it was in comprehension. She shook her head at the peaked arch over her head. The bridge. How had she never realized it before? Had she truly done such a consistent job of banishing the memories from her consciousness? It had always been the bridge. Always.

How high had it been? Twenty meters? Perhaps. Certainly, it didn't have the elegant lines designed by Ottoman architects. Upstate New York bridges were functional, sturdy, able to withstand the brutal winters. Her campus bridge was no exception.

The water below was not like the Neretva either, just a narrow ribbon of water at that point, crashing along the boulders. Here, there might be a chance of survival in the deep waters. On her campus, there was none.

Victoria shook her head. She hadn't thought about Derek in years. Even with all the years that had passed since the bridge, she wasn't sure she was ready to think about him now. There had been a reason for banishing him to the deepest recesses of her mind.

She'd changed afterwards. The playfulness was gone, the easy flirtation, a desire for connection. She concentrated on work, and work alone. She threw herself into her classes, her summer internships.

That was when she switched from economics to hotel management. Victoria's professors said she was born for it; so had all the owners of the hotels she'd managed since then. But she knew, deep down, it was simply her way of regaining control, of proving to herself that she could, following the night in which all had been lost so quickly.

Derek. Victoria closed her eyes and allowed her mind to sketch in the face she had banished from her memory. Blond hair, clean-cut, hazel eyes. Strong hands that always found an excuse to reach out and touch her shoulder, gently squeezing. The soldier on the bus earlier that day had brought back memories Victoria had worked so hard to bury long ago.

She breathed deeply and opened her eyes again, observing the bridge with the flow of people who continued to cross it. She shook her head and wiped a tear just spilling over. Shading her eyes from the sun, she looked up once again to the bridge looming above her, and forced herself to think back to that foggy night back on campus during her sophomore year.

Victoria's long, blond hair was pulled into a tight ponytail. She was aware of it swinging back and forth as she walked to the door of the coffee shop. She turned and waved at Lisa, reminded her of their plans to meet for lunch the following day. The coffee coursed through her veins and she felt satisfied she'd managed to jot down an outline for her history paper. It wasn't due for another week, but Victoria liked to be on top of things. She was never one to wait until the last moment.

She had only walked a block in the direction of campus, ready to return to her dorm and another hour of assigned reading before she called it a night, when she heard the sound of drunken men coming up behind her. It was last call and all the drinkers were simultaneously released into College Town, filling the silent street with their raucous yelling.

Victoria was in no mood to bump into drunken classmates or dorm mates, forced to make conversation with them as their eyes struggled to focus on her, trying to ignore how they reeked of cheap beer. The wind was biting and the fog kept visibility low, so she lowered her head and plodded on, concentrating on the reading before her.

"Victoria!"

She heard a drunken voice calling behind her, heard the footsteps running to catch up. Hands reached her shoulder and whirled her around. The fingers continued to clutch her shoulder and she remembered being annoyed to have this intimacy forced upon her. So close, she could see him clearly enough, despite the fog that hung thick in the air. Blond hair, hazel eyes. His eyes expressed everything he felt in his heart.

Derek had been her biology lab partner. If Victoria were honest, she never would have made it through biology without Derek. Derek was pre-med and a genius in biology and chemistry, whereas Victoria was barely scraping by in her science requirement. She worried about the class dragging down her grade point average, and Derek had been only too happy to step in and serve as her knight in shining armor: patiently tutoring her, explaining lab sessions as a teacher might walk a confused first grader through a new concept. And all along, there were the invitations to dinner or out for drinks, the casual brush of his leg or arm against her skin, the ever-present look of hope in his hazel eyes every time he looked at Victoria.

And why hadn't Victoria responded? Partly, because she wasn't accustomed to requiring help. Victoria had always been the star student. Derek's kindness and his patient explanations helped her, but also made her feel inadequate. It was so easy for him and such a struggle for her, and Victoria didn't like dwelling on those feelings.

Then, she imagined, it was his neediness when he was around her. That puppy-dog look of adoration in his eyes. It made her uncomfortable. It felt like too much pressure. She accepted his help, but thwarted his advances.

But on that foggy evening, he stood before her, a telltale glaze to his eyes from too many beers with his friends. His hands continued to grasp her shoulder, his fingers kneading softly. Victoria ignored the soft tingle she felt there, where his skin made contact with hers.

With the alcohol in his system, Derek was braver than usual. He didn't drop his hazel eyes from her gaze. She grew increasingly uncomfortable under his scrutiny, less certain of her convictions.

"Victoria," he said softly, "why can't you feel the same way about me? I'm crazy about you—you know that. I know I could make you happy." Keeping his hand firmly on her shoulder, he leaned towards Victoria and brushed her cheek with his lips.

Victoria didn't feel annoyed, as she would have expected. She felt her heart beat faster. Why had she always been so distant with Derek? Why had she always thwarted his attempts to get closer to her? He was handsome and bright. He was funny. He genuinely cared about her. Was it just pride?

He stood back and searched her eyes. She observed his prominent cheekbones, her reflection in his questioning eyes.

"Victoria, come back to my house—to the living room. I'll make you coffee. We can talk."

She was about to say yes, but something stopped her.

She'd blocked this memory out so long ago. What was it that made her hesitate? Why couldn't she have agreed? A chat and then she could have gone home, if she wanted. Or maybe she would have wanted to stay.

But it all came flooding back. She reached up and removed Derek's fingers from her shoulder, feeling their warmth, the life coursing through them, even as she dropped them away from her body. She shook her head and looked straight into those hopeful eyes. "No, Derek. You're drunk. Go home and sleep it off. I'll see you in biology class on Monday."

She remembered the swirling fog, and the wind rustling through the trees, the sound of the water pounding on the rocks below. The bridge just before them.

The goddamned bridge.

"I'll make you notice me, Victoria. I will." He reached out and grasped her shoulder once more, a brief squeeze before running to meet his friends. His voice through the fog. "Victoria, look at me! Say you'll come with me!"

Victoria ignored his voice and kept walking, but a nagging caused her to stop in her tracks. She heard the drunken laughing of his friends, her name carried by the wind. Her heart sank in her chest as she doubled back to the bridge. She didn't recognize the harsh edge to her voice when it emerged from her mouth. "Derek, get down from there!"

"I've never said no to you, Victoria … but now I will."

She heard the drunken laughs of his buddies as she came closer to him. His form took shape against the fog. Damn it, he was standing on the ledge, just as she'd feared.

"Derek, please get down." Her voice was softer now, fear strangling it in her throat.

"I'll just walk to the other side, show you what a hero I am. Then you'll have to notice me."

"Derek, you're drunk." She heard the desperation in her voice. "Please get down." She heard the asinine laughing of his idiot drinking buddies. He took one step, then another. Her heart was racing, as she pleaded silently for him to get down.

"You see, Victoria?"

Through the fog, she saw the flash of that smile, those hazel eyes gazing at her, instead of the edge of the stone bridge. *Get down, you idiot. What the hell are you doing?*

Another step. Another. "Almost there, see Victoriaaaaaaaa …"

She'd spent years repressing that memory, had almost succeeded, but now it hit her as hard as it had on that awful night. Derek stumbled, lost his balance and fell over the edge. She heard the sound of her name echoing down to the boulders below. Everything else was a blur. Her desperate screams, the wail of an ambulance. The rescue workers who climbed down, unable to do anything. Rescue workers took her away. Drips and medications. Her groggy thoughts. Snatches of scenes from that night that kept swirling back in her head.

Meeting Derek's parents was the worst. They visited her in the hospital. His mother cried, telling Victoria how much she had meant to her son, what hopes they had pinned on him, what a dear, sensitive boy he had always been. Derek's father stood behind his wife. His eyes were the same hazel color, but there was no life in them.

Don't you understand, woman? It's all my fault. If he hadn't been trying to get my attention, he would still be here today! Don't you realize I killed your son? He offered me his heart, and I looked right through him … as if he didn't even exist.

Victoria never said any of those words. The sedatives had the desired effect. Victoria did not attend the funeral. Her parents insisted she return home for some weeks, before returning to campus. She joined two other lab partners for biology, and the professor was forgiving for the rest of the semester. More forgiving than he should have been.

Victoria concentrated exclusively on her schoolwork. That's when she switched into the university's School of Hotel Management. She had a knack for it, a skill for controlling everything around her. Rather amusing, when she thought about it, since her own life was such a mess.

But the more she focused on her work, the better she felt. She kept men at a distance, shied away quickly if they got too close.

Even Daniele. Here she'd convinced herself all these years that it was her work and her drive, but it was her attempt to run from the trauma of her youth. From the guilt.

Still gazing up at the bridge, she picked up her cellphone and dialed the familiar number.

"*Ciao, Daniele. Sono io.* I'm here in Mostar ... Yes, it is beautiful. But I'm calling you because I need to talk. I have a lot of things to explain to you. Things I wasn't even willing to admit to myself. Can you come? .... You can? Oh, thank you. If you get a flight to Dubrovnik, I'll make arrangements for the hotel to pick you up and drive you here ... *Grazie, Daniele.*"

Victoria breathed in deeply and stood up, her eyes still on the bridge. She saw the young, blond child who had given her a scare earlier, now crossing over it, his mother's hand firmly in his own. From far above, the child saw her and he waved down.

She smiled and waved up at him, his hair catching the light as he crossed over the Old Bridge and disappeared into the golden light of the setting sun.

MOURNING

Milan

"OSSIGNORA," Maria sobbed, making the sign of the cross before fingering her rosary. "When I think of a woman—at your age—being left all alone."

Shawna watched Maria's enormous breasts heave under the heavy black fabric. *I shall go raving mad if she keeps this up all evening.* Shawna tensed her jaw and turned her gaze out the window. The rain pattered insistently against the window pane, nearly obliterating the view over the *Duomo*. Only the tip of the golden *Madonnina*, bravely peeking out from an opening in the thick shroud of fog, was visible.

Milan's dreary spring and the need to make arrangements were colluding against Shawna, holding her hostage in a gilded cage when she desperately needed to clear her head with walks in the fresh air. Shawna longed to wander Milan's streets and visit its dark churches, with their flickering candlelight. She wished to stand at the edge of the Navigli as the sun slipped from the sky, at the moment when the bars and restaurants lining the canals turned on their lights for happy hour traffic.

Instead, Shawna was a virtual prisoner in her fashionable

Brera apartment. She felt the towering walls, laden with their priceless art, close in on her as she wandered its grand rooms and empty bedrooms, while Maria wailed incessantly and a small army of household staff came and went.

The phone rang throughout the day. At first, Shawna insisted Maria answer and tell callers she was indisposed. But that could only work for a limited time. With the funeral approaching, Shawna had to speak directly with callers, arrange their attendance, listen to the ceaseless flow of well-meant condolences for Massimiliano's death. Her husband, her recently deceased husband, was seemingly known by everyone. By each day's end, she was exhausted.

She'd known, of course, and for quite some time. The doctors had been nothing if not honest with her. Even Massimiliano, while he was still lucid, knew the end was near. Her husband's excessive wealth meant that he could buy a comfortable exit. His last days would not be spent in some depressing, antiseptic-smelling hospital room.

The master bedroom had been fitted out with all the necessary equipment. Milan's best oncologists were on call. A team of nurses worked in shifts, their slim, young figures garbed in white as they bustled efficiently around his bed, ensuring his comfort. Massimiliano appreciated female beauty. Shawna knew he took pleasure in those attractive, ready-to-please faces around his bed as the end drew near.

Shawna hadn't had the heart to move back into the master bedroom after Massimiliano passed away. She tried the first night, but she slept poorly and decamped to a guest bedroom the following day.

Maria's unceasing wails broke her concentration, and Shawna observed gnarled fingers handling rosary beads. Suddenly, the old woman looked up, meeting Shawna's wide blue gaze with her own watery brown eyes.

"And to think," she wailed, "that I began here when Signor Massimiliano was just a young man. So young and handsome and full of life. And now," she trailed off, once again making the sign of the cross, "he is with our Lord." The last word dissolved in another wave of inconsolable sobs.

Shawna turned back to the window. The fog still hung thick in the air, but the rain was lessening. "I should go out and speak to Father Giovanni," she said, striding towards the entrance hall.

"Oh, no, *Signora* Shawna," said the old woman, following her. "Please let me go! You should not be arranging everything."

No, I shouldn't. You're paid to work for me. But her choice of words was different. "I'd prefer to do it myself. Massimiliano told me how he wanted everything at the funeral." She belted her coat and picked up the umbrella, nodding to Maria without making eye contact.

Her tension eased once she was out of the house and on the streets. The day was still grey. Shawna often thought Whistler could have painted his *Arrangement in Grey and Black* just as effectively by posing his mother on any Milan street during springtime. There wasn't much she missed about rural Alabama after nearly a quarter century in Italy, but Milan's dismal weather would sometimes make her pine for the sun and blue sky of her youth.

People scurried through the streets as Shawna walked past the Castello Sforzesco. She looked at window displays on the Corso Magenta, where she contemplated, and quickly dismissed, having an aperitivo at the Bar Magenta.

Continuing on to the Sant'Ambrogio Basilica, she paused at its twelfth-century portico and fourth-century basilica. Although she wasn't raised Catholic and didn't convert when they married, she'd been many times to services at this church with Massimiliano. He'd been baptized here at the basilica dedicated to Milan's patron saint. They'd attended services for Christmas, Easter, and Saint Ambrose's Day celebrations each 7 December, often acknowledging the same acquaintances they would see later in the evening for opening night at La Scala.

But her agenda, as she entered the church, was a solemn one. She proceeded through the dark interior to an office, where she inquired after Father Giovanni. The smell of incense filled the air, and Shawna took deep breaths, the familiar smell calming her nerves.

"*Signora* Shawna!" boomed the voice of a slight man, dressed in his robes. "Ah, my dear. You look as if you haven't slept in days. Come in, come in." He ushered her into his office.

When all the arrangements for the funeral service were finalized, Father Giovanni turned his kind eyes to her. "I've been thinking about you, and how hard these next weeks might be on you. This is an abbey in Liguria." He slid a brochure across the desk. "I have spoken to them about you. You're welcome to spend some days or weeks there, if you wish."

Shawna looked up quickly from the brochure filled with photos of a lovely abbey, set up in the hills, with the Ligurian Sea lying just beyond. She was certain her confusion was evident in her eyes.

Father Giovanni's baritone laugh calmed her.

"Don't worry. No conversion, I promise." He winked at her. "They arrange to host visitors wishing for a short retreat and some time to reflect."

Shawna looked again at the brochure. An abbey overlooking the sea, simple dinners in the refectory, the calming smell of incense in the abbey church, a few days away from her life in Milan. Perhaps.

THE CEREMONY WAS BEAUTIFUL, just as Massimiliano would have wanted it.

Despite Maria's wails throughout the week, she and the other household staff handled everything brilliantly: catering from Peck's, fine Tuscan wines from Massimiliano's own cellar. Her house was filled with her husband's friends and acquaintances, accumulated over eight decades, all mingling around the spacious dining and living room.

A grey-haired man in an impeccable dark suit approached her. "Shawna, what a beautiful service today. I just wanted to convey our condolences before I leave for my flight."

"Of course, Senator." She nodded politely. She had always been uncomfortable with Massimiliano's close friendships with so many politicians.

"I can hardly believe Massimiliano is gone." A worried crease disfigured his handsome, perfectly tanned brow. "I know it's indelicate to ask you so soon, but if you're thinking about selling Massimiliano's plane, I'm eager to purchase it."

She looked up quickly, then struggled to hide her surprise.

"And, of course," he lowered his voice, "I'd offer you a good price."

She nodded politely and signaled Maria to see him out. Fewer people remained when Leone barged through the door, pupils dilated, unsteady on his feet. Shawna clenched her fists beneath her Chanel sleeves, digging her nails into her palms, and staving off the panic rising in her chest.

Leone, Massimiliano's troubled son from his first marriage, had stormed off after the funeral service. He had, of course, been invited to his father's home following the mass. Admittedly, Shawna felt only relief when he refused, taking off like the pampered, spoiled child he'd always been.

Judging from his appearance, he'd found his regular pusher at *Stazione centrale* and squandered more of his father's money on what he called his "recreational habit."

"*Signore e signori*," he hollered, clinking on a wine glass. "I hope you're all enjoying my father's food and wine … and the company of my father's legal whore. Now that *papà* is gone, I'm sure she'll be available to service any of you. Do I hear any bidders?"

Calm down, thought Shawna, feeling all eyes upon her. A burly nephew of Massimiliano's immediately shuffled Leone away. The well-bred guests strained to pretend nothing had happened, taking their leave as soon as etiquette would allow.

Later that evening, Shawna approached Maria. "Please arrange for the car tomorrow. I shall be going for some days to an abbey for a period of quiet reflection. I do not wish to be disturbed."

Shawna turned on her heel to avoid the shock she was certain to see in Maria's eyes.

SHE'D SLIPPED THE DRIVER a thick wad of cash to keep him quiet, but Shawna was taking no chances as she asked to be let out at Genova's port. She lifted her own bag and click-clacked along the docks in her high heels.

When she approached the luxury yacht Massimiliano kept moored at Genova's port, young Leonardo was standing at attention on board and hurried to assist with her bag.

With a quick salute, he said, "My heartfelt condolences, *Signora* Spadaro."

"*Grazie*, Leonardo." She walked past him onto the boat, noticing he wore the ridiculous white uniform Massimiliano insisted upon, although it did enhance the Sicilian skipper's deep tan and dark eyes. "I'll want to rest ... and to leave right away."

"Of course, *Signora.*"

Shawna moved to the upstairs deck and settled deep into a lounge chair, melting into the plush pillows and feeling the tension of the past days ease away as the boat left the harbor. Shawna observed Genova's medieval turrets and towers fade in the distance. She forgot all about Leone's hateful words following the funeral, Maria's constant wailing and declarations that Massimiliano was a saint and, at the age of eighty-five, "taken away too soon."

Instead, Shawna concentrated on Liguria's stunning coastline. Her hair whipped in the wind, and she felt a sense of happiness and freedom she hadn't experienced in a long time, certainly wouldn't have felt hidden away in some abbey.

They'd never know back in Milan. After all, the boat was hers now.

Later, after they harbored at Portofino, Shawna sipped her Bellini. The *prosecco* bubbles tickled her lips, and the sweetness of peach brought a satisfied smile to her face. The San Martino church bells chimed, reverberating off the surrounding hills.

She gazed out over the crystal-clear blue water, its gentle waves capturing the golden sunlight. The oranges, yellows and reds of the picturesque, portside villas shimmered in the brilliant noon light. How she longed to own one of those villas, and to languish in the warmth of one of those sun-drenched balconies, a place to finally feel content and fulfilled.

"*Dai, Shawna. Sono pronto. Vieni giù!*"

Shawna turned towards the insistent voice, a flicker of anger momentarily marring her chemically preserved face. It dissipated just as quickly as her gaze fell upon the rippling muscles of the bare-chested young man emerging from the cabin's hold.

The sun glinted off the boyish, tousled curls of his ebony hair as Shawna admired his taut skin, his muscular build, the boundless energy she knew she'd experience when she followed him down to their swaying cabin.

Leonardo was no genius, that was obvious. But in the end, she was just a girl raised in the cotton fields of Alabama, albeit a comely one who'd been schooled on the finer things of life—and turned out to be a model student. She'd long ago determined that the few moments of stolen pleasure during furtive groping in the cab of Jesse's pickup truck would only lead to a lifetime of misery. And so, she'd vowed to reinvent herself.

Yet, even in her wildest imaginings, her younger, provincial self had never envisioned the levels of wealth and sophistication she would one day attain.

Not bad for a girl who came to Milan to flaunt her face and body on the fashion capital's catwalks. When her dreams failed to materialize, she'd adjusted her ambitions, working as a *cubista*—one of those scantily clad women who dance suggestively on a raised box for night club clientele—to pay the rent. She'd been ogled by Italian actors, soccer players, businessmen, and far too many politicians to recall. They'd invited her to the VIP lounge, where they'd sip expensive champagne and, as often as not, white envelopes flush with cash would be exchanged for stolen moments of intimacy.

Shawna had her regular admirers, as she chose to call them. The most insistent, her most ardent follower, was a wealthy manufacturer of luxurious fabrics for Milan's top designers. Massimiliano, who was forty-five years her senior, appeared to be living on borrowed time. She didn't hesitate when he proposed and promised to change her life.

After marrying Massimiliano, presiding over his fashionable Brera apartment, and hosting their privileged Milan soirées, everyone seemed to forget her less-than-illustrious "early career." Even powerful men whose furtive desires she'd satisfied on the velvet couches of the VIP lounge now kissed her warmly on the cheeks when they met at La Scala, or on the slopes of Cortina, or in fashionable Milan dining rooms.

And now, here she was. A woman of means, thanks to Italian inheritance laws, with no strings attached. Had she not longed for this day?

She had everything her long-frozen heart could desire: Leonardo waiting to entertain her that afternoon and, a few days later, once the will had been read and the furor died down, she would find herself in Paris with Sébastien. Not as young and unflagging as Leonardo, but, with his innate culture and sophistication, Sébastien could ease her entrée into the right Parisian society, just as Massimiliano had done for her in Milan.

And Shawna liked keeping all of her options open. Her marriage had taught her important lessons. Money could buy you anything. Or anyone. And the origins of wealth were forgotten far more quickly than one would imagine.

Shawna looked up at the cloudless blue sky over the bell tower and blew a kiss heavenward. "*Grazie,* Massimiliano."

Yes, she had used her husband, there was no denying that. But he had used her, too. For twenty years she'd paid her dues, never imagining he'd hold out so long.

Shawna walked toward the stairs, unbuttoning her dress and stepping out of it, scrupulously ensuring that her Fratelli Rossetti heels did not snare the luxurious heap of hand-spun silk.

The sun caressed her body. She looked down to admire her toned limbs and still-perfect curves, never compromised by the horrendous trials of childbirth, now encased in their lacy La Perla armor.

"When I think of a woman—at my age—being left all alone," she whispered to the gently lapping waves, a smile of satisfaction spreading across her face, before she descended down the stairs to claim her afternoon of pleasure.

MISSED CONNECTIONS
Florence

LAURA OFTEN THOUGHT ABOUT IT as she went about her housework.

It was never obsessive, as in *I can't believe the opportunities I squandered when I had the chance.* But a little voice lodged itself in the back of her mind and taunted her, causing her to question her decisions, before she sought to lose herself in the immediate tasks that kept her fingers busy and her mind concentrated.

It was better when the house was full of noise and activity, the nagging doubts held at bay.

Laura looked up from sewing Francesca's end-of-school-year play costume. The old backpack lay at her feet. A long life of travel, decades-worth of train trips and flights, had finally caught up with it. Split at the seams, it revealed a crumpled piece of paper that had been slumbering deep within.

Earlier that morning, Laura smoothed the paper gently on her lap. A sob caught in her throat. Thick black letters, scrawled in a confident hand, caused her heart to beat faster. A name. A contact. A wish.

A light breeze tousled her hair. She looked up. Swallows hurtled through the blue sky, unmarred by even one cloud. Just like a similar May day on a train, so many years ago.

LAURA PRESSED HER FACE to the train window. Brunelleschi's dome dwarfed the skyline, its red tiles distinct against the bright blue May sky.

Pietro had promised to take her to Florence that week, her first visit.

With her semester abroad in Brussels wrapping up, she'd come to visit him before her last weeks in Belgium and her return trip to Michigan. Now she wished she'd secured a summer internship in Europe, rather than her camp counselor job in Ann Arbor, yet again.

For Laura always erred on the side of caution, a shadow forty-year-old trapped inside an attractive twenty-year-old's body. Even the year abroad seemed out of character, too adventuresome for the cautious woman she strove to be.

Everyone sensed it eventually. Her classmates, her friends, past boyfriends. Laura was bright and pretty, but eventually others tired of her for what she lacked: that spark, that effervescence she noticed in girls she longed to count as friends, and in men from whom she instinctively withdrew.

That absence of a spark attracted her to Pietro. No one would call Pietro wild or spontaneous. No danger lurked within. Pietro was a shadow forty-year-old, too, with the added benefit of being Italian, and thereby, exotic to Laura.

The train pulled into the Santa Maria Novella station. She watched the people scurrying on the busy platform. "Firenze," she read aloud from the sign, trying to roll the "r."

"Not bad," said a voice beside her. "You must be here for Italian courses."

She detected an Irish accent. A tall figure hoisted his bulging backpack to the overhead rack. With his back turned, she observed broad shoulders, sandy blond hair, and sinewy arm muscles straining with the effort. When he turned, his bright blue eyes caught her momentarily off-guard. A hint of danger.

Laura offered a tight smile and returned to the book that had fallen open in her lap.

"*The Unbearable Lightness of Being.* Something tells me you're headed to Prague. The border guards ask you if you've read it before they let you in."

Laura met those eyes. She knew the type—the flirt, the dangerous one. "Yes, I'll be going to Prague with some friends, but I didn't know it was law. I'm sorry it's such a cliché for you." She narrowed her eyes. "Tell me, what does a worldly man such as you read while he's on a train?"

He smiled sheepishly, producing a comic book.

"*Dylan Dog,* I see. Perhaps you shouldn't be lecturing others." She flipped silently through its pages. "At least you get points for originality. It's in Italian. Or do you just look at the pictures?"

His smile was slightly crooked. It made him even more handsome.

"No points. Mum's Italian, so I'm Irish-Italian. It's not really hard to read in my *madrelingua.* What're you doing in Italy?"

"Visiting my boyfriend in Rome."

"Ah … an Italian boyfriend. I never recommend that." He offered the crooked smile once again. "Unless he's Irish-Italian, of course."

Laura couldn't help but smile, too.

"I'm Riccardo."

"Laura. Nice to meet you."

"So where did you meet your Italian?"

Clearly Laura would get no reading done, but truth be told, the words had been swirling on the page the past hour. It had been a long trip; she didn't mind company. "In Brussels during my semester abroad. Pietro was there for an EU accounting project."

"You live for excitement, don't you? You go to Brussels for your semester abroad and you find an accountant. Living life on the wild side, aren't we?"

"I happen to like Brussels, okay? It might not be Paris, but it's pretty nice."

"So why didn't you go to Paris?"

"Because I ... Listen, no offense. I just want to get some reading done."

She opened her book and pretended to read, but he'd hit a nerve. Laura often asked herself the same question. Paris had seemed big and daunting, an overload of the senses. Brussels was easier ... less risky. Just like Pietro.

And when you'd grown up like she had, in a house with all the chaos and drama you could handle from your unreliable, drunken father and spineless victim of a mother, safe and steady were damned good options. Brussels and Pietro were about as reliable as you could get.

"Laura, I'm sorry. I'm an ass. What can you expect when you mix an Irishman and an Italian?"

Riccardo smiled at her again.

She shook her head. "Okay. But no more digs."

He held up his hands. "Promise ... just one question. Name five famous Belgians."

Laura rolled her eyes. "As if I haven't heard this a million times. Brueghel *père et fils*, Jean-Claude Van Damme ... and *basta*."

"Ah, so you do have a sense of humor about your adoptive city."

She sighed. "You've interrogated me. What is it you do, Riccardo?"

"I'm an archaeologist. I'm visiting my mum in Naples, then I fly to Cambodia. The Khmer Rouge have mostly surrendered and archaeological missions are returning. I'll be up at Angkor."

Laura heard the excitement in his voice, noticed the spark in his eyes.

"I have friends there working on de-mining and setting up schools. Wanna see pictures?"

He looked like a child on Christmas morning as he passed her pictures. She saw photos of families crowded on the steps of huts on stilts, of some of the most adorable children she'd ever seen, skinny with bare feet, all standing in a one-room hut decorated with bright posters—a school Riccardo's friends had built. There were photos of markets, photos of scooters transporting live pigs splayed across back fenders. His face grew animated as he showed her the temples, explaining their history, the damage that time and war had wrought, the ever-present danger of mines.

Riccardo was the opposite of safe and reliable. He was passionate, risk-taking. Exactly the type of person she instinctively avoided. Yet, sitting beside him on the train, his leg brushing her own as he explained, with such raw passion in his voice, the work he would be doing, she felt her inner forty-year-old begin to fade.

"Why don't you come with me next week?"

Gazing at a photo of dawn at Angkor Wat, Laura didn't make the connection immediately.

"Excuse me?"

"Dump the accountant. Come to Naples. Join me."

She blushed.

"My friends need help with their school. I'll buy you the ticket—no strings attached. We can just be friends if you don't fall madly in love with me, but I'm guessing you will."

"You would imagine that, yes." Laura studied him. "And my last year at the University of Michigan?"

"Take a gap year. Learn Khmer. Get real-life experience. How long has the university been around? It'll still be there when you get back."

The train was approaching Rome. Riccardo pulled a piece of paper from his pocket and wrote his name, number and a message: "Take a chance. Join me on this adventure, Laura. We could be good together."

Laura stared at the words in silence. Her brain conjured up images of her father, a life wasted chasing dreams. But for the first time, she wondered what it would be like to live life as a carefree twenty-year-old, not to be so scared. She looked up to see those blue eyes imploring her.

The train pulled into the station. She slid the paper into her backpack.

"Think about it, Laura." He stood and kissed her on both cheeks. "I'll wait to hear from you."

Her skin tingled where his lips met her flesh. Laura stepped down to the platform in a daze. She waved at the blond-haired man observing her from the window and walked the length of the platform to Pietro. He stepped forward and kissed her, a lifeless kiss compared to Riccardo's lips brushing her cheek in the cabin.

"You must be exhausted after your trip. Hope it wasn't too miserable," he said in that even, business-like voice she used to admire.

"No. Not miserable at all."

She followed him into the metro station and felt a movement at her back. Confused, she turned around. "Stop, thief!" she yelled. A gypsy boy darted through the crowds.

"Damn it, Laura! How many times have I told you not to keep your wallet in your backpack?"

Laura sank to the dirty steps of Termini, rifling through the zipped compartment. Her wallet was gone, but so was Riccardo's paper. Tears streamed down her cheeks.

LAURA OBSERVED THE CRUMPLED PAPER in her lap. Riccardo's plea for her to join him. The thief hadn't stolen it. It had been trapped in the backpack's lining all these years.

The whole world had changed in that interval. She'd Googled Riccardo and saw photos of him with his wife, alongside their beautiful Cambodian-Irish-Italian children. He was a professor of archaeology in Cambodia, and, according to his website, the couple ran children's charities in Siem Reap. Laura squinted her eyes and tried to imagine her face next to Riccardo's. Her life of adventure.

Instead, she looked at the clock. Francesca must be picked up from school, Pietro would want dinner on the table when he returned. There was no time for daydreaming.

Laura folded up the paper and slipped it deep down in her lingerie drawer. She stepped out the door, and into her safe life.

THE RING

Bergen

VALERIA ADJUSTED HER GOGGLES, took a deep breath and launched herself off the edge of the pool. She plunged under water until she broke the surface, arching one practiced arm in the air. Breath-stroke-stroke-breath, stroke-stroke-breath.

Her muscles groaned with the effort. It had probably been a mistake to have raised all the weights at yesterday's gym session. She'd known she would pay the following day, but she still felt invincible as she cut through the water with strength and speed. *Take that, Carlo.*

She flipped and pushed off the edge, accelerating for the last length. She touched the wall as if she were in contention for an Olympic medal. However, unlike the genuine champions who basked in adulation from their fans, the senior citizens didn't flinch from their adjacent aqua gym class—flabby arms flailing joyfully to the rhythms of Gloria Gaynor's "I Will Survive."

"Okay, Federica Pelligrini," said a familiar voice in the next lane. "I think you're done winning medals for the day. What do you say about making moves to get back to the office?"

"Killjoy." She shook her head at Manuela's comment and pulled off her goggles before straining her painful biceps to propel herself over the pool's edge. Everything had been so much easier when she'd been sixteen. But no point in allowing her body to believe it could slide into middle-age frumpiness before its time.

She slipped her feet into flip-flops and wrapped the inviting robe around her dripping form. With Manuela beside her, they shuffled their way to the showers, trading the scent of chlorine for that of high-end beauty products.

Following a respite under the welcome shower jets, the women emerged warm, clean and fully de-chlorinated. Wrapping robes once more around their bodies, they made their way to the bank of hairdryers.

"I wish I could just tuck my hair under my hood," said Manuela. "But it's way too cold to go out like this. Why does Rome feel like Siberia this winter? And it sucks because I need to get back for my two thirty."

"What's the point?" asked Valeria, sliding the comb through her long tresses and working out the knots. "You know Marco's gonna make a big show about completely restyling the packaging, and the fireworks will only be some minor change to the color scheme or the fonts." She tossed down the comb and picked up the dryer. "Typical Marco. It's always the same. The more he hypes it up, the harder it is to spot the changes. What a waste of time."

Manuela had conquered her own battle with knots and was now drying her shoulder-length hair, with its complicated system of layers. "Anyway, you have no right to complain, *Signora* Going-to-Bergen-for-the-fifth-year-in-a-row. I wish I were headed to Norway tomorrow."

Valeria shot a pained look at her friend. "I wish you were, too."

Manuela caught her glance in the mirror. "Are you going to be okay? Will this be a distraction? Or will it just make it worse?"

Valeria held her friend's gaze as long as she dared, willing the tears away. Her voice was subdued under the roar of the dryers. "Yeah, it won't be easy to be back without him this year." She sighed. "But thank God he changed industries. Can you imagine me having to go back to face him there among the same crowds? People who haven't seen us in a year and would have assumed we were still together. The humiliation."

"No need for humiliation from your side." Manuela's eyes blazed in fury. "It's not your fault he can't keep it in his pants."

Valeria closed her eyes and sighed again. "Yeah, but it *is* my fault I wasted five years of my life with the *stronzo*." She clicked off the dryer and styled her curls. "I'm not getting any younger. And my sell-by date is becoming more pronounced every day."

"Aw, c'mon." Manuela finished smoothing her hair and applied her makeup. "You're being ridiculous."

"I wish I were. You wouldn't get it. You and Gianni have been together forever. A baby on the way." She looked down pointedly at the tiny bump under Manuela's robe. "You have *no idea* how people look at you when you reach our age and can't hold down a relationship. Like there's something wrong with you." She shook out the part in her long hair. "I'm a disaster. Two back-to-back serious relationships where the guy's backed out, without any heartache or regrets from his side. As if it had never really mattered. The woman no man wants. It's like other guys sniff it out, pick out that scent of defeat clinging to you wherever you go ... and they stay away. Far away." She placed the hairdryer down into its holder and began to apply her mascara carefully. Her big, blue eyes were one of her best features, and she always ensured her makeup and clothes accentuated them.

"C'mon. You're blowing things out of proportion."

Valeria twisted a perfectly behaved curl into submission, keeping her hands busy as her anger burned within. "It's not, though. I see it in their eyes as men are sizing me up. I can read their thoughts. Late thirties. Never been married, never even engaged. I've become expert in that look they cast over me. And it's not the same for men. Late thirties, forties, hell, even fifties and never married—they're just playboys out having a bit of fun, still allergic to settling down. More power to them, that's what people think." She took a deep, controlled breath. "For women—for me—it's entirely different. We're pathetic in their eyes. It would be better if I were divorced. Or even widowed. At least they'd see me as someone a man once wanted." She released her long-suffering curl. "Not the woman who's constantly jilted for someone better. Someone younger."

Manuela stopped her preening and caught her friend's gaze in the mirror. A brief look of pity etched itself across her face, before she transformed it into a tentative smile. "I know this blindsided you, but you can't get into a rut. He's really not worth it." She reached down for her friend's hand. "Tomorrow you'll be up with all those hot Scandinavian guys. You'll forget all about him." She looked pointedly at the clock. "Okay, pep talk's over. I need to get back for that useless meeting."

They returned to the lockers and dressed in silence. Wrapping themselves in thick coats and scarves and hoisting gym bags over their shoulders, they made their way to the door. Manuela stopped short in front of a homemade sign. "*Dio mio*. Look at this."

Her face was so close to the sign, Valeria couldn't read anything. Manuela turned back and wiped away a tear. "That is so incredibly sad."

"What is?" asked a bored Valeria.

"I left a valuable ring in the locker room yesterday," Manuela read from the notice. "I need to find it. My husband died in a tragic accident and I had a jeweler solder our wedding rings together." She turned back to Valeria. "There's a photo of the design. She writes, inside are our engraved names—Marek and Anežka. I'll offer any reward. Please help return this memory of my deceased husband to me. It feels like it's all I have left of him and our love." Manuela turned back, her eyes shining through a film of tears. "Okay, I know my hormones are all over the place, but that's the saddest thing ever." She sniffled. "Do you know what kind of names Marek and Anežka are?"

Valeria tilted her head. "Czech, maybe Slovak. Remember we had a Marek from Prague on an internship with us a couple of years ago?" She looked at the sign. "The notice is in perfect Italian." She peered carefully at the photo.

Manuela wiped at her eyes. "Oh, that poor woman. I hope she finds it."

She walked to the door. Valeria stayed a moment longer, examining the unusual ring in the black-and-white photo. She whispered, "I hope she does, too," before following her friend out of the locker room.

THE ONLY ADVANTAGE of being scheduled on the day's first flight out was that the pre-sunrise road to Fiumicino was virtually empty. Rome looked completely different in those early morning hours when only taxis traversed the city's deserted roads. Rome was most certainly not in competition for the City That Never Sleeps title. Although one had to wake up at an ungodly hour like she had this morning to discover how much sleeping the Romans apparently did.

After twenty minutes of traffic-free driving, the taxi arrived at the airport, where it deposited Valeria and her luggage. She maneuvered her way through check-in and the security check, ready to relax with a cappuccino before making her way to the gate.

Even with the caffeine, she'd still sleep on the flight. Some women, when dumped, found it hard to sleep. For Valeria, dumpee status always had the opposite effect. Tired all the time, she was ready to collapse in exhaustion the moment she returned from work, groaning at the sound of the alarm clock each morning, regardless of how many hours she'd slumbered.

How could Carlo have destroyed her like this, when they'd been talking about making things official? She'd done everything right. Giving him his space. Not too needy. Not too distant. Thoughtful gifts and home-cooked dinners. Listening in rapt attention to all his complaints about his work day, but never expecting him to be her sounding board, especially if a soccer game was on TV. And there always was. Technically, her position was more senior than his, but she'd always downplayed her role, pretending he had the more important job at the company. All that effort, and still he'd dumped her. For someone younger and even more pliable than she'd been. Five years together meant nothing to him. The absence of a biological clock did that to men, she supposed. He could take his time and wait to settle down whenever it was most convenient to him.

She stopped at a café and ordered a cappuccino, observing in silence as the barista foamed the milk and poured the froth into a perfect heart. She smiled at him and carried it over to the table, settling the coffee and her newspaper onto the countertop. Scanning the headlines, she saw more news about some virus spreading through some distant Chinese city she'd never heard of, people being locked into their homes to prevent its spread. If the photos were to be believed, they were barricaded in their homes from the outside. She shook her head at the brutality of it, thankful such things could never happen in Italy.

When was that upcoming trip to Hong Kong scheduled? Must be April. Plenty of time for this to blow over, just like SARS and the swine flu had in past years.

She scanned the rest of the front page. Yet more bad news. Way too early in the day to start depressing herself. At least she didn't speak Norwegian. The papers could be filled with the most tragic news each day and she'd be none the wiser.

She tucked the paper into her carrycase and leaned back in her chair. Lifting the cappuccino to her lips, she took a long sip and scanned the passageway. The same space, only a few hours later, would be filled with more businesspeople and families, racing to get to connecting flights. At this hour, the terminal played host to a mere trickle of human traffic.

She watched a little girl yawning and clutching a teddy bear to her narrow chest. Her tiny hand was clutched in that of her mother, who was barking orders into her cellphone. The woman's heels were clicking assuredly with long strides, the little girl clearly not up to the task of keeping up. Valeria watched the exhausted girl somehow break free from her mother's grasp, slumping to the shiny floor and placing her thumb in her mouth decisively. Her mother, without ever detaching her cellphone from her ear, scooped her daughter up with her free hand, perched her on her hip and clacked hurriedly away, never losing her stride.

Valeria followed the little girl's bouncing brown curls along the corridor. Her heart stopped when mother and daughter passed a tall man in an expensive camel hair coat, frantically tapping his phone. She placed her coffee cup down and tilted her head, but the man was turned at an awkward angle.

The expensive, designer coat had been a recent Christmas present. The thick, glossy hair. The broad shoulders. The confident stance. Surely, it couldn't be. Her heart raced. Her breath was ragged. She stared without moving a muscle, but when he finished texting, he turned to examine the departures board and she released the relieved breath she hadn't realized she'd been holding.

An older man than she'd imagined.

Not Carlo.

Thank God.

She took the final sip of her now-cold cappuccino and willed her nerves to calm. This was happening too often. Maybe Manuela was right. This conference would be filled with Scandinavian men. She should focus on that. A distraction.

Decisively, she stood up and placed a hand on her trolley. She had a plane to catch, and her mind would be clearer with another two hours of sleep on this flight. She walked with confidence towards her gate.

"WE HAVE BEGUN OUR DESCENT to Schiphol airport. Weather conditions on the ground are five degrees and foggy. We will soon arrive at our destination. Flight crew, prepare for landing."

Valeria's eyes snapped open with the captain's announcement. She glanced at her watch. She'd fallen asleep the moment she'd clicked her seatbelt in place and had slept for the entire flight.

The fake Carlo sighting had confused her, and the in-flight nap allowed her a chance to detach. Since he dropped the bombshell, every tall, dark-haired man appeared to be her ex. This had to stop. Carlo moved on without any regrets, why couldn't she?

Maybe Manuela was right. She needed this time away to shake her out of this lethargy.

She couldn't keep playing the victim. Yes, she and Carlo had been together in Bergen for past conferences, but that didn't mean she couldn't return and make it hers. Valeria without

Carlo. Women were few and far between at these events; surely, she could find some Scandinavian heartbreaker to take her mind off the man who so ungraciously dumped her. She straightened in her seat and looked down at the myriad of channels still visible through the fog. She could do this. She popped a mint in her mouth and sucked it as the pressure played havoc with her ears.

The familiar airport came into view.

SHE STEPPED OUT OF THE STORE with the ubiquitous white bag with colorful windmills that branded her an obvious tourist at Schiphol. Which she was. But her return flight stopped through Oslo, so now was the only time to stock up on her gouda cheese and tins of sickly sweet Siroopwafels—items she never even thought about unless she was passing through Schiphol airport, and then, apparently, could not live without.

It was still early, but Amsterdam's airport was in full swing. She glanced up at the departures screen and saw her gate number to Bergen had just appeared. Slipping the bag filled with cheese and syrupy, hard waffles into her carryall, she made her way to her connecting flight.

"MADAME, COULD I OFFER YOU a hot coffee to warm up, and siroopwafels?"

Valeria's eyes snapped open. She glanced at her watch and was surprised to realize they were probably now flying over Norway. She'd fallen asleep once again. At this rate, she would morph into Rip Van Winkle.

She shivered and turned to the flight attendant. "Why is it so cold?"

The blond woman looked momentarily pained. "We are so sorry. We have a problem with the heating. You must have fallen asleep. Good thing you were wearing your coat or I would have woken you to ensure you were well covered. Have a bit of coffee, it will help. I'll come back with refills."

She poured coffee into a paper cup and handed it to Valeria, who accepted it in her gloved hand before the flight attendant pushed the cart on to the next row.

"I was so impressed you could sleep in this cold. Probably made it more bearable," said a voice beside her.

Valeria turned to see a blond man beside her, encased in an expensive wool coat and a plush cashmere scarf wrapped around his neck.

"Here, may I help you with your tray?"

She smiled and nodded and he lowered the tray table, allowing her to place down her cup.

"Thank you." She turned to him again, struck by those arctic blue eyes and chiseled features. The musky scent she assumed was his cologne. He was remarkably handsome. Late thirties? Maybe early forties? The accent sounded Scandinavian, but perhaps she wasn't the best judge of accents in English. Her Italian accent dominated her otherwise precise English. People were often telling her how "cute" her cadence was, which she took as code for "difficult to understand."

"It really is ridiculous how cold this cabin is. I think you were already asleep when I sat down, but at first there was hope it might have adjusted once we'd gained altitude. Obviously, no such luck." He offered a crooked smile. "Welcome to Norway."

Valeria turned to the window and looked down. The plane was flying north along the Norwegian coast, dramatic fjords cutting in from the sea far down below her.

She smiled as she looked back. "Maybe the airline's trying to help out—get us accustomed to the cold?"

"Yeah, maybe." He smiled again and held out a gloved hand. "Nice to meet you. I'm Johan Karlsen. Hope this introduction to frigid Norwegian temperatures doesn't scare you off."

She reached out with her own gloved hand. "Valeria Napolitano. Pleasure to meet you."

"Ah, Italian. Where are you from?"

She took a sip of her coffee, the warmth working its way down her body. "From Rome. Born and bred. And you?"

"Oslo, but I've been working for years in Amsterdam. I love Italy. I pass through fairly regularly for work. I'm in finance."

"Then I'm guessing you're in Milan more than Rome."

He chuckled. "You would be right on that. Can't you have a branch of the stock exchange down in Rome? I'm living in Amsterdam and I'm in desperate need of vitamin D. What brings a lovely Italian lady like you up to Bergen?"

She felt a warm glow. Her ego had taken a bruising these last few weeks, and male attention felt like a needed balm. She gazed into the depths of those arctic blue irises, eyes a girl could get lost in. "Ah, it's an annual work trip. I'm up here for the North Atlantic seafood conference. Every year about this time in Bergen. I enjoy getting up, buying tons of warm Dale Norwegian sweaters and filling my tummy with your salmon. Then I make my way back to Rome, where I can actually afford a glass of wine."

His laugh boomed throughout the cabin. "Sounding like a local already. So, Valeria, I assume you work in the seafood industry?"

She nodded. "A little over ten years now. I'm director of marketing for Maren Seafood."

"The fish stick company. I think every kid grew up with those." He smiled. "Give my nephews a choice of salmon or Maren fish sticks, and they'll choose the latter, much to my sister-in-law's shame."

"Sorry for your sister-in-law, but thrilled to know we're penetrating the youth market, even in Norway. Yeah, true, we're most known for fish sticks, but we have a wide range of products. Anyway, each year, the whole Who's Who of the illustrious fish world turns up in style in Bergen. We always have to fight off the *paparazzi*."

He leaned in closer. "You're making it sound terribly glamorous. I almost wish I could abandon my job and join you. Need a finance director?"

She took another sip of her coffee and met his direct gaze. "I'll see what I can do. But you'd have to live in Rome. And we don't have as many grey, rainy days as you enjoy in Amsterdam."

He broke out in more booming laughter that reverberated throughout the cabin. Those eyes, that bone structure, the confidence, the inviting smile. He was so perfect. The chemistry was there, too. She wasn't imagining it.

But soon enough, conversation would turn to the fact that she was single. That she had always been single. Unwanted by any man. He was trapped in a plane, so he couldn't exactly run away, but the retreat would follow slowly, surely. Their flirty banter would be forgotten, replaced by an image of a woman unloved, uncherished by any other man. A member of the Untouchable caste.

Or maybe a woman worthy of one night of touching, as long as one could flee the next morning without so much as a backward glance. That was her fate in life, what Carlo's abandonment relegated her to, probably destined to grow worse as the years passed.

This banter with a handsome stranger on a plane with a faulty heater, flying over the dramatic coastline of Norway would be one of the precious memories she would conserve and replay endlessly in her mind as she sat, an elderly spinster, in her lonely apartment.

"It isn't getting any warmer in here, is it?" Johan asked. "Do you think we could get some more coffee?" He winked.

"Maybe I could plea for a splash of aquavit to warm us up?" He signaled the flight attendant and whispered something in Norwegian.

She returned a few moments later with the coffee that she poured into their cups. Looking around her like some Cold War era spy, she slipped a tiny, clandestine bottle from her apron pocket and poured a generous dose of Scandinavian spirits into their cups.

"*Skål!*" proclaimed Johan, tapping his paper cup against hers.

She joined in his Norwegian toast and took a sip, feeling the burn in her throat, followed by a growing warmth in her stomach.

"Does the trick, doesn't it?" he said, his face coming closer to hers.

"It does," she agreed, ignoring the wild thudding of her heart under all the layers of clothes. "Although I'm not sure I could grow too accustomed to a liqueur made from potatoes."

He laughed again. "Our peasant ancestors had to make the best of what God provided to them. Which certainly wasn't much." He took another long sip. "I'd say they most certainly met the challenge, while scoring points for ingenuity. But I understand it may be an acquired taste. A bit like my frozen homeland."

She turned to the window and looked down. They were flying lower now, and she could see the colorful homes clinging to the rugged coastline. That same coastline must be stunning in summer with those White Nights. Her seafood conferences always occurred in the winter. What might it be like to explore this rugged landscape with someone like Johan?

Warmed by the alcohol, she grew brave and peeled off her gloves, clutching long fingers around the steaming cup and delighting in the warmth it afforded.

When she turned back, Johan was staring at her hands, his head tilted, his brow slightly furrowed.

"What an exquisite ring. Are you married?"

Married? She dropped her gaze to the point Johan was examining with such attention. With the cold on the plane, she'd forgotten.

The ring.

Its intricate swirls encased her ring finger, showcasing her fingers' length, her perfect manicure. She looked up and met his gaze. Those arctic blue eyes examining her, different somehow. More interested. Seeing her as someone to be desired. Someone cherished by another man. Someone worthy.

She looked down again at the shining, golden ring and sighed audibly. Forcing herself, she felt her eyes glaze over with tears—the fetching kind that made her blue eyes sparkle, not the pathetic kind that turned her eyes red when the latest man escaped.

She turned back to him once more, pain etched on her face. She twisted her pretty lips into a sad half-smile. "Married?" She sighed again. Sadly, this time. "Not now." She paused deliberately, before whispering, "But I used to be." She turned back to the window. They had descended even lower now. More fjords were visible, day after day of the ceaseless energy of ocean waves carving away the rugged rocks, forging their path through a solid, immovable object. She turned back and covered her eyes with her ringed hand. "It's so … so hard." She tilted her face back towards him, so tantalizingly close. "I was one of the lucky ones. Married to my soulmate. Marek." She stifled a sob. "He was from Prague, we met when he came down to work in Rome. I guess you could say it was love at first sight."

She reached for the coffee cup on her tray table. Johan sat beside her in rapt silence. She felt his gaze upon her. Interested. Drawn to her. In awe. She closed her eyes and she could almost see the beloved husband she invented in her mind. She took a deep sip of her cooling coffee—the alcohol sharp.

"You know that love that's so passionate, so all-consuming that it sweeps aside everything in its path?"

He nodded, almost imperceptibly.

She heaved her shoulders, up, down. "That's what we had. Whirlwind courtship, small wedding. What's the point in waiting—when you know?" The word trailed off on her lips. She took a deep breath, gathering courage.

Beside her, Johan didn't move a muscle. He barely breathed, all his attention focused wholly on her.

"I ... I should have known it couldn't last. That I didn't deserve such happiness." She wiped away the tear that escaped. "He died in a motorcycle accident. Sudden. Unexpected. No time to say goodbye." She stifled a sob. Her chest heaved up and down as she gained control. She closed her eyes, watched Marek's form fade away into the ether. "His parents were devastated." She sniffled and looked up at him through her tears. "I didn't get out of bed for weeks."

She recognized the compassion in his eyes.

"I needed something to remind me of him. Of our love. I had our two wedding rings soldered together by a jeweler." She held her hand out steady, in front of her. She stroked its delicate design. It looked so pretty in the bright light from the window. "It means everything to me. It's all I have left of him and our love. I don't know what I'd do if I ever lost it." The tears flooded her eyes. She fluttered her eyelashes gently, then looked down again.

He covered her hand with his own, blanketing her in warmth. He laced his fingers between hers and squeezed gently. She fought the entirely inappropriate smile that was eager to emerge.

He shook his head. "That's terrible, Valeria. Poor you. How could you stand it?" He breathed in deeply. "You're very brave to pick up and continue after such a tragedy." He removed his hand and slipped a card from his breast pocket. "I know you'll be extremely busy with your conference. And I'll be meeting with clients, of course. But if you have time, I would like to invite you to dinner. I know a few local gems."

She took the card he offered her and examined it.

"That's my cellphone there. Call me tomorrow and let me know how your schedule is looking. Maybe tomorrow night?"

She sniffled again. "Maybe. I would like that, Johan. You're very kind."

"Not kind. The pleasure is all mine. I would enjoy dinner with you, continuing our conversation." He offered that crooked smile. "I am not always so lucky with my seat partners. A beautiful, fascinating woman."

She offered a tight smile and turned back to the window. The pilot announced their descent. The colorful houses of Bergen grew closer. The tall ships in the harbor. The fish market. She stifled a wider smile. *Beautiful. Fascinating.* A woman to be desired because others had before him.

The clouds parted and the sun blasted its stark Scandinavian light. Her ring shone with the bright sunburst, setting it aglow. The glimmering symbol of eternal love. She didn't fight the smile that broke free. Her luck was about to change.

SUPERSTITIONS
Milan

I GREW UP HATING my Oma's superstitions.

"Don't pass under ladders."

"Turn away from black cats."

"A broken mirror means seven years of bad luck."

During those childhood summers, I was shipped off to Freiburg, the little Black Forest town where my mother grew up but had long ago turned her back on.

My Oma seemed to always be recounting dreams of black crows. "That, Anna," she would say, pinning me in place with the sharp gaze of her watery blue eyes, jabbing my chest with one gnarled finger, "is the most fearful dream of all. It means someone will die. Mark my words."

After her funeral, I returned to my home of Milan, certain my ties with my mother's homeland would be severed now that occasional summer visits with my grandmother were rendered unnecessary. Fresh out of college and with a bit of money in my pocket, I relished the chance for longer summer holidays in exotic, sundrenched locales with my friends, without having to cut plans short and retreat from my friends to visit the sleepy German town.

I quickly forgot my Oma, my mind erasing her German-accented Italian, her Old World, peasant ways.

Until thirty years later, as I sit in the entryway of my chic Brera flat, crying over a shattered mirror. For a moment, it is her pitiless face that appears in a broken shard. A face I thought I had forgotten years ago. Those familiar, watery, blue eyes pin me to the spot.

The tears flow faster and I cradle my legs into my body, rocking in place. My sobs will not be heard by my own children, studying at their universities abroad, nor my husband, who spends most of his time waiting in international airport lounges, prepared to board a flight to his next business meeting.

No one will hear my cries of agony. My curses about the injustices of life.

For this afternoon my doctor confirmed my fear, validated the black crow that visited me in last night's dream.

SNAKE CHARMERS AND DONKEY CARTS

Marrakech

THE HAWKERS' CRIES FILLED THE SQUARE, the guttural sounds of Arabic throbbing in Manuela's ears. All around her, men yelled out in that strange language. Men were everywhere. They brushed past her in the marketplace crowds, and she shrank back. Unfamiliar smells filled the air.

She clung to Adriano's hand as they walked through the Jemaa el-Fna square, willing herself not to cry. A cobra reared up his ugly head, its black tongue flickering, only a few feet from where she stood. She bit her tongue to keep herself from screaming. The snake swayed from side to side as the snake charmer played music on his pipe. A fat man in dirty robes approached her with another snake, trying to wrap it around her neck.

She stumbled backward, afraid she might faint, but thankfully Adriano was pulling her away, toward the dark, labyrinthine streets of the souk. Here she would do battle with the scooters and the donkey carts, but at least there were no snake charmers poised to place a slimy, wriggling serpent around her neck in exchange for coins.

Manuela breathed in deeply. It was all too much. The blood coursed through her veins at double-speed. Her heart pounded in fear and revulsion. She leaned in closer to Adriano, his comforting solidity managing to calm her and provide her with the courage she lacked in this odd city.

"*Min fadlak,*" said a robed man, indicating his wares.

Manuela instinctively shrunk from his attentions, but Adriano stepped closer, examining the delicate lamps shining in the dark marketplace. Their intricate patterns cast colorful, elaborate illuminations through inky night sky. Even she could recognize its mystic beauty.

"*Kam else'er?*" said Adriano.

The two men began haggling over the price, and Manuela stood silently, a spectator to the show. Life was a spectacle here, but one she took no pleasure in observing.

Three days into her holiday in Marrakech, Manuela felt only anxious and confused. The streets were too narrow. She had to remain vigilant not to step in the droppings left behind after the donkey carts passed. There were too many people pressed too closely together. People stood so close when they spoke to you. Adriano told her it was rude to step back, but she couldn't help herself. The yells in Arabic sounded harsh and threatening to her ears. The sights and sounds, the colors and smells were too exotic.

Manuela could only relax when they returned to their riad in the evening, though even there she could not completely escape the lingering sense of foreignness. The wooden keyhole doors were too small, and she kept bumping her head on their frame. The sweet smell of spices filled the apartment with a cloying scent she was unable to banish, even after opening the windows for long periods of time in the hopes of airing the room.

She would step into the shower and rinse the city's dirt and grime from her body, before enveloping her skin in a soft robe. When Adriano pushed her gently down to the bed, a sense of familiarity would calm her, and she could temporarily forget all about the stresses of this chaotic city.

Yet each morning she felt drained and exhausted once again, unable to face another day, desperate to return home, where things were safe and familiar. She longed to hear Italian spoken in the squares, to enter a restaurant and know that familiar foods were on the menu, to be capable of conversing with the shopkeepers.

To belong.

But what could she do? Adriano seemed to thrive in this new environment. He craved exotic places. Where had he learned to count in Arabic? He and the hawker were aggressively shouting figures back and forth, and she saw the spark of excitement in Adriano's eyes. For her, this city was hell on earth. For him, an exotic tale out of *Arabian Nights*.

She breathed in deeply once again, attempting to quell the panic attack she could feel working its way through her body. The hawkers came closer with their oils and their soaps and their leather slippers. She closed her eyes and suppressed the desire to scream.

Back home, her days were spent cutting through the red tape of property purchases in Tivoli and placating demanding clients. Her hard-earned vacation was supposed to relax her, not cause greater stress.

She'd begged Adriano to go back to the Sardinian resort they'd visited this past spring, with its well-designed bungalows, soft, white sand beaches, perfectly ordered rows of umbrellas and beach chairs, and crystalline waters beckoning just before them.

Just smelling the salt air caused a sense of well-being to wash over her body. She'd thought Adriano would book the tickets for the resort, as they discussed. It was charged to her account, after all. Instead, he stopped off at her house with two tickets to Marrakech.

"You're going to love it," he said, kissing her on the neck. "It will be an adventure. I swear, you'll never want to come back to Italy."

She sighed. Not wanting to return to Italy wasn't the problem. It was Morocco where she never wished to set foot again.

THE MAX MARA DRESS had cost a small fortune. Manuela slipped it over her head. Soft fabric caressed her skin as it slid over her curves. She styled her long, dark locks, admiring their glossy sheen and the way they cascaded down over her shoulders, just like Adriano liked it. She examined her reflection in the mirror with an appreciative smile.

She'd ventured into Rome to buy the dress, thinking she would be wearing it at the outdoor dining space alongside a Sardinian beach. When she tried it on in the dressing room, she could almost feel the sea breeze against her face, hear the crash of the waves in the distance. She'd imagined sitting with Adriano under a bright moon and stars as they enjoyed their seafood platters and gazed into one another's eyes.

Instead, this evening they'd be seated on their riad rooftop restaurant, eating couscous. Again.

Manuela glanced down at her high-heeled, strappy sandals. At least tonight she only had to maneuver the stairs to the rooftop, and not the slippery, garbage-strewn streets of the medina. In Sardinia, the sandals would have been easily shed as they walked barefoot along the cold, soft sand of the moonlit beach.

As she sat in Adriano's arms, listening to the crash of the waves, talk would turn to why she couldn't move to Rome. What could boring Tivoli offer a young woman, when the throbbing rhythms of the big city lay just beyond?

Adriano never understood. She liked the tranquility. She liked her big house, walking through town to greet the people she'd grown up with. She despised the chaos and confusion of Rome. She hated Adriano's tiny broom closet of an apartment off the *Campo dei fiori*. "Two steps away from everything you could ever want," he always said. Not that she wanted any of it. Except him, of course. Most of the time.

She still harbored hope that she could bring him around. That he would come and live with her in her villa in Tivoli. He could commute to Rome. Lots of people did. Manuela had hoped their vacation in Sardinia would give her a chance to convince him of that. Surely, he would understand.

THERE WAS NO SOUND OF CRASHING WAVES in this landlocked, arid town. No cries of the seagulls as they circled overhead. Just the shrieking cries of the muezzins. The endless calls were amplified throughout the entire city, calling the faithful to prayer.

Adriano told her the mosques called the people to prayer five times a day, but to Manuela it seemed at least a dozen, maybe even more. And why did the first call to prayer have to be before sunrise? Each morning the blaring calls blanketed the city's loudspeakers and woke her. She was never able to slip back into the precious sleep that allowed her to escape this city for a few blessed hours each night.

Yet she smiled and nodded convincingly when Adriano asked her if the muezzins' calls weren't one of the most romantic and exotic sounds she could imagine. *Of course, Adriano, far better than the crash of the waves and the smell of clean, unpolluted sea air.* Sarcasm did not escape from her lips as she sank deep into the plush pillows, held Adriano's warm hand in her own, and gazed up at the same stars that were shining down on the Mediterranean shoreline where they would certainly spend their next holiday. She'd paid her dues. Literally and figuratively.

She could make the best of it. Manuela kicked off one of her high-heeled sandals. In the shadow of their table, she rubbed her foot under Adriano's khaki pants, with the promise of the intimacy that awaited them after dinner. Adriano was eagerly discussing the next day's excursion, and Manuela tried her best to block it from her mind.

Their couscous arrived at the table, and Manuela forced a smile. Only through great restraint could she lift a fork overflowing with couscous to her mouth, rather than hurling the dish over the terrace's edge and down into the dark depths of the medina. Surely the millions of stray cats that wandered Marrakech's dirty, twisting streets would eat this bland cuisine.

Only four more days to go and she'd be back in Italy, with a big bowl of pasta *al dente* and fresh *parmigiano* cheese piled on top. She hoped to never see couscous or tajine again in her life, but tonight she just smiled at Adriano as he raved about their dinner. She nodded her agreement as she took another insipid bite.

Adriano handed her her wine glass. "*Salute,*" he toasted.

Manuela took a sip of the Moroccan red. Not bad, but nothing like home. She sank back into the plush cushions, wine glass in hand. Adriano sat beside her, running a warm hand up and down her arm.

"I love your dress." He leaned closer and whispered in her ear, "Can't wait to take it off."

She giggled and looked up at the stars. When footsteps approached their table, she allowed her gaze to drop. It was not the waitress returning to check on them. A couple stood before them. In his cream-colored suit and canvas hat, the man looked as if he'd stepped off the set of *A Passage to India*. The woman at his side wore her flaming red hair up in pigtails, a sprinkling of freckles exploding across her nose. Her clothes hailed back to Morocco's golden era of glory on the western hippie trail.

What an odd couple.

"So sorry to disturb you," said the man. "But we heard you speaking Italian in the lobby this morning and we weren't in time to introduce ourselves. I'm Michele and this is Barbara."

"Ah, you're Italians?" said Adriano.

Manuela extended a hand as Adriano introduced her. She'd assumed they were English. The coloring, the unnaturally red hair, the clothes. But the accent was unmistakably from Lazio.

"Won't you join us?" Adriano gestured to the pillows on the other side of the table.

Manuela shot him a look, then suspected Michele must have seen it. She studied her plate of couscous with interest.

"Oh, we wouldn't dream of it," said Michele. "Please return to your dinner. We'll speak later." He took Barbara by the elbow and began to turn.

"You're not disturbing us," insisted Adriano. "Please join us. It's nice to meet someone from home."

Michele and Barbara turned to one another for a moment. Some look of understanding must have passed between them, because they both sank down to the cushions in unison, taking their places across from Adriano and Manuela. The waitress appeared, took their order, and descended to the courtyard kitchen.

"Where do you live?" Adriano asked.

"We don't live together," said Michele. He took off his Panama hat, and lay it down on the table beside him. "Barbara lives in Rome."

"Ah, so do I. Where?" asked Adriano, turning to Barbara. The flickering Moroccan lanterns caught the copper strands of her hair.

"Testaccio," she said.

Adriano smiled. "Nice area. Love the clubs there. I'm on *Campo dei fiori.*"

Manuela knew with what pride he conveyed that information to people they met. After all, he'd forked out a small fortune for rent on his little broom closet of an apartment, and on his irregular musician paychecks, it always seemed an absurd luxury to her. But as she watched Barbara's face transform with this news, she knew they'd get on. She'd responded correctly.

"Oh, you're so lucky!" Even her freckles seemed to glow with excitement.

"Barbara's an artist, and I think she's always dreamed of a loft on *Campo dei fiori* or Piazza Navona. One day, maybe." Michele smiled and patted Barbara's leg.

"An artist?" said Adriano. He sat up straighter on his cushions.

"Adriano's a musician," said Manuela. "He always has antennae for other artists." She smiled. "And finds *notai* terribly boring."

"You're a real estate attorney?" Michele leaned closer. "Small world. So am I. Where?"

"Tivoli."

"We're neighbors," Michele said. "Zagarola."

"Don't tell me. Let me guess. In the Mantegazza studio?"

"Yes. And you? Right in Tivoli? Which one?"

"Well, it's my father's," Manuela said in the shy, almost apologetic voice she used to announce she'd just stepped into her comfortable job thanks to daddy. "D'Andrea."

"You're kidding! The biggest studio in Tivoli, and all of the area. I envy you."

Adriano groaned. "Can you believe these boring lawyers? Tivoli's the center of the universe all of a sudden?"

Barbara laughed.

"Okay, okay," said Michele, with a good-natured shake of his head. "I think that the boring lawyers present get when we're being insulted."

Their plates of couscous arrived and Adriano poured wine into all their glasses.

"How do you like Marrakech?" asked Adriano.

Manuela saw how Michele sank back in his cushions, fidgeting with the napkin on his lap. Instead, Barbara leaned forward, a flush of excitement visible on her face, even in the flickering candlelight. "We *love* it! It's even better than we imagined it would be. I can see why the artists loved it here. The light's amazing. I just wish I could stay."

"I know!" said Adriano. "I feel the same. Maybe I can convince my band to come down. We should record here."

Manuela met Michele's bored gaze and a flicker of understanding passed between them.

"The only thing that really sucks is that we couldn't get into the day trip for Kasbah Aït Benhaddou," said Barbara. "It's only going tomorrow, and they told me the jeep is full. Can you imagine going out to the desert in a jeep, seeing the old Kasbah? I'm kicking myself for not having booked earlier."

"Sorry about that," said Adriano. "We're booked on that trip tomorrow. It would have been great to have you with us."

"Well," said Michele, taking a sip of his wine. "There's plenty to do here in the city. We wanted to go to the Majorelle Gardens tomorrow, maybe visit a hammam. I'm not too upset." He broke out into a wide smile. "I'd just get carsick bumping around a desert in a jeep."

"Oh!" said Manuela. "What a relief I'm not the only one. I've been dreading tomorrow's trip. I suffer from motion sickness.

I'm not planning on eating anything tomorrow, otherwise the trip will be a disaster. Sounds like you'd enjoy it much more than I would, Barbara. You should just take my place."

Adriano's mouth fell open, and she could see the pain she'd unwittingly inflicted. He'd been talking about this trip nonstop since they'd arrived.

Barbara's flushed face broke out in a smile. Her response was immediate. "Do you mean it?" Her voice rose an octave.

For a split second, Manuela wished she could take back her words.

Barbara turned her freckled face to her right. "Michele, honey. You wouldn't mind at all, would you? You and Manuela could go to the gardens. I even have the reservations at the hammam."

Manuela leaned into Adriano's warm body, feeling a tingle up her spine as he slid his hand around her waist. He still had that power over her. She looked up into his eyes. "*Amore*, is that okay for you?"

He leant down and placed a kiss on her forehead. "If you're sure, Manu." He straightened back up and sipped his wine.

She smiled up at him and cuddled closer. No motion sickness pills tomorrow. No vomit bag tucked discreetly into her sleeve. The Majorelle Gardens and the hammam sounded so much more civilized. "So, Barbara. All taken care of. I hope you'll enjoy your day in the outback."

"*Grazie, Manuela*," she said, lifting up her glass. "You've rescued my vacation."

THE STEAM WAFTED OUT from beneath the bathroom door, swirling upwards. Manuela lay on the bed, a light breeze from the open terrace doors caressed her body. The silky black lingerie was new, but Adriano was angry when they returned to their room. He'd stormed to the showers without even looking at her.

She hoped his anger would wash away with the city's dirt and grime. Backing out of tomorrow's excursion had been a risk, but this whole vacation set her on edge, just when she needed to relax. Monday she would return to her office and the towering stack of cases that awaited her. This vacation would do nothing to help her recharge. At least there was hope for the hammam visit rather than the jeep excursion.

The water stopped, and she waited silently. Finally, the door opened and Adriano emerged, wearing a white bath towel. He strode over to the terrace door, glancing out at the tower of the Katoubia Mosque before closing and locking the doors. He turned to Manuela, who lay on top of the sheets, but he barely registered her form.

"How could you bail out on me, when I had to organize so far in advance to arrange for that tour? Now I have to spend the whole day stuck in a jeep with a hippie Pippi Longstocking?"

Manuela attempted to pout seductively. Usually, it didn't take much effort to coax Adriano to bed, but tonight he seemed in no rush. She propped herself up on a pillow, sliding one leg over the other and patting the space beside her.

"I'm sorry, *amore*, but you know what a disaster I am on jeep trips. I'd ruin it for you. You can discuss art, mutual acquaintances in Rome. Anyway, think about me." She rolled her eyes. "I'll spend the whole day with the guy who pines away for the colonial past Italy never experienced."

The lines on his face were rigid, a slight twitch worked at his jaw. "And who's to blame for that? Serves you right after dumping me."

She turned and slid to the edge of the bed, then raised herself on her hands and knees, centimeters from Adriano. She arched her back and tilted her head. "I'd never dump you, baby. It's the desert driving I can't stand." She lowered her voice into a whisper and pouted. "How can I make it up to you?"

Adriano stood still for a moment before allowing his towel to fall to the floor and closing the short distance that separated them with a single stride. "I'm sure you'll think of something."

THE NEXT MORNING, Manuela woke to an empty pillow. She vaguely remembered Adriano kissing her cheek before he left their room that morning at five.

Almost eight, read the alarm clock. She and Michele hadn't made firm plans as to what time to meet. She'd shower and have breakfast, maybe knock on his door if she didn't see him in the breakfast room.

As she entered the tiled courtyard, its central fountain gurgling peacefully, she recognized Michele's profile as he gazed up at the mosque's tower. His golden hair glistened in the sun. He looked so different without his Panama hat and colonial garb. He wore jeans and a blue polo shirt that stretched tight against a muscular chest. She squinted her eyes to be certain it was the same man she'd eaten dinner with an evening earlier.

He sensed her observing him and turned towards her, a smile lighting up his face as his gaze caught hers. He stood and strode across the courtyard. "Manuela, my date for the day!" He kissed her on both cheeks, before leading her by the elbow back to his table. "I insist. We've both been deserted by our *innamorati* today. Join me for breakfast and help take the sting out of being dumped." He held out a chair for her.

"You," Manuela stuttered. "You … uh … you look so different from last night."

He smiled and looked down, appraising himself before his gaze caught hers once again. "Well, I didn't have my artist girlfriend to dress me in that ridiculous colonial garb this morning, did I?" He tapped one hand to his chest. "My natural state, if I'm not being dressed up as performance art."

Manuela placed her napkin over her lap. "I must admit to preferring conventional Michele."

Michele tapped her forearm and she felt the fleeting warmth of his fingers against her skin.

"It seems we have much in common. Ah, here comes the waiter with our mint tea. I may not have warmed to Marrakech, but this is positively addictive."

"I agree with you there."

The waiter set out an additional cup for Manuela, then lifted the teapot high and poured the golden tea out of the spout in an elegant arc of glimmering liquid.

Manuela smiled and lifted her teacup. Catching his gaze, she moved in to clink cups. "To Marrakech."

"To Marrakech. Let's conquer the Majorelle Gardens and the hammam while Barbara and Adriano do battle with the Saharan sands."

"Who got the better deal today?"

Michele winked. "I know I did."

Their food arrived and they enjoyed their Moroccan pancakes with honey, the rich yogurt, and delicate croissants. The water gurgled in the fountain and the sun warmed their shoulders.

Maybe today wouldn't be as tiresome as she'd imagined.

"NOW HERE'S A PLACE I could live!" Michele stretched his arms out wide, a big grin stretched across his open face.

The sky was a perfect cornflower blue, not a cloud in sight. It served as a colorful backdrop for the electric blue buildings and the lush green trees and cacti.

"It *is* beautiful," agreed Manuela, "but it's the sense of peace I treasure most. Just beyond those walls is all the pollution, and filth, and chaos of the city, but here it feels like I've wandered into paradise. So perfect and tranquil."

Michele chuckled. "So I take it Morocco wasn't your idea either?"

"Are you kidding? I wanted Sardinia. I'll return to Tivoli with more accumulated stress than I had when I left."

"Hear, hear! A woman after my own heart. My grandparents are from Sardinia. We have a villa there and I go each year. Barbara insisted we break with tradition on this holiday. And I've regretted giving in from the moment I arrived and stepped in donkey manure on the street."

He twisted up his face in a comic grimace, and Manuela laughed. "I know, the medina's awful, isn't it? For me, the breaking point's the grubby snake charmer who keeps trying to slip a viper around my neck. And I'm supposed to pay for the privilege?" She sighed. "Adriano loves every moment of it. I spend my days worrying I'll have a panic attack."

Michele hooked his arm in hers. "There's safety in numbers. Let's go brave the hammam together. You can close your eyes and pretend you're drinking *mirto* along some white sandy beach."

"If only," sighed Manuela.

They walked toward the Majorelle exit to emerge into the big, scary, chaotic city just outside the protective garden walls.

MANUELA BEGAN BREATHING FASTER, leaning her body closer into Michele's. "But this *can't* be right. We took a wrong turn at that little hovel back there."

Michele studied his map, flipping it over from side to side, looking in vain for street names. "What's the point of a map in the medina? There's no chance in hell you'll ever actually find anything anyway in this giant labyrinth."

Manuela looked down at her expensive leather shoes, caked in a layer of unidentifiable filth. Shoe shiners kept approaching her, requesting some coins for a polishing job. But what was the point if she'd just attract the street filth to her immaculately polished shoes once again?

"Oooh, Michele, look! Look at those women covered in black. It looks like they're carrying baskets. It must be a market. Let's ask there. Someone must know how to get to the hammam."

"Manuela, wait."

But Manuela was determined to make their spa appointment. She barged into the gaggle of women shopping. "Excuse me, Bains de Marrakech? Bains de Marrakech?" She heard the squawking of a live chicken the amused shopkeeper was holding mere centimeters from her face. She instinctively stepped back, but not back far enough to see the glint of a blade and the quick, precise movement of the sharp edge slamming down on the chicken's neck on the countertop. A fountain spewing red.

Manuela's eyes grew wide in fear. She gasped and stumbled backwards. Strong arms wrapped themselves around her waist and pulled her to her feet. "Manu, let's go. There's a taxi stand over there," said Michele, in an authoritative voice that calmed her frayed nerves.

She allowed him to lead her by the hand like a lost child.

TWO HOURS LATER, Manuela lay flush on a massage bed as a masseuse kneaded her muscles and rubbed the local *argan* oil into her skin. She breathed in deeply and closed her eyes, trying to conjure up screeching seagulls and familiar white sand beaches.

The Bains de Marrakech, she had to admit, was a spectacular find. She and Michele had divided into the male and female hammams, followed by a massage. With every moment spent here, her tension drained away dramatically.

She feared having to step out that door again into the scary world beyond, so she tried not to think of it. *Breathe in, breathe out. Gentle waves breaking onto the Sardinian shore.*

SHE AND MICHELE emerged from the taxi in Jemaa el-Fna. He paid the driver and stood next to her, tucking her arm firmly under his and pulling her body tightly against him. She knew he felt the need to shield her from the chaos raging around them, and she wasn't about to argue.

They walked through the narrow, twisting streets that led them to their riad. They chattered nonstop about the sense of well-being they felt after emerging from the hammam.

"Really amazing," gushed Manuela. "I wish we had something like that in Tivoli."

"Looks like someone will have to get back more often."

Manuela made a face. "Let's not exaggerate."

They stepped into the lobby and asked Sherif, the robed man at the reception, if the desert tour was back.

He shook his head slowly. "I am afraid there have been some difficulties with the jeep. A breakdown. They will have to stay the night, but everything should be fine for their return tomorrow morning."

"Tomorrow morning?" Manuela and Michele asked in unison.

"I AM SO GLAD they recommended *La Maison d'arabe* to us. And so pleased you wore that beautiful dress again. You're a vision." Michele's eyes sparkled in the candlelight.

Manuela felt a tingle of pleasure. She smiled and looked down. "Unfortunately, it's the only elegant outfit I brought." She looked around at the refined courtyard dining, the illuminated pool, and the lush vegetation. "This is beautiful, just what the doctor ordered after the change in plans."

"Just because our boyfriend and girlfriend decided to desert us for the desert, doesn't mean we have to rot away bored at home. Plus," he leaned across the table to her, "I have it on good authority that this place makes a mean pasta carbonara." He observed the grin that broke out across her face. "If I have to face one more night of couscous, I'll go insane."

Manuela shook her head. "You won't get any arguments from me. Pasta it is—about time."

The waiter took their order and returned with a bottle of red Moroccan wine.

"To the start of a beautiful friendship," said Michele, raising his glass.

Manuela sipped her wine and smiled. "I just adore *Casablanca.* But if I love that film so much, shouldn't I like the real Morocco?"

"I don't see why you should," said Michele. "It's not as if any of the film was actually shot in the real Morocco. It was filmed in some Hollywood studio set, all comfortably air-conditioned, or fanned by servants, or whatever they did back then, and catered with hamburgers and milkshakes for lunch. The actors and producers probably never stepped foot here either."

"But." Manuela leaned in closer, her brow furrowed. "Is there something wrong with me because I don't appreciate exotic holidays? It's just…" She began folding and unfolding the napkin on her lap. "Adriano always calls me provincial. Says I can't spend my life seeing the same beaches of Sardinia, going to the same little towns in the Dolomiti to ski." She placed her hands on the table and met Michele's gaze. "Do you think he's right? Should I make more of an effort to expand my horizons? Does it make me boring?" She didn't like the little-girl quality her voice had assumed, but she didn't drop her gaze.

Michele leaned in, bringing his face closer to hers. Manuela watched the flicker of the candlelight playing with the taut lines of his face. He was so handsome now that he was dressed simply. Yesterday, beside eclectic Barbara, he'd seemed a mere caricature.

"Just because our other halves feel life's an elaborate checklist, and that they have to have X number of exotic destinations under their belt to impress everyone at the next dinner party, it doesn't mean you have to feel bad if that's not what you want."

He placed his hand over hers and she felt a spark.

"I've spent every summer at my grandparents' villa at Stintino," said Michele.

"Stintino?" Manuela's eyes grew wide. "Oh, I love that beach. I go all the time."

"And we never met? Maybe we built sandcastles together as kids?" He smiled. "The point is, it's a place I love returning to each year. I know the people. I know the beach. It never fails to cheer me up, and relax me. I always return home feeling recharged. Why should I feel guilty for forging that kind of bond with a beloved place?"

He removed his hand from hers to sip his wine. Manuela felt its absence.

"Now my girlfriend informs me I'm supposed to shell out a fortune to go to Ibiza, or Fortaleza, or Phuket. And I don't even know why. Those places mean nothing to me, and I don't like bragging rights. If that makes me provincial, so be it." He raised his glass. "To provincialism."

Manuela raised hers. "To provincialism."

The waiter returned with their plates of pasta.

Michele smiled. "And if that isn't perfect timing, I don't know what is."

They ate and discussed their work. Michele was passionate about his job, and eager to learn about Manuela's. Adriano never took any interest in her work. He routinely deemed it boring, yet she heard in-depth recounting of the gigs his band played in dingy, underground clubs where only a handful of fans showed up. It was nice to be sitting across from someone who took an interest in real estate law and could appreciate what she'd achieved.

"You're so lucky to live in Tivoli," said Michele. "I'd love to work there."

"Really? You don't aspire to a studio in Rome?"

Michele shook his head. "I *hate* Rome. Barbara keeps trying to get me to move there, but an occasional afternoon walk is enough for me. I'd go crazy living there—the chaos, the smog, the traffic, the prices. The Romans." He rolled his eyes. "Barbara and Adriano excepted, of course." He smiled. "Although, I suspect Adriano is about as Roman as Barbara." He winked. "She's from Rieti."

Manuela laughed. "Adriano's from the extremely provincial Frosinone. But he'll kill me if you repeat it. He likes to pretend he's a Roman, born and bred, with a family tree dating back to the time of the Empire."

"Your secret's safe with me."

The piano player returned, passing by their table. Michele hissed to him. "Hey, Sam, over here."

The man looked at him quizzically.

"Sam, you played it for her, you can play it for me." Michele placed a thick wad of dirham into his hand. "If she can stand it, I can! Play it!"

The man bowed slightly. "As you wish, *Monsieur*." He strode to the piano, and sat at the bench. The first notes of "As Time Goes By" filled the courtyard.

Michele stood next to Manuela and held out his hand. "*Madame*, would you do me the honor of this dance?" He led her to the edge of the pool, illuminated from within. Placing a firm arm around her waist, he led her. It had grown late, and there were only a few fellow diners, but Manuela didn't feel embarrassed to be with Michele twirling around the makeshift dance floor.

"How did you learn to dance so well?"

He grinned. "My mother was a dance instructor. I was the only boy in Zagarola who had to skip out of soccer practice on Tuesdays and Thursdays to waltz around with middle-aged women at my mother's studio."

"Well, I am impressed."

He twirled her and pulled her back in close, never dropping his gaze. "Then it was worth it."

The strains of "As Time Goes By" did battle with the call of the muezzins as Michele twirled Manuela in his arms, the Moroccan lanterns casting their magical glow over the scene. She didn't try to block out the grating cries with imaginary sounds of the seagulls and rolling waves. There was something harmonious, magical even, in the muezzins' calls to prayer that evening. When Manuela thought back to Marrakech, this was the moment she'd remember.

"A WHOLE NIGHT AWAY somehow makes it okay?" Manuela knew she was shrieking, but she didn't care who heard. "Don't give me that bullshit about being a man with needs that you couldn't control."

Adriano sat on the bed and sank his head into his hands, silenced for a moment. "I know, Manu. I feel terrible about it.

But I'm honest enough to tell you. I could have kept quiet and you'd be none the wiser."

Manuela paced back and forth with bare feet, clenching her fists to fight the urge to throw heavy objects at Adriano's head. She could feel the blood coursing through her body with each frenetic heartbeat.

"What the hell, Adriano. *One* bloody day! And with the woman you called a hippie Pippi Longstocking. Just couldn't control those urges, eh?"

He dropped his hands and looked up at her. "None of this would have happened if you hadn't backed out at the last minute."

Manuela's mouth dropped open. She raised a clenched fist to her chest. "So now it's *my* fault you screwed Barbara? I'm supposed to be with you every minute of every damned day if I want to ensure you don't jump other women if you're unattended for a few hours?"

He shook his head and ran his fingers through his tousled, black hair. "That's not what I meant, Manu. It was a mistake. I'm sorry." There was a spark in his eyes as he looked up at her. "But you're so … so provincial. The whole world is big and scary for you. It gets boring having to deal with that. Can't you ever have any sense of adventure? If you had just come on the trip, it would have been us under the stars at the Kasbah."

The rage swirled through Manuela's body, and she felt the violent urge to throttle Adriano. Humiliating her like that, then sitting there on their bed and blaming it all on her. Was *this* worth fighting for?

Manuela closed her eyes, took a deep breath and allowed her heartbeat to slow. When she spoke, her voice was calm and controlled. "So says the worldly boy from Frosinone. Maybe I was blinded by the fact that you're a musician, although generally one gets paid for one's work before he can claim it's his profession. But honestly, Adriano. You've always been a shit." She lifted her suitcase from the closet shelf, and began filling it slowly and methodically. Her penchant for order meant that everything was folded in neat, little piles, perfectly positioned for an emergency getaway. "You'll be forty and still playing in hellhole cellar-clubs without getting paid. You and Barbara did me a favor."

Adriano's mouth dropped open. The glint in his eyes now reflected his fear. "You don't mean what you're saying. You're just angry."

She left him there to pack up her makeup case in the bathroom, placing it in her suitcase and then zipping it up. Adriano hadn't moved from his spot on the bed.

"You're right on that count," she said in a calm voice. "I *am* angry. But not at you, at myself. I deserve better." She placed her purse over her shoulder. "As of this moment, I'm done bankrolling you. You can settle the bill—I'm guessing that will clear out your life's savings. I'm checking into the *Maison d'arabe* for the remaining two days of the vacation from hell. I may as well take advantage of the pool and the spa there." She threw his e-ticket on the bed. "I'll make sure my seat reservation is changed as far from you as possible. I'd like this to be goodbye, no need for future contact." She smiled. "Unless, of course, you and Barbara strike it rich and need a real estate attorney to handle your purchase of a villa in Tivoli. I'll even give you a discount, for old time's sake. *Ciao*, Adriano."

"THANK YOU, Sherif. *Monsieur* Bonardi will be checking out on Saturday, as planned. I need a little time alone at the spa to relax."

Sherif raised one questioning eyebrow, but said nothing.

Manuela pulled a business card out of her wallet. "Sherif, if I leave my card and a message, do you have an envelope, and could you ensure it's delivered to *Monsieur* Michele Nardi?"

"Of course, *Madame*." The play of a smile tugged at his lips. He handed Manuela an envelope.

On her card, she wrote: "Call me when you're back. I'll invite you to lunch. M."

She hesitated, her pen still poised over the card. Quickly, she scrawled below. "We'll always have Marrakech."

Dropping it in the envelope, she sealed it and handed it to Sherif.

"*Merci, Madame. Bonne journée.*"

"Oh, it is already, Sherif. One of the best days of my life."

With a smile and a wave, she lifted her suitcase and walked confidently to the Jemaa el-Fna to hail a cab.

CAVES
Matera

WHEN RICK ENDED IT FOREVER, just six months before the wedding, Amanda couldn't have cared less.

Yes, there was the nonrefundable catering deposit to consider. True, the invitations they ordered three weeks ago had just been delivered, their elegant, gold-embossed script announcing the happy event that would never take place. The dress would be a problem, to be sure.

Yet those were only fleeting thoughts in Amanda's mind as she took in the sweeping panorama from her balcony with a fierce determination to finally enjoy the trip. She turned as she heard Rick take a breath, ready to deliver a lengthy speech in his authoritative management consultant voice—the one he used with clients who paid exorbitant rates for his services— about how they had made a mistake, how it was better to admit it now and move on.

Rick prepared himself for tears. He prepared himself for pleading. He had, undoubtedly, already done a dry-run of his speech. Perhaps he'd even prepared a well-organized PowerPoint presentation with which to practice, like the ones he delighted in creating for his clients.

What he wasn't prepared for was Amanda's indifference.

"Okay, Rick. Reception can find you a taxi for Bari, where you can catch a train back to Rome," Amanda said as she entered the room from the balcony, rummaging through her purse. "I almost forgot, your return ticket to New York." She shoved it into his hands. "When I'm back, I'll arrange to pick up my things from the apartment."

She stifled a sigh of relief at the thought of vacating the pretentious, sterile apartment they shared—the one expressly designed to impress others.

Making eye contact when she handed him the ticket was a mistake. Rick looked like the spoiled kid he often was, angered his speech hadn't received the reaction he expected. Rick didn't do well outside his comfort zone. This trip had demonstrated that rather clearly.

"Goodbye, Rick," Amanda said in a clipped tone as she turned and stepped back out onto the balcony. A moment later, she heard the hotel room door slam.

Not a moment too soon, she thought as a smile played on her lips. The sun was slipping low in the late afternoon sky and casting its golden light off the *Sasso Caveoso.* A magical city of caves.

AMANDA HAD LONG DREAMED of visiting the southern Italian town of Matera. Now, thanks to Rick's unexpected announcement, she had three days to explore it in peace and blessed solitude, to allow its magic to envelop her.

Amanda barely suppressed a smile as she laced up her stylish walking shoes and left the hotel, treading carefully on the slippery cobblestones. The climb was steep, the stairs well-worn from the footsteps of generations of residents. Amanda stopped occasionally to catch her breath and admire the view.

Two years ago, when she was thirty-two and nursing a broken heart after a slew of disastrous romances, Rick was hired as a consultant at the firm where she worked. He was brash and confident. Her friends and colleagues encouraged her to return his attentions and, following their advice, she eventually did.

At first, she'd been happy, but that quickly changed. Soon she noticed that Rick never abandoned his winning presentation voice or the sports references he favored—they were the same ones he used at work, at dinner parties, even in bed.

She scrimped and saved to invite him on a pre-wedding trip, then listened to his endless complaints in Rome and Naples about the lack of organization, the slow service, the way those cities could never hold a candle to New York.

Amanda walked up the steps to the *Duomo*, stopping every few moments to catch her breath at the views of the *Sasso Caveoso* below. She examined the cave homes haphazardly constructed on top of one another, amazed that the steps she tread on formed the roof of someone else's cave home. The whole town was a harmonious jumble of construction, like the card houses she'd constructed as a child.

She made her way to the pedestrian *Piazza Pascoli*, where she stopped for an espresso and quickly abandoned her book, preferring to observe the children playing street soccer, young couples walking hand in hand, and old men standing in clusters, hands gesticulating wildly, fully engrossed in their conversation. In a small town like this, these same men must have gathered together in the same way for almost a century. How could their conversations and arguments still be so passionate?

Amanda felt pleasure as the late afternoon sun warmed her face and shoulders. She sipped her coffee and smiled at the empty seat beside hers.

The handsome young waiter handed Amanda the bill. Pointing to her book, he spoke to her in heavily accented English. "You like Carlo Levi? Are you English or American?"

"American," she answered, meeting his dark eyes framed by impossibly long eyelashes.

"You're a long way from home."

Amanda noted the flirtatious smile of a young man accustomed to female attention. "I'm running away. It seemed a good place to get lost." She met his smile and paid her bill, tipping like a New Yorker.

He grinned at her generosity. "*Grazie, Signorina.* Stay as long as you want. Beautiful women are always welcome here."

Amanda slipped her book into her purse and walked away, casting a last look over her shoulder at the young man who was carefully observing her departure. His gaze did not drop as her eyes met his.

Could I really stay here, Amanda wondered, *make a clean break? Not just the wedding, but my life, too?* Her mind clung stubbornly to the idea. Returning to her firm to market more useless products to unsuspecting consumers had long ceased to interest her. Maybe she could find a little cave apartment to rent, find work at a local language school. Start over.

AMANDA WALKED THROUGH THE CAVES until she reached the *Santa Lucia alle Malve* cave church. She allowed her eyes to adjust to the dark interior before she looked at the twelfth- and thirteenth-century frescoes adorning the cave walls.

Amanda stopped short before the image of Santa Lucia draped in oranges, reds and blues, her chalice raised. Her soulful eyes, arched eyebrow, and delicate face glowed in the candlelight. Amanda felt inexplicably drawn to the image. Her heart beat faster as she stood alone before the painting, observing the chiaroscuro effect of the candlelight on the cave wall fresco.

Her solace was soon shattered as a large tour group squeezed into the dark cave. Judging by the accents, a senior tour group from England. They clomped into the silence in their sturdy walking shoes. Spiderwebs of varicose veins showed beneath the hems of inexplicable capri pants. The Italian sun had not been kind to their pale skin. Amanda observed the army of beet red faces, sweating brows and peeling shoulders as the northern visitors swarmed around her. She backed up to avoid being enveloped by the crowd.

Amanda heard the voice of the Italian guide hushing the group. She heard the sing-song cadence of his accented English as he explained the cave church's origins in the eighth century. She moved to nearby frescoes to examine them, but her ears perked up when she heard the guide turning his attention to the fresco.

"Here we see the third-century saint, Santa Lucia—Saint Lucy. When she refused to enter into an arranged marriage with a pagan, she was denounced as a Christian. Before she was beheaded, her eyes were gouged out." Amanda turned to see him indicating the chalice she had just been examining a few moments before. "Traditionally, Santa Lucia is depicted holding a chalice that contains her eyes." Despite the groans and snickers emerging from the group, Amanda inched closer, eager to join them, eager to see better. "Today, Santa Lucia is the patron saint of her native Siracusa. She is also the patron saint of the blind and those suffering from impaired vision."

She ignored the sounds around her. She stood transfixed before the fresco, examining each minute detail. The group drifted away to other frescoes, and eventually they followed their guide out of the church.

The silence was a welcome relief. She stood motionless before the image of Santa Lucia for a long time before turning her gaze from the fresco and opening her wallet. Dropping coins into the offering box, Amanda lit a candle. She extracted her plane ticket from her purse. Holding it over the flickering flame, she watched the fire devour the paper, transforming it into ashes that fluttered down onto the cave floor.

As the bright light cast a glow over Santa Lucia's lovely face, Amanda noticed a slight smile she hadn't seen before. When she blinked, it was gone.

Amanda turned and left the church, shading her eyes as she emerged from the dark cave, momentarily blinded by the bright sunlight. Taking a deep breath, Amanda smiled before walking down the steps and into Matera's fading rays of golden sunlight.

HEAT WAVE

Rome

THEY CALLED 2003 the hottest summer on record. It wasn't just Rome; the heat wave crippled all of Europe. Daily temperatures soared into the nineties and past 100. Grass turned yellow, then brown. City dwellers fled the oppressive heat in droves. The rare air conditioners to grace Roman apartments droned on all day, working on overdrive.

Headlines screamed out about the alarming numbers of the elderly dying during that brutal summer. Politicians in France and Italy criticized their opponents for failed social policies, and talking heads questioned a society that left their elderly relatives alone in sweltering homes while their affluent children and grandchildren frolicked at the seaside or in mountain resorts.

Graham warned Melanie that she should stay in London until the fall. In London, he reasoned, she could count on his mother to help with the baby during the first months. Yes, London was also hot that summer, but still far better than Rome. New to his position, Graham was not entitled to leave. In fact, with so many staff members away, he was shuttling back and forth to Africa on missions. How could Melanie move to Rome, only to be left all alone with the baby?

Melanie kept giving in to Graham, seeing him on his infrequent weekends back in London. Her days passed uncomfortably, a virtual prisoner in her mother-in-law's suburban London home.

"No, my dear. You evidently lack a maternal instinct. It's far too hot to take the baby out in the pram today," her mother-in-law would say, with a scolding look in her eye Melanie was growing to know all too well. Then she would pluck little Helen from the carriage and sweep the baby off to the makeshift nursery.

As Melanie stood alone at the entrance, she gazed longingly at the world outside, a wry smile spreading across her face as she thought, *I almost made it this time.*

Melanie had never been to London before, never even been to Europe. In all honesty, barring a school trip to Washington, D.C., a long-ago family vacation to Orlando, and a handful of day trips to see shows in New York, she hadn't ever travelled much outside of western New York. The day exotic Professor Graham Downes walked into her office, she could barely gather up the courage to speak to him.

Her job in the SUNY Binghamton administrative offices included facilitating paperwork for new professors. She'd been in touch with the economic development professor from London, emailing him information, arranging for his hotel, passing on housing details and setting up appointments with a rental agency to see properties. His emails were friendly and chatty, asking her opinions about various parts of town, about life in Binghamton. When she joked that it would be dull for him after London, he responded that he refused to believe it if all Binghamton residents were as lovely and helpful as she.

Melanie looked forward to the elderly British gentleman's arrival on campus. Yet her voice failed her when she realized, a moment after he stepped into her office and introduced himself in his charming British accent, that he wasn't at all old. Or rather, his youthful face belied his forty-seven years. Melanie found her voice some moments later, but she would kick herself afterwards for sounding like such a simpleton. She didn't hear from him again after welcoming him that first day and assumed he had pegged her as the reliable but dull secretary. He would hardly be the first.

That's why Melanie was so surprised to receive a visit from him two weeks later. He walked through her office door with a large bouquet of tulips, apologizing for not having returned earlier to thank her.

"It's been so overwhelming, with a new school and a busy course schedule. I did manage to find a house, however, precisely in the neighborhood you recommended. I'm ever so grateful. Tell me, Ms. Richards, would it be considered cheeky to thank you by inviting you to lunch?"

Melanie had absolutely no idea what "cheeky" meant, but she shook her head immediately and managed to thank him.

That lunch was the happiest day of her uneventful twenty-eight years. She listened to Graham—he had been cross when she tried to call him Professor Downes—recount his studies in economics, and his field research in Africa and Asia. He had seen and done so much that she felt insignificant in comparison. She was certain she would only see him passing by on campus after their lunch together, but Graham surprised her when he asked to see her again.

Soon they were spending evenings at one another's houses and romantic weekends at quaint inns she'd always dreamed of visiting on the Finger Lakes.

When he asked her to marry him, during one of their weekend escapes, she was overwhelmed.

"It would only be fair to tell you, Melanie. I'm much older than you, and I would like to have children sooner rather than later."

She nodded solemnly before forcing herself to smile. "Of course, so would I," she said, before sinking her head into his chest so that he could not detect the lie in her eyes. For, unlike her friends and colleagues, Melanie had never been maternal. She'd dreamed of a man in her life—though never one as wise and worldly as Graham—but that dream never included children.

Yes, she cooed and smiled alongside the other secretaries when a colleague brought in a new baby, for that's what one was expected to do. But she never understood all the fuss. And she never imagined that she might one day have to give herself over to a tiny, helpless little being who relied utterly on her for his or her survival.

As boyfriend after boyfriend slipped through her fingers, Melanie even wondered if she might meet someone later in life, past her childbearing years. When she met Graham, she half-expected that he would feel he was beyond the need for children. But of course, he had selected a young wife, one who should be more than capable of bearing and caring for babies. Melanie remained in his embrace as long as she could, so that he would not detect her fear.

Graham's mother was not pleased with his choice. That was clear at the wedding and at the painful meeting between the in-laws, where neither side could find anything to say to the other. Soon after Melanie discovered she was pregnant–or "fallen pregnant," as Graham said– Graham learned that he had been selected for a position with the United Nations in Italy.

"Rome?" asked Melanie, finding the one-syllable word horrendously difficult to pronounce. "Tell me you mean Rome, New York."

Graham laughed. "No, my dear. The one in Italy, I'm afraid." He took her by the hand and placed his other hand on her growing belly. "Just think of it. We'll have our baby in Rome!"

Melanie did think of it. Day and night. Her blood pressure ticked up accordingly. They came to an agreement to move temporarily to London, where Melanie would have the baby, and then Graham would go on to Rome to set up the housing before Melanie and the baby arrived. When Roman rents turned out to be more expensive than Graham imagined, he suggested economizing in London by moving in with his mother.

"Just temporarily, mind you. You'll have the baby, and then a month or two later you'll come to Rome."

Melanie bit her lip as she thought of the disdainful look her mother-in-law always seemed to reserve expressly for her. But the fear of having a baby in a country where she didn't even speak the language scared her even more. London it was.

"GRAHAM, I BOUGHT THE TICKETS today. Helen and I arrive in Rome on Tuesday. I'll have you know there's no arguing with me on this." Melanie's voice was uncharacteristically firm over the phone.

When her mother-in-law criticized her that morning for the umpteenth time about her lack of maternal instinct, Melanie tucked little Helen into the baby sling and practically sprinted the three blocks to the travel agency. Sweaty and breathless, she joyfully booked her ticket to Rome for the following week.

"Darling, if you're sure. The flat is lovely, but there's no air-conditioning. The landlord has promised to install it, but the waiting list for installations this summer is endless. I wasn't expecting you 'til September."

September! God, she'd never make it that long. She might even strangle the old woman—or herself. "Don't worry, Graham. Helen and I will be fine. It will be a good chance to explore shady parks." She forced herself to sound confident. "We'll manage."

MELANIE'S ROMAN MORNINGS started early. She would join Graham for breakfast before he walked to the office, then she would nurse Helen, change her diaper, and pack the diaper bag, careful to include a blanket, book, sandwich, and plenty of water. Afterwards she headed off to the Celimontana Park to stake out a shady spot under one of the Mediterranean pines dotting its elegant lawn.

That day was no exception. Helen napped most of the morning and Melanie was free to read her book, lifting her eyes up occasionally to admire the Ancient Roman baths of Caracalla in the distance as she listened to the hum of the cicadas.

It was too hot to explore Rome that summer. When Melanie tried, she balked at the asphalt sticky under her sandals and worried that, despite her hat, Helen's fair skin could burn. This fear caused Melanie to retreat as quickly as she had set out.

It was better to spend her days at Celimontana, as she saw a handful of other mothers doing. They sat together in clusters, laughing and chatting in Italian. Melanie glanced at them longingly from under her long eyelashes. One had even made the effort to come over to her blanket one day; Melanie apologized for not speaking Italian.

"Your baby, how is she called?" asked the woman in stilted English.

"Helen."

"Helen?" said the woman, wrinkling her brow. "Ah, *certo—*Elena!"

"Yes, Elena, in Italian." Melanie smiled encouragingly.

There was a long silence before the woman smiled politely and indicated her friends. "I must to go. My *amiche.*"

"Yes, of course," Melanie said, masking her disappointment as the pretty young woman stood up and pushed her stroller towards the animated group.

I must learn Italian, thought Melanie, *or I risk being dependent on Graham.*

GRAHAM HAD FOUND A BABYSITTER through work and she joined her husband for dinner a few times at colleagues' homes. Graham hoped that these outings would result in friendships for Melanie, but Melanie always felt so dull and under pressure to perform at those dinners. They spoke about work, throwing about acronyms and discussing people she didn't know. They wanted to know what her opinions were on European politics, famine in the Horn of Africa, or the fate of Kosovo, and she spent those dinners feeling as if she were being tested. And failing.

Conversation would turn, for her benefit, she realized, to motherhood. But even there she lacked charisma. Graham was far more witty and knowledgeable about early child development, even if he spent so little time with Helen. Melanie couldn't even make a success of that. She observed her own dullness through the eyes of Graham's colleagues, and it depressed her.

Helen stirred from her nap and wailed for milk. Despite her ineptitude as a mother, at least Melanie had learned Helen's nursing cry. Sweat pooled between her breasts, dampening her nursing bra, but she draped a large scarf over her shoulder—observing that she was the only one to display such modesty in Rome and feeling envious of the less-inhibited Italian mothers—before unhooking the detachable cup and positioning Helen. Helen latched on greedily. She constantly demanded the breast and Melanie, fearful that she could offer her daughter so little else, found pleasure in at least providing nourishment.

As she looked out in the distance, she heard a sound beside her and turned to see a very old woman hovering above.

"My dear," said the woman in English. "May I be so forward as to ask to join you?"

The woman's English was accented, but her diction was precise. She walked with a cane, yet was still unsteady on her feet. Her wrinkles were deep, her wispy white hair pulled up in an old-fashioned knot on her head. Her brow glistened.

"But of course, where are my manners? Here, let me make space on the blanket." Melanie slid over, disturbing Helen, who voiced her disapproval before swiftly returning to the breast.

The woman lowered herself with great difficulty, groaning as she positioned herself beside Melanie. Melanie heard the woman's labored breathing and was angry at herself for not having helped her.

"Oh, my dear. Do not grow old."

Melanie felt embarrassed. Was she meant to respond? Luckily, the woman changed topics.

"This is the hottest summer I can remember, and I can remember many of them. My flat is too hot, and I pass my days out here."

"Like me," smiled Melanie. "And Helen, of course."

"I have seen you out here with your little girl. I heard you speaking English to her once."

"Yes," Melanie nodded. "We've just moved here for my husband's work, and Helen and I are trying to adjust. I'm Melanie, by the way."

"A pleasure, Melanie, I'm Lucia."

The older woman offered her hand and Melanie shook it awkwardly over Helen's head. Once again, Helen had fallen asleep at the breast. Melanie lay her down, then fumbled under her shawl to arrange her bra and button her sundress.

"She's lovely," said Lucia, gazing at the sleeping baby. "But I never see you looking happy, like other new mothers. I wonder if it's all been harder than you expected."

Melanie startled. She was on the brink of denying it, when she changed her mind. She was so alone. She couldn't admit her failure to her friends back home, her parents, or Graham. Obviously not to her mother-in-law, who would only weaponize Melanie's failure. Maybe speaking it aloud would help.

"I'm afraid it is," she said, averting her gaze from Lucia's sharp grey eyes. "Harder than I imagined. Although maybe the real problem is that I never imagined it. I always envisioned the man without the baby." She whispered, "I'm not sure I'm cut out to be a mother."

"Oh, my child," Lucia said, fanning herself with a magazine. "Not everyone is—at first. But you seem like a smart young woman, and I'm sure you will learn to love your daughter. We always assume maternal instinct sets in the minute a baby is born, perhaps even as the baby is growing in the mother's womb, but I don't think that's true for every woman."

The woman's voice was kind, the first kindness Melanie heard relating to her glaring ineptitude. A fat tear slipped from Melanie's eye and ran down her hot cheek. The old woman handed her a handkerchief.

"Melanie, I think it helps to admit it. And to work on it each day. You cannot set yourself up to be a failure simply because something does not come naturally to you." Lucia gave

Melanie's hand a gentle squeeze. "I think we may just have something in common ... and it's not youth."

Melanie looked at the old woman and offered a faint smile.

Lucia took a deep breath. "I was not a natural mother either. Nothing I did seemed right, and I had a difficult mother-in-law who constantly criticized me and took great pleasure in declaring I did everything incorrectly." She shook her head at the memory. "When my husband accepted a job in Edinburgh, just after the War, I was happy to escape my mother-in-law. But I was miserable there my first months. I didn't speak the language; I didn't have friends. And I was certain I was doing everything wrong raising Antonio."

Melanie watched her closely.

"It was in a park one day when an elderly Italian lady approached me. She told me she had observed me with my baby over the past weeks and that I had to stop being so hard on myself, that motherhood was a job I still needed to learn, and that I would." Lucia turned to look at the younger woman. "She was the first to give me hope. And she was right."

Melanie hoped her eyes expressed all the gratitude she felt for the older woman's generous words. "Where is Antonio now?"

The old woman stared down at sleeping Helen, her face so angelic in repose.

"He died. Ten years ago. Just two years after my husband."

"I'm so sorry, Lucia," Melanie said, her voice soft.

"It's so unnatural to lose one's child. A parent wishes to go first. But I will join them soon."

The two women sat in silence, until Helen stirred.

Each day after that, Melanie looked forward to the park. Graham was away on missions, but she and Lucia would share her blanket and a picnic lunch and chat, both eager to escape their sweltering homes and the loneliness palpable within those walls. Melanie felt her confidence as a mother grow, alongside the burgeoning love she felt for her daughter.

One August morning as suffocating as the rest, Melanie and Helen awaited Lucia at the park. Lucia was uncharacteristically late and Melanie began to worry.

When a group of the regular young mothers passed by, one stopped to speak with Melanie. "I've seen you with the elderly lady," said the woman, wheeling her baby stroller back and forth. "I'm sorry to have to tell you, but she lives in the building next to mine. Her cleaning woman found her early this morning. The ambulance came, but it was too late." She observed the tears form in Melanie's eyes. "I saw you two were close. I'm so sorry." She turned her head to the group of mothers settling under a nearby tree. "Would you and your baby like to join us?"

They called 2003 the hottest summer on record. Twenty thousand elderly Italians died that summer, including one who changed Melanie Downes' life.

BALINESE TRADITIONS
Ubud

THE WARM AIR OF THE TERMINAL hit Giovanna's face as she exited the plane. Walking toward the baggage collection, she saw her reflection in the mirror. Her lean frame, long, dark hair and olive skin contrasted with Pietro's robust build, blond hair, and rosy skin. The juxtaposition caused her to smile.

They didn't belong together.

That's what every confused stranger's glance telegraphed to her before asking if the boy was her son. Some simply assumed she was the nanny, telling her how adorable her charge was.

Back when Jake was beside her, no one asked those questions.

Pietro's tiny hand clutched hers anxiously. His body pressed close to her leg as she made her way to the visa counter. These past months, he never let Giovanna out of his sight, even to go to the bathroom. He crawled into her bed night after night. Exhausted as she was, she never had the energy-or the heart, really-to insist he return to his own room. She couldn't bear to add to the young boy's suffering.

"Two visas, please," she said to the uniformed woman behind the counter. "I don't have any rupiah. Do you take euro?"

"Yes. Forty euro."

Giovanna took the visas the woman handed her in exchange for the bills, then made her way to passport control, followed by a long wait at the baggage carousel. As they waited, Pietro's eyes grew larger and increasingly worried. His lips trembled; tears threatened to burst from his eyes.

"Oh, *amore*. It's been a long flight. You must be exhausted." She knelt down and stroked his cheek. "As soon as we collect our bags, we'll find the taxi outside waiting to bring us back to the hotel. You'll feel better after a good night's sleep."

"I want our own house, *mamma*. Not a hotel. Why are we here?"

Why are we here, indeed? Hadn't she asked herself the very same question, at least a million times? If her own doubts weren't enough, there were those of her parents and her sister, her colleagues, her neighbors. No one could understand it. Not even Pietro.

She looked deep into those clear, blue eyes, with their flecks of white around the pupils. Jake's eyes. She sighed deeply. "It's where we're meant to be, *tesoro*." She forced a smile. "You'll love it. I promise."

A few minutes later, dragging two suitcases behind her and managing long strides despite Pietro clinging to her, she emerged from the humid terminal into the sweltering day. Hundreds of Indonesian faces stood before her, each with a placard bearing a name. Panic welled up inside of her. She looked frantically around the solid wall of unfamiliar name cards, seeking out her own as the pressure on her leg grew tighter. When she glanced down, she saw the tears streaming unchecked down Pietro's soft cheeks.

"Okay, we came. Now can we go home, *mamma*?"

WOMEN WASHED CLOTHES in roadside streams. Bare-breasted women worked beside men in the rice paddies, flocks of ducks waddling or swimming around them. Wood carvers worked at makeshift workshops along the road's edge. Women carried enormous baskets balanced precariously on their heads. Young children rode astride scooters that zipped dangerously between the cars. Giovanna screwed up her eyes each time one of the young boys attempted a dangerous swerve around moving vehicles.

She turned from the window to Pietro's body extended across her lap. Exhausted from the jetlag and his tears, Pietro had fallen asleep just outside the Denpasar city limits. She stroked his blond locks absently.

What on earth *was* she doing? Giovanna had made so many questionable decisions in the past months, but on this trip, she had held firm. Jake had wanted this, and therefore, so did she. She screwed up her eyes as they barely passed a scooter driver before swerving back in—the driver no more than a day over nine years old.

"HERE WE ARE," announced the driver. He turned and observed the sleeping boy. "You take care of him. I'll ensure your bags reach your bungalow."

Giovanna smiled and nodded, lifting Pietro as she walked into the reception office.

A man in a sarong and traditional headpiece welcomed her, checked her in and then accompanied her to her bungalow. She lay Pietro gently down on the single bed, removing his sandals. He snored gently, his angelic face in perfect repose, a vision of innocence in his exotic new surroundings.

"If you need anything, Madame, please do not hesitate to call. Breakfast is served from seven to ten in the open dining room beside your bungalow."

"Thank you so much. Goodnight."

"Goodnight, Madame."

Giovanna bolted the door behind her as the hotel worker left. She extracted her toothbrush from her backpack, brushed her teeth and shed her clothes, not even bothering to locate her pyjamas. She glanced at her watch—still on Bologna time. She tumbled into bed, watching the progress of a gecko scurrying up the bungalow wall as her eyes grew heavy.

SUNLIGHT SPILLED THROUGH A CRACK in the heavy draperies. Giovanna observed its pattern through one wary eye. She turned to the clock on the bedside table. 8:30. On the bed beside hers, Pietro was still asleep at half past eight. Still in his own bed. She couldn't remember a night of unbroken sleep in the past five months, and here they'd both slept for twelve solid hours. The miracle of jetlag.

She rose, pushing aside the mosquito netting, aware of the whirr of the fan above her head. The tiles felt cool and smooth under her feet. Quietly, she made her way to the bathroom. She splashed cool water on her face and dabbed her face dry with a plush, white towel.

Despite the rest, her eyes were slightly bloodshot. Faint purple shadows spread under her eyes, the result of too many sleepless nights. She rubbed her index and middle fingers from her nose outward along her left cheekbone, trying to recall the radiance of her skin that disappeared months ago.

Maybe this vacation would help restore the old Giovanna.

PIETRO SAT IN SULLEN SILENCE at the breakfast table. At her urging, he ate a bowl of cereal, then gazed blankly at his place setting.

Giovanna worked hard to fill the silence. "Did you hear the roosters this morning? There are quite a few ... Look up there, honey. See the people out in the rice paddies? Shall we take a walk up there later this afternoon? ... There's the start of the jungle, over there. Peaceful, isn't it? What a change from the city. ... There's a shuttle bus going into town in a half hour. Would you like to go and see the monkeys?"

She was aware of the forced joviality to her voice, sounding almost manic to her ears. But Pietro's vacant stare caused familiar panic to well up inside her. When he slipped into this state, Giovanna responded with forced chatter. It was absurd, she knew it was. Still, his silence terrified her.

Later that morning, Giovanna bought their entrance tickets to the Monkey Jungle, then peeled out extra rupiah notes to buy bananas for Pietro.

The bananas didn't last long. The most aggressive monkeys gathered in rowdy gangs at the entrance gate, intimidating each new visitor. Pietro didn't stand a chance. Petrified by their aggressive grunts and how they edged around him, he quickly rid himself of the entire bunch and buried his face in Giovanna's skirt. She placed a hand on his shoulder, feeling his body tremble through the thin cotton of his T-shirt.

"*Mamma*, let's go away," he sobbed.

"Oh, Pietro, honey." She channeled her most calming voice. "Don't worry. They can be a bit aggressive when they want food, but they'll be okay. I promise."

"No," he wailed into her skirts. "They want to hurt us."

"No, baby, they really don't. Take my hand." She maneuvered his body away from her leg. "Do you see those men in green down there, wearing the Balinese sarong? They're here to make sure the monkeys behave, that they don't become too naughty with the visitors. They'll look out for you. And so will I." She met her son's gaze and saw the pleading look in his eyes. He was scared about more than the monkeys. Would she be able to look out for him like he needed? She didn't know, but she forced a confident smile and pulled him gently onto the entryway path. "Come on, *amore*. You'll love it."

They wandered the sacred Monkey Jungle's shaded paths and watched the macaque monkeys run alongside them, swing from the trees, and scurry up statues or temples. Pietro delighted in the monkeys who sat beside carved monkey statues. He watched a mother macaque scoop up her young and place him onto her stomach, carrying him along on her journey.

When he came upon a wading pool, he stopped short to see the monkeys jumping from the branches to splash in the cool waters. He delighted in their naughtiness. He observed as they chased one another, as they fought, as they cannonballed into the water, then shook out their wet fur, hitting the spectators.

Although she might have been mistaken, Giovanna may even have witnessed the ghost of a smile on Pietro's face. "You like them, don't you?"

"I do." He nodded. He was silent, watching two monkeys rolling over one another in a fight. "Dad likes monkeys, too. He should be here with us to see them."

Giovanna felt a lump forming in her throat. Her tongue felt dry. She nodded silently, afraid her voice might fail her. "You're right, darling. He should," she managed in a voice that almost sounded normal.

PIETRO STARED AT THE CARP flittering through the lily pads. The giant koi pond stretched before the ornate Pura Taman Saraswati temple. Giovanna admired the drama of the temple—its orange color, its intricate carvings and elegant spires. It looked so tranquil, surrounded by water. She breathed in deeply, feeling a sense of peace.

"Madame, your Nasi Goreng."

She turned her eyes from the temple to face the waiter. "Thank you."

"And you, young sir. Your fish."

"Thank you," Pietro said quietly, eyes downcast until the waiter left. "Do people in Bali always sit on the floors, *mamma*?"

"No, honey. But it's comfortable, isn't it? Sitting on these mats, with the view of the pond and this temple."

He nodded solemnly, looking like a wizened seventy-year-old rather than the seven-year-old he was.

Giovanna remembered that playful spark in his eyes, the one that had disappeared. Would it ever return? She so longed to hear once again that joyous, high-pitched giggle, to witness that boyish enthusiasm, to watch his whole face light up when he smiled. Instead, he sat before her, a faint frown of concentration on his face. She knew if she tried to speak with him, he'd provide monosyllabic responses, preferring to be left in silence. Their days were punctuated by silence now.

She sighed once again and looked across the lily pads to the carved gods draped in black-and-white-checked sarongs. A Balinese girl was placing offerings of flowers on their pedestals, the look of devotion evident on her face. Giovanna wished she could believe in anything that fervently. All she felt was hollow inside.

"*Mamma*."

She turned to see Pietro's pinched face observing her. "Oh, did you finish already?" How had he managed to finish when she hadn't even touched her meal? "Would you like some fruit? Some ice cream?"

"No, thanks. Could I lie down on the mat and rest while you finish your lunch?"

She saw that distant look in his eyes. "Of course, darling. Just lie down there and close your eyes. Your body is still on Italian time." She began eating her fried rice. Within a minute she heard gentle snoring from across the table. The monkeys must have worn him out.

Turning back to the temple, she saw a woman who looked Indonesian taking a photo of a tall, blond foreigner. The man mugged for the camera and the woman laughed. He stepped toward her to retrieve the camera, but took her in his arms instead, spinning her around and kissing her. She laughed, but gently pushed him away as she looked around her. He took her tiny hand in his as they strode to the temple. Giovanna watched her indicating the statues and explaining something to him.

The waiter returned to clear her plate and she ordered fruit and tea. When she turned back, the couple was leaving the temple. She observed their departure with something like regret.

Years ago, walking hand in hand under the porticos of Bologna, she and Jake must have looked similar, his tall, muscular frame dwarfing her lanky figure. His blond hair glistened in the sun, announcing to the city his foreignness. She'd loved when his huge, rosy hand gripped around her tiny fingers.

He'd come for a year to study at his school's Bologna center during his master's degree in international relations. She was in the city completing her degree in Italian literature when they met at a student party. She'd almost bowed out when a friend invited her. The city was swarming with loud, drunken American university students. Willingly spending an entire evening with them at one of their parties seemed senseless. But it was there she met Jake. They'd seen one another across a crowded room, and, like the old cliché, she fell victim to the thunderbolt. So did he. By the end of the year, he'd changed his plans for a doctoral program in America for one at the University of Bologna, eventually getting a professor position at his old university's Bologna center.

She looked down at her wedding band. That party had been fifteen years ago. The Bali trip had been a surprise Jake arranged months ago for their small family. She and Jake had always wanted to come here. They cancelled a scheduled trip soon after the 2002 bombings. A few years later, they cancelled a second time when Giovanna discovered she was pregnant and the mere mention of travelling halfway around the world exacerbated her already debilitating twenty-four-hour morning sickness.

And now, years later, she was finally in Bali. She and Pietro. Alone.

THE CROWDS GREW DENSER as they walked down Monkey Jungle Street. Giovanna clutched Pietro's hand tighter as they weaved their way through the crowds. She kept a careful eye on the uneven sidewalks.

A policeman in a yellow Day-Glo vest blocked her with his arm as she tried to cross the street. "No crossing now. Ceremony is beginning."

"What ceremony?" she asked, but he'd already moved on.

Music grew closer, the joyful notes of unfamiliar instruments filling the air. To her left, a group of young men dressed in identical red short-sleeved polo shirts, sarongs of various patterns and flip-flops approached, playing stringed instruments, drums, and a gong. Pietro observed them, wide-eyed, but when the drum grew too close, he covered his ears and winced. At the intersection, they spilled into the next street. Cars waited patiently behind the police barricade lines.

"Maybe it's a parade," said Giovanna, bending low to speak in Pietro's ear.

"Look, *mamma*." Pietro's voice rose with excitement. "There's a parade float."

Pietro had seen small-town American parades when visiting his American grandparents. She turned to see what Pietro's finger was indicating. It did indeed look like a parade float, with colorful layers arranged on top of heavy bamboo poles. On top was a large, papier-mâché white bull, a young man riding on top and waving his arms in the air. At a signal, a group of young men dressed in yellow-colored sarongs heaved the float up, resting the bamboo poles on their shoulders.

"Oooh!" exclaimed Pietro, switching from Italian to English, the language spoken with his father, but one he'd been using more frequently with Giovanna. "How can they carry that through the streets? Isn't it heavy? What are they celebrating, *mamma*? Is it a holiday?"

The old Balinese man beside him clutched Pietro's shoulder with his long, bony fingers. Giovanna observed the deep crevices in his face, his wispy white hair, and wondered how old he was.

"Not quite a holiday, lad, but almost," he said in accented but precise English. "It's a cremation ceremony, and it brings together the whole community."

Pietro's big blue eyes widened as he looked up in confusion. "A cremation ceremony?" The music grew louder and Pietro turned back to the street where a group of colorfully clad women walked behind the float. Enormous baskets of fruit and flowers were perched high on their heads.

The old man observed the women, too, before turning his attention back to Pietro. "Yes. Three people in our community have died. In our religion, we wait and allow their spirits to mingle with the elements: with the earth, air, fire, light and water. Only then can we cremate them so that their souls can return to live again, perhaps within a baby about to be born to the same family."

Pietro frowned, a furrow forming between his brows. He looked so much like his father when he was up late writing an article or preparing a lecture. When did Pietro learn to adopt the same expression? Or had he always done it and she'd never noticed before?

"People can come back as a baby? Into the same family where they used to live?" The furrow grew deeper. His voice took on a breathy quality.

The shadow of a smile formed on the old man's face. "Yes. That is what we believe."

Pietro remained silent, turning back to see the street celebration, the swirl of colors of the mourners dancing to the raucous music. Giovanna pressed against him, feeling the tremor of his shoulders. The sunlight caught the glint of tears in his eyes. She shouldn't have brought him here.

How could they free themselves from the crowd, when they could move neither forward nor backward, hemmed in by the throngs of celebrants, observers and tourists? But now Pietro was looking up at the old man, and the sadness transformed into a glow. He no longer looked distraught. Was that a smile brightening his damp eyes?

He reached up and tapped the old man on the arm. "Is it just your religion, or can the dead come back for other religions, too?"

Giovanna caught her breath. His little face looked so earnest. His blue eyes burned with a hope she hadn't seen in so long.

"My daddy died, and I miss him. My auntie is expecting a baby. Could my daddy's soul come back to us in that new baby?"

The naked longing was painfully evident in his voice. Giovanna swatted away a tear.

The old man glanced at her nervously, then bent down as far as his frail frame would allow. "It's a mystery to us all, but we can always pray, can't we?"

A wide grin broke out across Pietro's face, the first smile she'd seen since that awful dash to the emergency room five months ago. His glowing face turned up to hers. "*Mamma*, did you hear? Daddy might come back! Now we just have to wait for *zia* Lina's baby to be born."

She felt her heart breaking all over again at the idea of pointing out what the priest had already explained to Pietro: that his father was in heaven, that he could hear Pietro's prayers. His eyes examined hers, waiting for her affirmation.

"Yes, my dear." She took a deep breath. "Maybe. We'll have to wait until the baby is born to see."

He smiled up at her, looking even more like his father. He leaned into her, throwing his arms around her waist in a hug, and she leaned down to meet his embrace. His rosy skin against her olive skin. Her long, dark locks tumbled over his tousled, blond curls. They didn't belong together, and yet they did.

The music grew louder, the dancing more frenetic. They both turned back at the cremation ceremony, a classic Balinese tradition, mother and son, thankful to be a part of it.

GENDER EQUALITY

Brussels

"WELL, THAT'S JUST RUBBISH, if you ask me."

No one wanted to ask Sven anything, but that never stopped him from perching on his beloved soapbox.

His fleshy face grew red from exertion. The spark in his piggy eyes lit up as Francesca observed that petulant smile she knew all too well spread slowly across his face. God, she always had the worrying desire to smack it off his face when it appeared.

All was in place for his moment of glory. For Sven loved nothing more than sharing his enlightened worldviews with the rest of the staff, secure in the knowledge that his opinions were the only ones that mattered.

"Are you kidding me?" Sven sneered and made eye contact with all those around the table. "Review the resumés and work plans for staff who haven't been promoted in the past ten years? Especially if they're women? What kind of half-baked gender policy is that?"

His snort of disdain reverberated off the tasteful taupe walls of the executive meeting room. There it was, that annoying half-smile again. Francesca restrained her hand under the table, afraid her fist might have ideas of its own if she allowed it free.

When she'd left Naples behind eight years ago, she'd been convinced an international working environment and enlightened northern views would make her career so much easier. But that was before meeting Sven, and countless other cookie-cutter models. She forced herself to concentrate on the inane words issuing forth from Sven's fleshy mouth.

"And what kind of lesson is that, for crying out loud? Let's just reward mediocrity, for Christ's sake. If you ask me ..."

Calm, Francesca. Don't let your face give you away. It was hard enough to attend these meetings each week as the token woman, forced to watch the male management ensure their privileged fortress did not fall under attack by the *hoi polloi*.

"If you ask me," Sven droned on. "Anyone who has remained in the same position for *ten years*, clearly deserves to be there. He or she simply lacks initiative, good old-fashioned gumption. And I'll go one step further ..."

She clenched her teeth as his chubby hand pounded down on the table to emphasize the brilliant observation he was just on the cusp of delivering. Francesca thought of the generations of peasant stock who toiled away in the unforgiving fields of Scandinavia. All that sweat and back-breaking labor, the years of sacrifices ... and for what? To spawn the likes of Sven, who now sat at the head of this meeting table feeling so superior.

"I'll suggest that they're damned lucky to even *have* a job in this economy. Instead of complaints to personnel ..." He fixed Francesca with his icy gaze. "They should be thanking us. After all ..."

Damn it, the petulant-little-boy-smile had returned. Couldn't she just pitch him out the window and get it over with? Just one quick shove, followed by a brief splatter on the busy Brussels streets below.

"... you know what they say, the cream always rises to the top."

She noted the polite laughter in the room in response to his booming, confident belly laugh. *Of course, Sven. Pure coincidence that your wife's uncle became Prime Minister, and overnight you moved into this position. Everyone knows your talent had nothing to do with your meteoric rise. The cream always rises to the top, my foot ...*

When Francesca raised her eyes, Sven was looking squarely at her.

"Oh, Francesca. There's some staff appreciation event tomorrow. The big boss wants a woman on stage to give us a little pep talk, tell us all about the rosy outlook for women working here." He rolled his eyes and offered his can-you-believe-the-crap-I-have-to-put-up-with? smile to all the men sitting around the table, before turning his gaze back to her. "You're from personnel, go cook up some figures and make us look good tomorrow. Hehehe ... Okay, folks. Meeting adjourned. Back to work."

"WELL, YOU *ARE* IN CHARGE of personnel, Francesca. I would assume presenting the gender balance of your organization would be part of your job," Philippe said, as he poured wine into their glasses.

"That's not really the point, is it? I'd be happy to present the situation. Our hiring practices are atrocious. Yes, of course we're international, that's obvious. But we seem to always recruit from the same tennis and golf clubs. It's been ages since we've hired a talented woman based on her merits, not her connections ... and it's certainly not that we don't receive enough impressive CVs. The promising women we do have languish in the lower-graded positions, while every male moron shoots past them up the ladder."

Francesca could already feel the headache coming on.

The headaches began soon after she'd been "promoted" to the personnel position. Francesca had been happy in her job as an economist, overseeing European development projects in Africa. But she'd long ago hit the glass ceiling, watching a string of dim-witted men being named senior economists as she slaved away, thanklessly, in her windowless office.

When the agency was criticized for its lack of female promotions, the personnel position was quickly offered to Francesca. Nothing had changed in the year she'd been in the position. She proposed mentoring programs for female hires, direct recruitment for internships through the local universities, job rotation schemes. All her suggestions sat untouched on the desks of upper management, while she was carted out at meetings as a shining example, in a skirt and heels, of changes afoot.

A title and an office with a window seemed a small exchange for the frustrations accompanying her new position.

Francesca picked up her glass and took a long sip, the wine soothing her nerves as it worked its way into her bloodstream. She cut a piece of her steak. "What pisses me off most is that he ordered me to get up and lie through my teeth during some stupid staff day they've invented. Then I have to field questions."

"Sven's a bastard anyhow," Philippe shook his head and reached for the remote control.

The European Cup match was about to begin. Francesca panicked for a moment when he pointed the remote at the television and pressed the "on" button, realizing she had his undivided attention for only a few seconds more.

"Even he has to realize he's only there thanks to his wife's connections," said Philippe.

"The thing is, he really doesn't," she said. "He's managed to convince himself that he somehow deserves it. He is a man, after all …"

But Philippe was no longer listening. The notes of the first national anthem sounded in the stadium, the soccer players stood with their hands resting on the shoulders of the young children who had accompanied them out to the pitch. Millions of male eyes across Europe and beyond—including Philippe's—were locked onto their television screens.

In living rooms across Europe, wives and girlfriends simply dissolved into thin air, mid-sentence.

Francesca took another long sip of her wine. Her husband would resurface in another two hours. For now, she needed to concentrate on how to not make an ass of herself at the staff event the following day.

FRANCESCA ENTERED HER OFFICE, shedding the fitted jacket that restricted her breathing and kicking off her pumps as she sank down into her desk chair. She clicked into her email.

A moment later, she desperately searched the carpeted floor with her toes to find her cast-off left shoe as Sven's hulking figure filled her doorframe.

"Not exactly the rosy picture I was hoping for, Francesca. I thought you women were good at dotting your 'i's with flowers and constructing the convincing fairytale from nothing."

Sven crossed his arms over his adequate belly. He'd put on weight in the last few months. Perhaps she should be grateful for her ho-hum career advancement.

"Not *quite* what I was expecting when I asked you to speak today." Sven's eyes narrowed.

Francesca successfully located her shoe. She rose and walked around the desk, standing before Sven and crossing her arms across her trim stomach. She met Sven's beady little eyes with a confident stare.

"What were you expecting, exactly, Sven? Should I have lied? I told them we were making progress … and, between us, we all know what a load *that* is."

Francesca saw the set of his jaw change. She sensed his anger.

"You know, not everyone is as pleased as I've been with your promotion. You have to demonstrate to the naysayers that you're more of a team player. In the future, if you're not able to do what I request, just let me know in advance." He paused and she sensed the danger in his angry glare. "I can always find someone else who can deliver."

He turned his bulky frame to leave, but paused at the doorway and looked over his shoulder. "I'm not as cynical as you are, Francesca. I know I have a lot of talented women working under me."

She gave him a tight smile before he turned and walked out the door. *I'm sure you do, Sven. But all the work that Sheila from accounts does "under you" does not reflect what most women associate with professional development.*

Francesca returned to her desk and slumped down in the chair, kneading her temples with her fingers. Her headache had returned.

THE NEXT DAY, Francesca sat at her desk, speaking to several young women from the organization. She'd been charged with developing the new gender policy and wanted views from a wide range of staff members. Before she met with senior staff, Francesca was eager to consult with the most junior women, whose solid academic credentials and impressive skills didn't seem to be translating into tangible career growth. The session had just gotten underway when Sven barged in without knocking.

"What's going on? Planning a hen night?"

Francesca bit her lip and breathed deeply through her nose before speaking. "What can I do for you, Sven?"

"Bit of an emergency, actually. Ladies, could I ask you to clear out?"

They picked up their purses and filed out. Effectively undermined in thirty seconds flat.

"I've been summoned for an urgent meeting outside, and you know Françoise is home on sick leave. I've had to send that worthless little temp packing."

It probably didn't help the poor girl's chances that, although highly skilled, she was unattractive and about as round as you are.

"I'm in a bind. The Commissioner should be stopping by later this morning and I'm also expecting a delivery. It's important."

Francesca tilted her head, examining him closely. "Please tell me you're not saying what I think you are. You want me to be *your secretary* this morning?"

"Just for a few hours. Put a follow-me on your phone line and check your emails from Françoise's desk."

"You're serious?" Francesca could hear her voice rising. "I imagine you've already asked Helmut and Carlos before approaching me?"

"Damn it. The old sexism charge. I'm asking *you*."

His eyes made it clear he wasn't really asking. And Francesca knew that the more junior Helmut or Carlos would never be expected to do the same. Wouldn't even accept had he deigned to ask them.

"Are you a team player or not?"

It was the cold stare that got her. She knew she couldn't risk riling him again. Silently, Francesca reached for her purse, cursing herself for her inability to tell him to go to hell. She followed him and slinked into the secretary's work station, trying to ignore the looks cast her way across the open space.

"Now," said Sven. He looked at his watch, not bothering to meet her gaze. "Commissioner Durand shouldn't arrive earlier than noon, and I'll be back by then. If he does show up earlier, just get him a coffee and keep him chatting. You're good at that sort of thing."

Fetch his coffee? Francesca felt her blood pressure rise, sensed the telltale throbbing behind her eyes.

"Now, the DVD should arrive special delivery. My wife will be stopping by to pick it up at eleven sharp. The video producer at my son's soccer match promised to get it here by half past ten, at the latest."

"Your son's *soccer match*?" Francesca struggled to control the hard edge in her rising voice. Several colleagues swiveled their heads.

Sven noticed it, too. His look was harsh. "Shhh. Keep it down, will you? I suppose you think it's beneath you, but this is what teamwork is all about." He turned his back to her and muttered a sarcastic thanks.

A waft of cologne filled her nostrils as he strode away. *Important meeting outside. Yeah, right. It's a quick rendezvous with Sheila in some sleazy little hotel. Philippe would kill me if he knew I got roped into this again.*

Francesca tried to concentrate on finalizing documents, answering emails, and ignoring the smirks as staff members passed by her new work station. She imagined the cracks being made about demotions and tried, as best she could, to push them from her mind.

Just before ten-thirty, a delivery man came, collected her signature, and handed her a manila envelope. "*Merci,*" she said, before flinging it aside.

The flap must have been secured poorly. A plastic case crashed to the floor. "Damn," she said. Picking it up, she observed the cracked case. She removed the DVD from its container, hoping it wasn't damaged, and popped it into the drive. *Let's see the reason I'm stuck here playing secretary all morning, waiting for the fat little Viking's shining moment of glory, his shot at benchwarmer stardom.* For little Sven—she'd never bothered to learn his real name—was built like a graceless bull. Just like his Dad.

The DVD charged in the computer player. She heard distinct groans emitting from her speakers, and she popped her headset into the jack when heads swiveled her way. She'd probably only made things worse. Her colleagues would think she spent her office hours watching softcore porn.

Francesca slipped the headset on, rummaging through her purse for her tissues. But this wasn't background noise or sports groans. *What the hell was it?* Her eyes flicked instinctively to the screen, and she immediately felt the urge to vomit.

She blinked twice. There, on her computer screen, was a flabby, naked Sven kneeling on red silk sheets and pounding on his chest like a gorilla. A stethoscope hung around his neck. She rubbed her eyes in horror. *Please say this is a sick hallucination. I'd rather be going out of my mind than seeing this for real.*

But even after rubbing her eyes, the horrifying images still flickered on the screen, the nauseating sounds of Sven crying, "Oh, baby!" filled her ears. And there was Sheila, in all her silicone glory, wearing some sexy little G-string and—*what the hell was that?*—a white bustier with a little red cross on it, a pert little nurse's cap perched high on her bleached-blond hair. *Oh, yuck!*

"Come to the doctor!" Sven bounced up and down on the bed with mounting excitement, and Francesca feared she would retch all over poor Françoise's perfectly organized desk. This was just too much to take. Sven was hateful enough with his clothes on. No woman should have to be exposed to this.

She popped the DVD out of the player, and slipped it back into its manila envelope.

Still, as disgusting as it was, Francesca felt the first stirrings of respect for the woman she'd written off as a peroxide-headed bimbo. Blackmailing the boss. She had to hand it to Sheila.

When she looked up, Sven's elegant wife towered over her.

"Oh, hello! You startled me." Francesca struggled to stand up and shake hands, willing her voice to remain calm. "How nice to see you again."

"Oh, Francesca. Tell me this isn't the effect of the layoffs Sven wanted to implement. It's all he ever talks about at home these days. You haven't been downgraded, have you? I told him how much I value your work with the agency. I just want you to know this has nothing to do with me." Her big blue eyes were almost childlike in their innocence.

Francesca was confused for a moment. Her mind raced. *Layoffs? Sven was restructuring? Come to think of it, she had heard rumors, although she'd been quick to dismiss them. Why, that little bastard!*

She smiled at Sven's pretty wife and prayed her voice would sound genuine. "Oh, no. Just being a team player today and helping out." She ensured her smile appeared perfectly sincere as she picked up the manila envelope and handed it to Sven's wife. "Here you go. Special delivery that just arrived. Sven gave me strict orders that you watch it right away. No need to wait for him. Said your little star is the next Ibrahimović."

"Thank you, Francesca," said the cuckolded wife with a smile.

Francesca watched her walk to the bank of elevators. A delivery man exited the elevator before Sven's wife entered. He turned to admire her tall, regal figure. The doors closed. The delivery man approached Francesca's desk and she noted a smile of appreciation still on his lips. Sven's wife had that effect on men. Why she had chosen Sven was a mystery to everyone.

"Special delivery. A sports DVD." He read from his clipboard. "I'm told it's urgent." He handed Francesca a packet. "Could I ask you to sign here?"

"With pleasure," said Francesca. She scratched her pen across the paper and hummed a tune. Her head hadn't felt so clear in ages. There was no gnawing pain lurking behind her eyes, no pressure at her temples. She breathed in deeply, then looked into the deliveryman's eyes and smiled as she handed back the clipboard. "Don't ever forget that the cream always rises to the top, okay?"

WINE & BEAUTY
Milan

DUSK WAS FALLING on the Navigli, ushering in its moment of splendor. As the purple fingers of light faded in the metropolitan sky, the dirt and grit of the canal district were masked by the darkness, while sparkling lights strung along the canals reflected in the water and enhanced its beauty.

It was a place where tourists stopped and stared as they passed, enthralled by its charming corners and bustling restaurants and bars. The Milanese, young and old, gathered tightly together for *aperitivi* and the endless chatter that reverberated off the colorful canal-side buildings before absorbing into the gentle flow of the water. Leggy models, wealthy bankers and businessmen, society matrons and eager economics students from the prestigious neighboring university all rubbed elbows in the densely packed bars.

Café Navigli was similar to many establishments along the bustling Naviglio Grande. Discreet tables within, a gaggle of canal-side tables scattered haphazardly outside and along the canal. Its happy hour never failed to attract a diverse crowd.

Simonetta stood beside her co-worker, Roberta, as the

evening crowd began to trickle in, only to be replaced by the dinner crowd at a later hour. The raucous student table had been placated for the time being. No matter how many times she served those cliquey crowds, Simonetta shook her head in wonder that these were society's elite students. Although she would have liked to have studied herself, this crowd always left her feeling closer to her parents' firm working-class conviction that higher education was useless, even potentially dangerous, and absolutely to be avoided at all costs, lest one become lazy and entitled. For the first time, instead of rolling her eyes, she wondered if her parents had a valid point. Even if these economics students probably wouldn't be struggling to pay the rent in a few years' time…

"They're going to be loud and obnoxious all night, aren't they?" whispered Roberta, casting a wary eye over the student table.

"Afraid so," said Simonetta. "What else is new under the sun?" She sighed. "At least we know they'll escape the minute happy hour prices transform at the dinner hour." With almost two years under her belt, Simonetta could handle the Café Navigli in her sleep, but the owner had done well to hire Roberta. She was a quick learner and had settled in well during her first month, under Simonetta's diligent tutelage. Moreover, Simonetta enjoyed her company. Something she couldn't say for the numerous waitresses who had cycled in and out, rarely worth the effort to train.

The sloshed students were calling out to the waitresses, and none too politely. Simonetta flashed a tight smile. "Don't worry, I'll handle the Masters of the Universe this time. You stay here to meet and greet so we fill those remaining tables."

She made her way to the table where the students pummeled her with their orders, handed her their empty trays of appetizers and asked for more—gleefully fending off the need to cook tonight. She smiled patiently, ignored their baser comments, and carried out their wishes with her usual detached efficiency.

This job was supposed to have been temporary, a way to escape her parents' little village, their desire for her to join them on the assembly line of the local factory, and the chance to live in the heart of it all in stylish Milan. Who knew the heart of it all was so damned expensive? The money she had been trying to stash away was never enough. Unlike her parents, she did want to study. Wanted to start taking classes at Milano Statale to become a teacher, even if she knew she'd have to balance coursework with a heavy load of working hours to support herself. Leonardo moving in had slowed her progress and slimmed her wallet. Starting this autumn wouldn't be feasible, but surely in another year …

She went up to the bar with the drinks order and Carlo winked at her. "Are they behaving themselves? Should I water down their drinks to keep them docile?"

She laughed. "No worse than normal. Still stuffing their faces, so I'll replace their hors d'oeuvres. Wouldn't want the little trust-fund kids to starve to death. I'll be right back for the drinks." She made her way to the kitchen where the food was piled high, well stocked for the invading happy hour army. She replenished the trays and made her way back to the students, distributing the trays across the long table. "I'll be right back with your drinks."

When she returned from ferrying the orders, she stood at the hostess stand, reviewing reservations. With several large tables and every place setting fully booked, it would be a late night.

Roberta sidled up beside her. "Not sure if I'm ready for the chaos tonight."

Simonetta smiled at her. "You'll be fine. You eased in a lot faster than I did, back when I started."

"Yeah, well, desperation is a big motivator. I need the money because my parents can't help me out with paying for my classes. I've got my last exams in a month, then I'll be happy to squeeze in as many hours as I can to save up lots this summer." She paused to say good evening to regular clients taking their leave. "Anyway, all set for this autumn, when we'll be fellow students."

Simonetta felt her cheeks burn and she glanced down at her order pad with intense interest. She could feel Roberta's gaze boring into her.

"Don't tell me Leonardo's still freeloading over at yours."

Simonetta sighed. "Yeah. Eight months and he's never gotten around to paying any rent. And now he's talked me into lending him money for expensive camera equipment." She fingered the edge of her order's pad. "But he says he'll pay me back soon." The magma of Mount Vesuvius boiled within, and she whispered, "But I don't have enough money to start in the fall. It will have to be next year."

Roberta huffed loudly. "Simonetta, I get he's a charming guy. Good-looking, fun. But I know the type. He's using you. You know you'll never see that money again."

Simonetta looked into Roberta's hazel eyes, burning with rage, while her face remained implacable. "I'm starting to realize that. At first, I was understanding. Photographer's assistant is precarious, but now he's off on fashion shoots all the time." She took a deep breath. "And damn it, why should I kill myself waitressing to pay for his equipment when he's already living rent-free? He knows I'm not exactly rolling in money."

Roberta squeezed her hand, and her warm fingers felt comforting.

A man signaled for service and Roberta squeezed tighter before pulling away. "I'll get this." She approached the table with a broad smile.

God, Simonetta knew she sounded like such a hick speaking to Roberta, who'd grown up in Milan and saw through people like Leonardo so much better than she ever had. Roberta had met him once in her first days at the café, when he'd picked Simonetta up after a late-night shift and chatted a while with Roberta.

The next evening, Simonetta had been eager to hear her co-worker's assessment of her live-in boyfriend, not expecting her terse critique. "Good-looking, I'll give you that. But a definite player. Rather full of himself. Watch your wallet with that one, and make sure you get his half of the rent up front."

Simonetta had reeled from this cool assessment. Little did her new co-worker realize Simonetta had never seen a cent of rent money. Or grocery money. Or utility money. There were even occasional withdrawals from her ATM card, if she were foolish enough to leave her card lying around. Of course, Leonardo always claimed it was an emergency, and he'd pay her back. Something that never happened.

Slowly, month by month, the money she'd stashed away to start her studies had dwindled away. And now, she was back at square one. Simonetta twisted one long chestnut lock with her index finger. Roberta had been right a month ago, and she was right now. Leonardo was charismatic, and good-looking, and, yeah, good in bed, too. But how long could she finance her live-in boyfriend who was clearly using her?

Roberta returned to her place and glanced at her watch. "Forty minutes to the dinner shift." She grinned. "When all hell breaks loose." She placed a gentle hand on Simonetta's arm, truly worrying her hair by this stage. "*Bella,* you know you're doing that a lot more lately. If I had your gorgeous hair,

I certainly wouldn't risk always twisting it like that—I'd be afraid it would start falling out in clumps."

Simonetta shook her head, but placed her hand by her side. "Yeah, you're right. Just trying to get my head around how to get back on track for school next year."

"So are you finally ready to tell Leonardo to pay up what he owes or take a hike?"

Simonetta sighed. "And if I'm afraid of being alone?"

"Someone like you? You'll find someone better. You're smart, and funny, and gorgeous. Gorgeous always helps."

Simonetta shook her head. "Roberta, he works with models all day. He's surrounded by the most gorgeous women in the world. It's obvious he doesn't think I can compare to that."

"Then he's an ass. Find someone who appreciates you." She leaned in closer. "Believe me, I've met my fair share of conceited men. Milan specializes in them. Cut your losses now and get rid of him. Next year at this time, you'll be preparing for your first semester at college." She lowered her voice. "You deserve it."

The words spun in Simonetta's head. She knew Roberta was right. Ever since she'd met her, Roberta had an uncanny knack for being right, for chipping away at the little tower of lies and justifications Simonetta had constructed to rationalize her foolish choices. She watched two women approach the café. Beside her, Roberta stood ready to move, but Simonetta placed a hand on her arm, and whispered, "I'm fine. I'll go."

She took two drink menus and made her way to the women.

The taller, blonde woman addressed her. "*Buona sera.* We have dinner reservations, but we thought we'd come a bit earlier and enjoy a drink along the canal before we move to our table."

"Of course," said Simonetta. "Would you like to sit here?" She indicated a table right along the canal's edge.

The woman turned to her friend, who nodded, and they took their places at the table.

The blonde woman settled into her chair, looking out over the water. Simonetta admired the intricate, upswept hairstyle and wondered if she could manage the same with her thicker locks. Her gaze slipped down to the gorgeous Prada dress the woman was wearing. She'd seen it in the magazines, and the belted, twill design hugged the woman's figure in all the right places. The delicate petal color flattered the woman's complexion. How many months of rent would she need to save up for a dress like that?

Her gaze slipped down to the wedding ring and the expensive tennis bracelet encased around one delicate wrist. A shockingly large ruby surrounded by diamonds staked its claim on her right-hand ring finger. Finance husband, most likely. They always flocked here to drink expensive wines and chatter together, seemingly fresh from the salons and garbed in their impeccable clothes. Captured snippets of these conversations seemed to revolve exclusively around spa trips, jets to exotic destinations and reservations to exclusive Milanese restaurants. A parallel life to the penny-pinching version she lived.

As her mind took flight, Simonetta realized both women were looking up at her quizzically. She smiled sheepishly. "Sometimes I get lost for a moment with this purple light that falls across the Navigli. I was just admiring it." She moved to hand the women the menus, but the blonde waved it away.

"No need. We already know what we want. Could you bring us a bottle of Gaja Chardonnay?"

"Of course," said Simonetta. "I'll be back in a moment." She should have pegged them as the type to drop a few hundred on happy hour drinks. Now she'd have to constantly be on call to refill their glasses. When she passed Roberta, she murmured, "The Gaja, can you set up the tableside ice bucket?"

She hustled in and Carlo retrieved the bottle and prepared it alongside two glasses on an ornate tray. She brought it out to the women, lowering it to the makeshift table Roberta had positioned there for her and placing the two glasses before the women. Carefully uncorking the bottle, she poured a small amount into the blonde's glass, twirling the bottle upwards with a practiced wrist. She suppressed a smile. Back in her little village, she'd only known the wine you bought directly from local producers in jugs you supplied from home. Here in Milan, the café owner had insisted she attend sommelier classes. Although she couldn't afford the bottles she recommended, she could expertly pour and pair any dish with the perfect wine.

The blonde gave a discreet nod, and Simonetta poured into the blonde's glass before moving on to her friend. She then tucked the glass into the ice bucket Roberta had prepared tableside, covered it with cloth, folded up the makeshift table and took her leave.

After stowing the table and tray away, she stepped beside Roberta, whispering, "If they don't polish that off right away, we'll move it in when they dine. Don't worry, I'll keep an eye on refill duty."

"Thanks. I can't manage that bottle twist like you can. And those women look like they'd flog me alive if I spilled a drop, which I would absolutely do." She cracked a small smile.

"You'll get the hang of it. I did." She gazed at the two women, the lights shining down on them from the streetlights and café illumination being switched on as evening descended. The blonde whispered something to her friend, who threw back her head in joyful laughter before whispering something back like a cheeky schoolgirl. Both sipped from their glasses, looking glamorous on their spot along the canal. *Look at them, with their perfect clothes and thousands spent on hair and spas.*

Bet they wouldn't be agonizing over rent payments or affording college. The more she observed, the more resentful she felt.

When she noted the wine level diminishing, she stepped over to quietly pick up the bottle and to refill the glasses.

The blonde appraised her with a cool glance, muttering a quiet "*Grazie.*" Simonetta nodded and retreated.

The loud college students were beating a hasty retreat, after having settled their bill with Roberta. The crowds passed along the roads and the stars were beginning to sparkle in the night sky.

"You know, Simonetta," said Roberta beside her as they she started clearing a nearby table. "Sometimes lives can appear perfect from the outside. Yeah, those women have amazing clothes and probably tons of money, but who says their lives are so much happier?"

Simonetta offered a wry smile. "You know, you're probably right. What do you want to bet they'd jump at the chance to change places with us?" She chuckled and grabbed a wet dish cloth, cleaning the table Roberta had just cleared. "One has to expect that when leading such glamorous lives, after all. Everyone envies us. They want to be us." She shook her head and applied elbow grease to a stubborn stain.

LUDOVICA WASN'T OFTEN in the Navigli, even if, years ago, she'd lived here. In a run-down little apartment over these same cafés, to be exact. She looked out onto the Naviglio grande. She'd forgotten, but it really did look spectacular at night. All the grit and grime carefully hidden away in the romantic twinkling of lights strung across the waters, all the blazing streetlamps and lights from cafés and restaurants, the strolling crowds and their ceaseless movement.

She looked down at her Prada dress and shuddered. Her husband had, unusually, accompanied her shopping that day and insisted, but she no longer had the youth to pull off dresses like these. She shook her head in frustration.

Peals of laughter sounded behind her. Those raucous students a few tables over were obviously from Bocconi. Speaking with the hubris of the young whose wonderful lives stretched far ahead of them, all the glories still to behold. Or so they thought.

Reality would hit later.

Back when she'd been in their place, studying economics and reveling in thoughts of her boundless future, she'd thought just like they did. She hadn't factored in a handsome, young finance executive sweeping her off her feet and luring her away from her hard-fought banking position. She'd braved work after their son, but he'd insisted she leave after the birth of their daughter. And she'd relented. Now their kids were grown, but she'd never returned to work. Would anyone even want her now? With a rapidly changing workforce, dinosaurs were hardly in demand.

It didn't help that her husband was constantly regaling her with tales of the fascinating female executives he met at work conferences. Long ago, he'd ceased to find her fascinating. Instead, she seamlessly slipped away from corporate meetings and into the full-time role of household manager, his personal secretary, and organizing their dinner parties.

Across the table, Natalia was clearing her throat, and Ludovica looked momentarily lost. The waitress was beside them uncorking their Gaja. Her gaze met Ludovica's before she poured a taste into Ludovica's glass. Ludovica swirled the golden wine, wafted it below her nose and took a decisive sip, before nodding to the young woman.

She observed the waitress in silence as she poured for Natalia, then placed the bottle into the ice bucket and covered it with the serving cloth before quietly retreating.

Natalia held up her glass and Ludovica responded in kind, then they both sipped their wine.

Natalia was the first to place down her glass. "You're awfully quiet tonight. Is something bothering you?"

Ludovica played with the stem of her glass. "Is anything *not* bothering me? It seems to be my constant state."

"Is Federico behaving badly again?"

"If by behaving badly, you mean having it off with his barely-out-of-braces secretary, then yes. Federico is indeed behaving badly." She turned away to gaze across the canal, at a young couple on the opposite bank nuzzling one another under the flickering lights. They'd see how long that would last. She closed her eyes, took a deep breath and returned her gaze to meet her friend's troubled expression.

"I'm so sorry. I don't know how you put up with him." She placed a gentle hand over Ludovica's.

"Nor do I, to be truthful." She shook her head. "When the kids were younger, it was for their sake. Though goodness knows if the sacrifice was worth it."

Natalia grimaced. "Oh, no. Is it Samuele? Is he back in rehab?"

Ludovica wiped a tear away with her index finger. "Twenty-two years old, and his second round. You remember what he was like when he was young. I still don't know where we went wrong."

"Honey, it doesn't necessarily mean you went wrong. They grow up. Go away. Make choices ... too few of them good. That's not up to us, we can only be there for them. I'm going to guess Serena's not any better."

"Oh. You know. Just wrapped up in herself. Barely calls or visits, unless she needs money. Seems to keep taking the same exams over and over, so no idea what's going on there." She took another fortifying sip. "Has only contempt for me. Only *papà* is good enough for her."

"It'll pass. Remember how horrible Marta was for a while? It sounds terrible to say about your own kids, but I always took longer to answer my cell when I saw she was calling. I knew I'd feel awful for a whole day after those conversations." She reached up and swept a lock of hair behind her ear. "But I have to assume it was a phase. You saw her last week at lunch. She's so much more stable now. Loves her job. Finally has a nice boyfriend."

"I know. She seemed so much more mature when we all went for lunch." Ludovica took another sip of her wine, then sat in silence as the eager waitress ran over to top off their glasses. She offered a tight smile when the waitress retreated, and picked up on her earlier conversation. "Believe me, Marta is who I'm pinning all my hopes on. I'm praying this is just a phase. For both of them."

Natalia nodded. "It is. I'm sure. They'll come back to you. *La mamma è sempre la mamma.*"

Ludovica proffered a sad smile. "Let's hope they remember that. Goodness knows I've lost so many hours of sleep over them and their problems, when they barely spare a thought for me."

Natalia nodded knowingly before leaning forward. "And how's your dad doing?"

"Heart attack number two." Ludovica shook her head. "God, I know how hard it's been for him ... well, since *mamma* died ... but he needs to start taking better care of himself. Too much wine, too many cigarettes. He says he's too old to change." She traced her finger around the top of her wine glass. "I'm getting down to Bologna as often as I can, but no luck trying to get him here where I could help him daily."

"It's hard to pick up and move after such a long time. Plus, he probably doesn't want to lose the memories of her. Anyway, let me know next time you're heading down. I'll take a day off and we can call Maria, all have lunch together."

Ludovica smiled. "I haven't seen Maria in years. You're right. We should. Remember when we all used to come out to the happy hours here a gazillion years ago? Escaping from homework and projects?"

Natalia chuckled. "Those were good times. I miss them some days. Everything seemed so much easier back then."

Ludovica took another sip of her wine and looked thoughtfully to one side. "Do you see those two waitresses? How they're chatting quietly to one another? Probably poking fun at us and the other clientele."

Natalia glanced over. "What about them?"

"God, don't you just wish you could go back again? Look at the one on the left. Our waitress—glowing with the radiance of youth. Look at those gorgeous chestnut curls. I'd kill for hair like that. Look at that perfect figure. Bet she's not torturing herself with diets and hours at the gym. Expensive creams and potions to ward off wrinkles and cellulite. All that effort for an indifferent husband." She shook her head. "Come to think of it, Federico's secretary looks somewhat similar. She probably has no idea how good she has it. How perfect her life is now before all the complications start to weigh down on her." She stroked her tennis bracelet. "I dunno. If I could change places with her now, I'd do it in a heartbeat."

Natalia shook her head and smiled. "It was kind of fun when we were living in our little hovel here in Navigli, taking classes at Bocconi. Meeting guys who were all wrong for us. Never sure if we could scrape together enough money for rent. You're right. I guess we didn't appreciate it at the time. Didn't know how good we had it."

Ludovica shook her head. "How about a long weekend? Want to get up to Forte dei Marmi this weekend? I'll message Federico we'll head up Friday."

Natalia took a sip from her glass. "Tuscan seacoast escape sounds perfect. I'm sure I can get away for the weekend, and throw in a Monday. Almost like old times." She laughed. "But luxurious."

Ludovica texted away.

"Listen, while you're making plans with Federico, my bladder's about to burst. I'll just pop into the ladies' and be right back." She stood up. "Maybe we can shift over to the dining room. Age is catching up with me. I can't drink without eating anymore."

Ludovica looked up and smiled as her friend stood and left the table. Her phone pinged and she read the message. "Business meeting, my ass." She signaled to the waitress, who approached her with those glossy chestnut locks and effortlessly supple body. Damned youth. Ludovica looked up. "Could you help move our ice bucket and glasses inside? I think we'd like to start our dinner now."

Simonetta nodded and called over Roberta. The two women cleared the table and ice bucket.

Ludovica called her husband. "Federico, are you honestly telling me you have a business meeting *this weekend* in our beach home?" She closed her eyes and rubbed the bridge of her nose, fending off an impending headache. She fought to keep the familiar rage from creeping into her voice. She stood and walked toward the restaurant entrance. "Yes, well, we certainly wouldn't want you to miss out on closing those important business deals. Your secretary will clearly have everything well organized for you. Be on top of you all weekend long and help to take the tension away." She fought to keep the venom boiling up inside her. She sighed. "I never get to spend significant time with Natalia. If we can't have the Tuscan house, then we'll head up to Paris. Have Jacques air out the apartment. We'll fly up Friday night and stay through Tuesday." Now she would have to buy tickets, convince Natalia to add on a day to join her for a Parisian jaunt, but it beat sitting around and wondering what Federico and his bimbo were getting up to in the Tuscan villa. The furnishing–the bed–she'd chosen transformed into their playground. How could Federico do this to her? She returned to her seat, slumping into it.

"*Signora*, are you alright? Everything is arranged at your table. The wine is chilling, and the maître d' is ready to seat you, as soon as you're ready. I will be following to serve you."

Ludovica looked up at that heartbreakingly fresh and lovely face and smiled faintly. "Of course," she said distractedly, casting a last glance over the Naviglio. "The important thing, of course, is having the wine." She turned back to the waitress and smiled sadly. "You know, don't you, it's what makes us beautiful."

The young woman's forehead furrowed in confusion. Ludovica wanted to reprimand her for making faces like that. The wrinkles would come soon enough. No need to hurry them along and ruin a fresh, unlined face. But she said nothing, hoping Federico's mistress was also unwittingly hastening her own aging process. She looked up, momentarily confused. It wasn't Federico's tramp, but the young waitress. "Do you know E.M. Forster?"

The waitress looked confused, the deep furrow still there. "The author? Yeah, kind of."

"He wrote beautiful things about Italy and the Italians. In one of his novels, he has his characters traveling down to Italy. He speaks about the northern Europeans being ugly and drinking beer. He describes the landscape changing as their carriage passes into Italy, and he comments on the people, too, contrasting them with the less appealing northern Europeans. He says when he passes into Italy, the people cease being ugly and drinking beer; instead, they begin to 'drink wine and be beautiful.'" She looked out on the Naviglio once more before standing and positioning her purse on her shoulder.

The waitress stood in stunned silence. Here was Ludovica, oversharing once again. She gave a tight smile. "I always enjoyed that line." She smoothed down her expensive dress, the one she didn't even like. "Guess I can feel I'm doing my part—drinking wine, I mean." She shook her head. "My special tribute to beauty." She walked alone towards the entrance.

SIMONETTA STOOD FOR A MOMENT IN STUNNED SILENCE, until Roberta approached and handed her a warm dishrag.

"What was that all about?"

"No clue. Something about upholding Italy's standards of beauty by drinking expensive wine."

Roberta chucked. "Well, to be fair, she and her friend do that pretty well. We can be grateful for their selfless service."

"I overheard her phone call." Simonetta shook her head. "What a spoiled woman. She was browbeating her husband because she couldn't get the Forte de Marmi beach villa this weekend. Horror of horrors—she's headed to their Paris property. I hope she'll survive the injustice of it all."

"Do I hear a subtle hint of envy?"

"No, you hear a whole, towering heapload of envy." Simonetta took the dishrag from Roberta's hand and began to violently scrub down the tables while Roberta set to work emptying the ashtrays. "You know, a woman like that probably has no idea how good she has it. How disgustingly perfect her life is. Everything she could ever want right at her fingertips. A perfect life." She scrubbed harder at a stubborn food stain on a tabletop as Roberta wiped down the chairs. "I dunno. If I could change places with her now, I'd do it in a heartbeat ..."

The noisy, animated chatter of departing happy hour crowds formed a steady hum that reverberated off the colorful canal-side buildings and absorbed into the gentle flow of the water. Night fully descended onto the Navigli, with its inky black sky resplendent with sparkling stars and a full moon. Combined with the lights and laughter, all the grit, grime and ugliness of the city were fully hidden from view. Only the romantic façade of perfection remained.

Simonetta and Roberta picked up their dishrags and made their way into the restaurant for the start of dinner service.

BITTER HARVEST
Orvieto

ALLISON SAT AT THE DESK, staring at the number scrawled in familiar handwriting. He'd always favored his expensive fountain pens. The thick, black ink looked so bold and authoritative against the white page.

"Twenty-one?" she said, shaking her head. She was helpless to stop the flow of tears that cascaded down her cheeks once again.

THE PRIEST'S BARITONE VOICE could not fill the cavernous cathedral, but that did not stop him from trying. At first, Allison attempted to listen to his comforting words, but her mind quickly drifted.

She concentrated instead on Giuliana's warmth beside her. Allison's arm rested on her shoulders and she felt each distinct tremor of her body as she sobbed through the mass. At least the Italians did not have open caskets at their funerals, a tradition from her own culture she'd always despised. She was relieved a corpse in a coffin would not be the last image her daughter retained of her beloved father.

Allison pulled Giuliana closer. If only she could absorb the pain for both of them, and leave her daughter lighter. Giuliana's shoulders slumped. Tears flowed from beneath her closed lids. Allison had to get Giuliana back to Milan as soon as possible. The distraction of classes and exams would help. Staying home would suck the life from her.

Allison tried to focus once more on the priest's comforting words, but her brain was unwilling to concentrate. Instead, her gaze wandered to the chapel's Signorelli frescoes. Terrifying blue and purple devils beat and strangled the damned, their naked bodies contorted in pain. One winged devil carried a woman on his back, his ugly, horned head turned to gaze at her, her hands clutched firmly in his own. Pain and confusion marred her face, the golden locks of her hair fluttered in the wind as the devil transported her to the depths of the underworld and the angels looked on. Just beside her, another winged devil dropped his naked charge through the air, his body plummeting headfirst down to the writhing mass of human misery. The Last Judgment.

For over five hundred years, generations of Orvieto residents had gazed on this fresco—and thought what, exactly? That they would be far away from this misery in the company of the angels? Or did something in their lives lead them to suspect those winged devils might be transporting them below for the hereafter?

It was in this chapel, before this very fresco, that a young Allison—in Orvieto on a study abroad program—first met Guglielmo. In a burst of optimism, Allison had purchased a sketching pad and pencils. She sat in the silence of the Chapel of the Madonna di San Brizio on a sunny October morning, attempting to sketch the horror of the scene before her. But a semester in Italy could not work miracles, and Alison had never been talented in art. Yet with youthful bravado, she attempted, again and again, to capture the scene before her.

Two young men interrupted her solitude. The taller one, with thick brown hair and green eyes, described the fresco to the other. He gestured grandly to the figures, speaking in an Italian too rapid for her to understand, save a word here and there. When he turned to her and smiled, she felt her cheeks burn. She quickly returned to her sketching, allowing her long hair to fall over her flushed cheeks.

Footsteps approached. When she looked up, the tall, young man loomed before her. The white teeth of his smile appeared so bright against his tanned complexion.

"May I see?"

He hadn't even attempted Italian with her, she noted with disappointment. Her Italian was atrocious back then, but she always appreciated the chance to at least try.

Allison nodded and the young man leaned closer, studying her sketching, examining the writhing damned she'd tried to capture. Finally, he looked up and met her gaze. Allison felt the inexplicable need for his approval. His lips twitched upwards and she felt her heart soar for a brief moment, before he opened his mouth and issued a full-throated laugh that echoed throughout the chapel.

Her daughter's frail body trembled beside her, and Allison's thoughts returned to the funeral. She squeezed her close, just as she had when Giuliana was a girl and needed comforting. If only things were so easy now.

THE CORNFLOWER BLUE SKY and bright sunlight were at odds with the crisp chill in the April air. Allison worried about the effects of the sudden cold snap, but the vineyards were far from her mind as she made her way to the various tables to speak with her guests.

Giuliana was surrounded by friends and aunts. Allison felt less guilty about leaving her alone, and could concentrate her attention on all those who returned home with them after the funeral service.

Half of Orvieto seemed to be wandering the grounds of the old stone house and sharing memories of growing up with Guglielmo. Allison listened to tale after heartfelt tale, nodding in all the right places, but her emotions were still so raw. Ever since the day the officers showed up on her doorstep to tell her about the traffic accident on the A1, just a few kilometers away, Allison moved through her days in a fog.

She thought about the doorbell ringing back on that evening, how certain she was it was Guglielmo surprising her with a bouquet of roses before taking her to dinner. She tucked a stray lock into her upswept hair and checked herself one last time in the mirror, smoothing her dress. It had been expensive, but the soft fabric clung to every curve perfectly, and she'd wanted to look stunning on her twenty-first wedding anniversary. She leapt to the door and opened it wide, her smile quickly fading when she saw the policemen. The expressions on their faces said everything their lips had not yet uttered.

Allison shook her head, attempting to banish the memory. She looked out over the vineyards glowing under the bright afternoon sunlight. Soon enough, she'd be consumed by work among the vines as the late spring and summer sun ripened the grapes.

Guglielmo had been returning from Vinitaly, the annual wine fair, where he'd reached agreements with foreign distributors. He'd sounded so excited about it over the phone. Now Allison knew she would soon be working to meet those demands.

She twisted her wedding band nervously. *You'll have to handle it all alone for the first time. How will you manage?* She heard footsteps, and quickly hid her fear to turn with a smile and welcome another neighbor's reminiscences about her deceased husband.

LATER THAT EVENING, after the last guests had taken their leave and the sun set beyond the rolling hills of the vineyards, Allison and Giuliana sat together on the couch. The television was switched on, but Allison hadn't processed any of the news. She kept thinking about how she would retire to her room, all alone. For the first time since the accident, things seemed final. Guglielmo was buried in the Orvieto soil, and life would simply continue, whether she was ready or not.

"Mom, I don't have to go back, you know." Her daughter's voice was soft, uncertain. It was the halting voice Allison remembered from Giuliana's childhood, not the confident tone of the strong young woman who'd emerged just a few short years ago. "I can arrange with the school, defer a year. I could stay and help you with the harvest."

Allison turned to face her daughter, brushing a long, blond lock off her forehead. Giuliana had inherited her own fair coloring, but for all the rest she was her father's daughter. Her confidence, her knack for figures, even her expressions were all Guglielmo.

Allison attempted a smile. "No, honey. I can't let you do that. You worked so hard to get there, and I want you to get back up to Milan by the end of the week. It will do you good to be back in classes."

"But will you let me know if you change your mind, Mom?"

Allison kissed her daughter's forehead and pulled her in tight. "I can manage alone, *amore*. Your *papà* was so proud of you getting into Bocconi. He would have been the first to want you to return."

She caressed her daughter's back as the sobs intensified. They remained that way for a long time, Giuliana's crying drowning out the sounds of annoying television game show applause.

TEMPERATURES DROPPED. Allison couldn't remember a September so cold since she'd moved to Italy, and she worried the cold snap would anticipate the harvest. She wrapped her wool sweater tighter around her shoulders as she spoke on the phone to Guglielmo's tax advisor.

"I'm sorry, Allison, but I need all the information about the equipment Guglielmo bought six months ago. How strange of him not to have sent it to me. Sorry to put more on your plate, but I really need you to find those documents."

Allison groaned inwardly. In the five months since Guglielmo's death, she'd been buried in work, and in handling the financial side of the business, something she'd always been pleased to pass off to Guglielmo. Italian taxes and regulations intimidated her. Now she had no choice but to learn this aspect of the business, too. She took a deep breath. "I'll look for them, Alberto, and let you know as soon as I find them."

Allison hung up the phone and ran her hand across the top drawer of Guglielmo's desk. The only drawer for which she hadn't found the key. She'd been avoiding it, foolishly thinking Guglielmo would be back to open it himself.

She knew it wasn't true. Of course, she knew it. Yet something in her still resisted tampering with his things. Forcing the drawer somehow felt so final.

Sighing, she went to fetch the toolbox.

"*CIAO, AMORE.* Luana's in for a bit of fun. What about you? Leave your contacts and when you want to meet, and I'll get back to you as soon as I can ..."

Allison ended the call before the voicemail could beep. She stared back at Luana's name and number in Guglielmo's agenda.

Thick black letters announced 7 April 2012. The day before their twenty-first wedding anniversary.

The agenda was filled with a long list of women's names and numbers stretching from the eve of their first wedding anniversary in 1991 to 7 April 2012, the day before their twenty-first. One day before his death.

A different woman every year, their names and phone numbers meticulously recorded by her ever-methodical husband. All in Verona, apparently. Vinitaly often fell around those dates, but not always. Yet he always seemed to have an excuse—meetings with possible clients before or after the wine fair. How had she never suspected anything?

"Twenty-one?" She shook her head and the tears streamed down her cheeks once more.

THE LIGHTS FLICKERED over the Navigli, points of yellow reflecting on the canal's night-black waters. Giuliana sat at the outdoor table across from her mother. Her after-dinner espresso cup clattered to its saucer.

"So you're just abandoning the vineyard?"

Allison sensed the accusation in her daughter's words.

"Not abandoning it. Marco will be the managing director. He was always *papà*'s right-hand man."

"*You* were always *papà*'s right-hand woman."

Allison nodded and sighed as she watched all the young people walking along Milan's canals.

"So you just wake up one day and decide to move to Rome and manage Meaghan's wine bar? This all seems so sudden. Can't you just give me a reason?"

"Honey, I could give you twenty-one reasons, but I really don't want to go into that. You'll just have to trust me. I need to do this."

The confusion on Giuliana's face was evident, but Allison could tell she wouldn't argue anymore.

"I want you to be happy, Mom. I thought you would be back home. I appreciate that at least you won't do anything drastic until I decide if I want to take over things at the vineyard after I graduate."

They walked back to Giuliana's flat in silence. Allison noted the coolness of the kisses her daughter placed on her cheeks.

"Coming up?"

"No, *amore*. Not this time. I need to catch a train." Allison shifted her overnight bag to her other shoulder. "Next time, okay?"

Giuliana nodded, and Allison stroked her cheek. She'd let her daughter get used to the idea.

Allison reached the metro stop that would take her to the train station, where she'd board the *Freccia rossa* to Rome.

As she descended to the metro, she tapped Guglielmo's agenda, nestled in her coat's breast pocket, and smiled. *In the end, you made things easy for me. Some women mourn for years, but you've given me twenty-one reasons to start my new life.*

TEA INSTEAD OF COFFEE

London

BIG, CHILLY RAINDROPS splashed the lenses of the sunglasses she'd optimistically slipped on when leaving her flat this morning. Eleonora pushed them up over her hair and observed the storm clouds directly above. Fat, grey clouds always threatened rain in London. How could people stand it?

Teacup in hand, Eleonora moved inside, casting an apologetic glance at the waitress. The Brits constantly apologized. In Naples, no waiter would question you for ducking inside from a storm.

"Sorry, I'm late."

Yet more apologies.

Julian slipped into the seat beside hers, peeling off his raincoat and running his fingers through his wet mop of hair. He certainly wouldn't have sunglasses tucked away anywhere on a day like today. In fact, Julian might not even own a pair of sunglasses. She'd certainly never seen him wearing any.

Blinding rain lashed violently against the glass now. Yet another dreary Saturday. She sighed. "No Hyde Park today, I guess."

Julian observed her with that bland look of boredom Londoners perfected. "Only *you* could plan an April picnic. You're not in Italy anymore."

"Really? I hadn't noticed." She turned away from him and rolled her eyes. She watched the wind whipping through the trees, heard the distant pounding of thunder.

Closing her eyes, she tried to remember blue skies, the warming sun on her face on Piazza San Domenico Maggiore. Sitting around outdoor café tables with her friends before her classes, sipping foamy cappuccino, delicate layers of *sfogliatella,* delivered to their table fresh from the oven, melting in her mouth.

Noise and chaos swirled around them. The scooters weaved expertly along the edge of the tables. People laughed and spoke over one another, gesticulating wildly with their hands to make their points.

Her friends around the table, catching up on the latest football scores. Conversation would invariably turn to their own precarious lives, worried they'd be unemployed forever. Giuseppe complaining about his third year slaving away in a legal studio, still no paycheck in sight.

Lavinia grumbling about having to handle all the exams and student appointments for her professor, with no hope of moving into a university position herself. Although, she pointed out with a resigned look on her face, her professor was quick to ask her to withdraw her candidacy for *ricercatore,* thinning out the competition for a position miraculously won by a dimwitted young man with mediocre grades and no publications to his name. But one lucky enough to have an uncle in local politics.

Giancarlo asking Eleonora for the umpteenth time why they were both studying economics, when they'd only be jobless after graduation anyway.

She remembered the stunned silence around the table that summer morning when she announced her job offer abroad, in faraway London. The envy that shone in the eyes of all her friends. The friends whose calls and text messages grew more infrequent as the months marched on and her London life took its roots. Yet another of their young friends who'd fled her hometown in exchange for work.

Rain instead of sun. Order instead of chaos. Employment instead of joblessness. Tea instead of coffee.

Eleonora opened her eyes and observed the storm that now raged outside, probably flooding Hyde Park as they sat sheltered in this sad café with its drab décor and grey clientele.

She plucked the sunglasses from her head and tucked them deep within her purse. Who knew when she would be needing them again?

She thought of her empty chair at the café on the Piazza San Domenico Maggiore. Thought of it absorbing the strong rays of Mediterranean sunshine, the sounds of lilting Italian, the laughter and banter from the joyful crowds.

Slowly, she sipped her tasteless tea, willing herself to like it. "I know I'm in London now." She offered Julian a weak smile. "What shall we do today?" she asked, before forcing herself to take another sip of insipid tea, chasing pesky memories away.

FLYING FORTRESS
Valdosta

LUCILLA WAS CERTAIN her heart would explode. She groaned and collapsed onto Jake's broad chest, listening to the thundering beats of his heart. Her breaths came in ragged pants as she traced his well-defined pectorals with one finger. "You saved me a trip to the gym today." She looked up into those shining green eyes and grinned. "If you can muster up some energy after breakfast, we can have another go and you'll save me from the gym all week."

He wrapped his muscular arms around her and chuckled with his deep-throated laugh. "You'll be the death of me yet, Lucilla." He nuzzled her neck. "But a sweet death, at least."

She rolled off of him and propped herself beside him in bed. She cast him the dismissive once-over she'd reserved for each of their meetings, at least before they'd transitioned from bitter rivals to energetic lovers a little over a month ago.

"You come over last night and shamelessly bed me. Not once, but twice, I might add … and yet you can't even make an effort to pronounce my name correctly?"

"Aw, sweetheart. How's a country boy like me supposed to handle Italian pronunciation?"

He winked and, despite her better judgement, she felt her heart melting.

"Darlin', you need an easier nickname if you're fixin' to work here long-term."

"I think you can handle it." She eased in closer to him and whispered. "Double consonants. Pronounce them twice as long. Lucilla, Loo-chill-la."

"How 'bout Lucy? 'Kay—see from that look it ain't gonna cut it. How's this for Eye-talian?" He winked. "Loo-chill-la."

She laughed and gave him a peck on the cheek. "Not bad for a Georgia boy." She didn't note that the Georgia boy had studied up at Vassar, and seemed to slip in and out of his just-a-guy-from-the-cottonfields-of-Georgia accent at will.

He wrapped strong arms around her. They lay still, allowing their thudding heartbeats to slow. Outside, the crickets were chirping up a loud chorus as the morning temperature began to soar. Although the shutters were firmly closed, the glass pane above the windows angled out at the sky. Lucilla observed the Spanish moss delicately floating in the gentle breeze. Six months here and she still took pleasure in watching the Spanish moss swaying above as she lay in her bed following her early morning alarm, delighted in their exotic form in the dusky evening light. She'd sent hundreds of photos back to her parents in Florence, knowing it would make her dad nostalgic for his youth.

Jake nuzzled into her right cheek, kissing her bare shoulder. "Anyway, with Richardson as a last name, I would have imagined your parents would have come up with an easier name. Your dad's from Savannah. He'd get how hard it is for us."

Lucilla smiled faintly. "He hasn't been back in ages. He's probably more Italian than my mom at this point. He thought

I was insane for taking this job offer and coming back to the place he couldn't escape fast enough."

"Ah, no. Savannah's the big city compared to Valdosta. He's right to wonder what his darlin' daughter's doin' out here in the swampland and cotton fields." He slid his arm out from under her and rolled on top of her, his lips tantalizingly close to hers. "Gettin' up to lord-knows-what trouble with the bad-news local boys."

She leaned up to give him a quick peck. "Well, he had that part right, at least." She slid out beneath him, slipping into a silky robe on the chair beside her bed. "I don't know about you, but after that workout, I'm in desperate need of a coffee and some breakfast."

He slid up to the edge of the bed, reaching for his boxers. "Music to my ears Loo-chill-la."

"*Perfetto.*"

He kissed the top of her head. Scooping her up, he carried her to the kitchen and deposited her in a chair at the kitchen table. "Don't wanna be blamed for being sexist. Where are your coffee filters and coffee?"

She indicated the cabinet and as he prepared the coffee, she arranged the cereal, milk and fruit on the table. She looked over to where he was measuring out the coffee. "Wow, a girl could get used to this."

He pressed the button and turned back with a smile. "Heck, you were living in Italy before … not sure I can compete with that." He sat across from her.

"You're doing just fine."

"Gettin' used to our backwards ways?"

"Not backwards. It only took me a little getting used to. I was kind of shell-shocked when they let go of all the new hires at RAI. I hadn't planned on coming back to the States after college. And certainly not to Georgia."

"Hey, I can get you feeling bad leaving a job you loved in Rome, but after four years of college in Indiana, you're not gonna to convince me Georgia's a step down."

"It's definitely not." She placed a hand over his. "I've found the company to be superior."

He smiled and stood, turning his sculpted back to her to pour two cups of coffee before placing a steaming mug before her. "I'm glad to hear it. And miraculously, we both have the day off—finally a whole day together. And a second night." He leaned across the tabletop to brush his lips against hers in a gentle kiss. "About time."

"Couldn't agree more. But it's not like we can go out. Someone might see us."

"True. Wouldn't want the paparazzi chasing us. Did I get those double consonants to your liking this time?" He winked. "Next time we get a whole weekend, I need to swoop you away somewhere far from prying eyes."

Lucilla sighed. "That would be fabulous." She took a sip of her coffee, savoring the comforting flavor and the caffeine working its way through her system. When had she become someone so dependent on stimulants to start her day? It seemed only yesterday she'd teased her Italian mother about how she was a monster in the mornings without her daily espresso. Time—the great equalizer. "But what are the chances we'll both have the same days off?"

Jake nuzzled in and kissed her throat. "We'll make it work."

She leaned back and laughed. "Always the optimist."

"Hope so. If you can still stand me by summer, maybe you can join me visiting my mama at her place out on Sea Island for the Fourth of July. She decamps for most of the summer, but she always puts on a big show for the Fourth. Would be a great chance to meet her." His eyes were soft.

"Not much pressure there, Jake. What would the doyenne of Valdosta think about it if you brought back a girl who is very clearly not a local? Half foreign, even."

He grinned. "I think she's given up on that. At least, I hope she has. I'm sure she'll love you ..."

Lucilla forced a grin, but her throat constricted and she placed down her coffee cup. Mrs. Peters was formidable, to say the least. Lucilla had crossed her path at the charity functions she was frequently forced to attend. No matter the cause, Mrs. Peters was at the center of the activity, her opinion sought out by all the local women. She'd identified Lucilla immediately as an outsider, and her greetings were consistently cool. And that was before Lucilla had even started seeing Jake in secret. Now the cool reception was bound to be magnified.

Jake was deluding himself if he thought his patrician mother would welcome Lucilla into her home, the largest mansion in Valdosta, with its pretentious Greek columns, perfectly placed magnolia trees and expertly tended flower gardens. Lucilla doubted she'd be any more welcome in the Grande Dame's Sea Island summer retreat, probably in the family since the English settlers' first arrival on Georgian soil. She knew about these Southern matriarchs from her father's tales and she did not share Jake's sense of optimism on her warm welcome into the fold.

But she smiled noncommittally and squeezed Jake's hand. "That would be nice." She kissed his lips gently, retreating and drinking in that deep green gaze. "So, what are the plans for today now that we're virtual prisoners? I wish we could take a dip in the pool, but someone's bound to see us and'll blab."

He shook his head. "Oh, woman of little faith. Then again, I'm fine with being locked inside all day with you and trying to find some way to entertain ourselves." He stroked one finger up her thigh, brushing under the silk of her robe and sending a tingle through her body. As she anticipated what would follow, she groaned at the ring of his cellphone over on the kitchen counter.

His hand stopped on her thigh and he grimaced. "You're gonna kill me, but I gotta take this." He shook his head, almost imperceptibly. "They'll just be checkin' in. I'll just be a sec."

Famous last words in their profession. He grabbed his phone and walked into the living room, the sound of his voice muffled through the glass door.

A few moments later, he returned, looking sheepish.

"No. I know that look. You *promised* this time …"

"I know, babe." He leaned in to give her a kiss. "I was supposed to be covered today. They owe me a day off, but I need to take this assignment."

At least he had the decency to look guilty. As he should. She should grill him on the assignment, but they had already agreed it was off limits. For either of them. She shook her head. "You will return here tonight with the most exquisite gourmet dinner you can scrounge, an expensive bottle of wine, and a bouquet of red roses." She crossed her arms over her chest and pinned him in place with her most severe look. "Otherwise, you're not getting through the door."

He pulled her into a tight embrace. "You're the best, Loo. Chill.La. I'll be back early. Promise." He pulled back. "Look on the bright side. Without me, you can get out to the pool for a swim and quiet time."

She shook her head. "Not exactly the together-time I was banking on." She tucked her legs under her and took a sip of her coffee. "Be off with you. You'll make up for it tonight."

With another quick kiss, he sprinted out the door.

She leaned back in her seat and drank more coffee. This was not at all the day she envisioned. What was the point of a relationship when you had to sneak around, and barely even saw one another? Today would have marked the first time when they had an entire day and two nights together, and already it was ruined. What was the point? Leave it to her to become entangled in an impossible relationship.

She stood up and poured more coffee into her mug, before returning to the table. From the window she observed the Spanish moss still dancing in the treetops. Soon enough the gentle breeze would transform into a sultry, sweat-inducing heat. Maybe she could grab her abandoned novel now gathering dust on her bedside and head out to the pool to divide her day into swimming, reading and dozing. It's not like she didn't deserve a lazy day.

Lucilla drained the last of her coffee, placed her mug in the sink and retreated to the bedroom, with its rumpled sheets recalling images of their energetic lovemaking only a short time earlier. She shook her head. *Just shower, Lucilla. Run those errands and then head back to the pool to relax.*

As she made her way to the shower, her cellphone buzzed. She clicked in and read the message twice before fully comprehending and typing in a response.

So much for a day off, she thought as she stepped into the shower.

IN HER SHORT TIME in this community, she'd been countless times to the Air Force base. The press officer raced to her car window, welcoming her once she passed the guard gate.

"So glad you could make it, Lucilla. They told us it was short notice. Sorry 'bout that. Park the car over there." She indicated a lot. "Lieutenant Masterson is waiting for you, and he'll accompany you." The young woman smiled brightly. "Enjoy your day! It's a unique experience."

Too bad I was anticipating an entirely different unique experience, she thought as she pulled away. Maneuvering into a spot between two large pickups, she locked her car, although it seemed unnecessary on this heavily guarded base. Who would abscond with her vehicle?

She turned to see a young, black man in a perfectly pressed blue uniform. She quickly took in the razor-sharp creases and spit-shined shoes, before smiling at him.

"Welcome, Ms. Richardson. I'm Lieutenant Masterson. It's a pleasure to meet you." He glanced down at her shoes, seemingly relieved not to see heels. "It's a short walk. I'll accompany you there."

"Thank you, Lieutenant," she said as she fell into step beside him.

"I saw your first name is Lucilla," he said, with perfect pronunciation. "Is your family Italian?"

"My mom is. I grew up there."

"I love Italy. My last base was Sigonella."

"Lucky you—I adore Sicily." They fell into easy banter in Italian. Unlike most soldiers based abroad, he'd made real efforts to pick up the language, even adopting a faint Sicilian cadence and an overreliance on the *passato remoto* verb tense that made her smile.

They turned into an airstrip and both fell silent before the expansive metal glimmering in the bright sun.

He tilted his face up, raw admiration transforming his face. "She is a beauty. I'll be honest. I'm envious you're going up while I'm stranded on the ground pushing papers today. It'll be an amazing experience." He smiled at her. "They don't make birds like this anymore."

She gaped at the huge, olive-colored monolith glistening under the bright sunlight, the four old-fashioned propellers that would guide them on this journey. At least she hoped they could still get the job done. The huge, clear nose of the plane, with its transparent eye, where the gunners would have been seated back in the war.

"How is this even able to function, so many years later? Are we sure it's safe?"

"Good question, but yes, you can be sure it's safe." He gazed up at it with shining eyes. "It's thanks to the Indian Air Force. They bought these up and were using them for years. They flew them, trained in them, maintained them and kept them in operation all this time." He shook his head. "Incredible, isn't it? And come here." He led her to the side of the plane, where a busty blonde bombshell was painted, her long, shapely legs stretching down. He grinned at her. "They obviously liked our WWII pinups, because they kept her well-maintained, too."

She laughed as she gazed up at the painted model. What this busty, pinup mascot must have witnessed during her lifetime.

"Hey, Lucilla," a familiar voice called.

Both Lucilla and the lieutenant turned to see a tall, broad-shouldered man approaching them at a quick pace. He wore khaki pants and a sporty hunter green shirt. The sunlight glowed on his wavy chestnut hair. His green eyes shone with excitement.

"Mr. Peters, I'm sorry there was no one to accompany you to the airfield. I got carried away describing this amazing aircraft, and I should be getting back to see to the others." He turned back. "I see you and Ms. Richardson–despite being rivals–are already acquainted. Although," he turned to Lucilla and winked at her, "you should know the correct Italian pronunciation is Loo-chill-la."

"So I've been hearing …" The man muttered.

"I need to get back to the others. Wishing you both a pleasant flight."

"*Ciao, Tom. Ci vediamo al ritorno,*" said Lucilla, with a smile for the young officer.

With a wave, he was gone.

"What the hell's going on? What're you doing here? And why are you flirting with an officer you just met?"

"Jake, it's still early. Calm down." She rubbed a hand over her eyes. "I wasn't flirting with him. He was based in Italy and speaks some Italian. I imagine I'm here for the same reason you are. Day off, but got called in for an assignment."

He furrowed his brow. "So we're both going up?"

"Looks that way. May the best man–or, preferably, woman–win." She smirked.

He shook his head. "It's not a competition, you know."

"Isn't everything?" She laughed. "Of course it isn't. Just teasing. Anyway, you owe me an expensive takeout dinner tonight to make up for running off early, so I win either way."

He smiled. "Okay, I obviously wasn't expecting this, but yeah. At least we have tonight to look forward to ... after our day off."

"Hey, what's going on here?" A heavyset young man in jeans and a Georgia Bulldogs shirt came up to them, lugging a heavy camera. "Hangin' out with the enemy, Lucilla?"

"Would seem that way." She turned to him and smile. "Zach, you've met Jake Peters before, haven't you?"

"Not in ages." He shook hands. "We played against each other on rival football teams back in high school. Saw you're back on Channel Seven. Happy to be home?"

"Yeah, it's strange being back after so long. But good. How 'bout you? Commuting from Thomasville?"

"Nah, married a local girl, so living in Valdosta now. God help us, if we have a son, he'll have to play ball here."

Jake laughed.

"Sorry, but can I steal my journalist away for a chat before we head up?"

"Yeah, sure." Jake looked around him at the small crowd that was forming on the airfield. "Have to find out where my cameraman's at. See you both later. And Lucilla ..." He winked.

Lucilla's heart fluttered. He wouldn't dare say anything compromising, would he?

"You're still in time to say something if you change your mind. Might be a bit too rough for a delicate lady like you. Once we're up in the air, it'll be too late."

She rolled her eyes. "Worry about yourself, Jake. I'll be fine."

Lucilla and Zach stood in silence until Jake was out of earshot. "Insufferable snob," muttered Zach. "Always considered Valdosta royalty, living large up in the big house and lording it over the peasants. Can't stand that guy."

Lucilla watched Jake's retreating form, shoulders back, confident gait. "Is he really that bad? I mean, he's pretty full of himself, but he seems harmless."

Zach groaned. His freckles were even more pronounced in the bright sunlight. "Not you, too, Lucilla. My wife had a major crush on him all throughout high school—before she did much better, obviously." He grinned. "Anyway, careful. He's the competition, and if he senses weakness, he'll crush you. That's just how his kind are. Wouldn't be gettin' too friendly, if I were you."

"Fair advice. Now should we get a stand-up here before we start preparing for flight?"

He handed her the microphone and stepped back to set up the tripod and camera, framing her against the bomber's nose.

"We're here at Valdosta's Moody Air Force base on a spectacular day for flying—and, as you can see here behind me, we have a very special flight planned for today. This is one of the few examples of the WWII bombers still in operation— the B-17s—more commonly known as 'The Flying Fortress.'" She took a step back and touched the side of the plane. "It's thanks to the maintenance of the Indian Air Force that this plane is still in operation—and we'll look forward to testing her out on our flight today ... and getting a taste of what the soldiers experienced back in WWII."

She stood immobile for a few seconds, then placed down her microphone. A small group of journalists had gathered around.

"Hey, Lucilla. Good thing you did your stand-up now. You may not be up to it after our flight." A short man in cargo shorts doubled over and pretended to vomit.

She cast a withering gaze at Matt, a columnist from Valdosta's biggest paper. All around her were only men. Damn, she'd be the only woman on this flight, and they'd all be on her if she showed even one sign of weakness.

Two Air Force officers approached the group and called everyone to attention. "Thank you for joining us here today. We don't often have the honor of flying such impressively maintained WWII bombers. We'll be taking off in a short while and we'll fly down to northern Florida before turning around and coming back to Moody Base—estimated time of arrival sixteen hundred hours. On to a delicate topic." He grinned, scanning the audience, but his gaze lingered longest on Lucilla. "Let's just say these old planes are a lot different from what we're used to today. They're not pressurized cabins, and believe me, you'll notice that awful quickly. You'll be flying low, but it's still gonna be pretty rough up there."

He nodded to the young female officer beside him and she began distributing bags to everyone.

"Ladies and gentlemen. I urge you to each take a handful of these. You're in for a bumpy flight, and better to be prepared if you're not feeling well. We don't want to have to hose the cabin down afterwards. Save us the work." He grinned.

When the officer reached Matt, he took two. "Hate to say no to a pretty lady, but I won't be needing these. Better to give a stack of them to the person who'll need 'em most. Right, Lucilla?"

"Yeah, whatever, Matt," she responded.

Matt elbowed Jake. "Get a load of your rival TV reporter. How long do ya think the girlie'll last without losin' her lunch? Five dollars says she'll lose it at take-off."

Jake chuckled, and Lucilla shot him a withering gaze.

"Uh-oh," said Matt. "Looks like the competition is miffed with you, man." Matt whipped a notebook out of his pocket. "I've got five dollars on five minutes. Winner takes the pot. What about the rest of you?"

Lucilla looked on in horror as the crowd put in their bets. She slipped her vomit bags into her purse and turned away. Her gaze caught Zach's, who seemed far too interested in the ongoing betting pool for her taste. "Don't you dare," she worded silently. He tagged along behind her. "C'mon. Let's get some b-roll of the plane before we take off."

He chuckled. "Worried you might not feel well afterwards?"

She shook her head. "Not at all, Zach. I'm more worried about how you'll be feeling."

"You can't take everything personally. You're the only woman here. It's natural you'll get a bit of ribbing."

She rolled her eyes. "I get ribbing by the bucketload. All the time. Here, get this angle here. Gorgeous with the sun hitting the wing. And be sure to get a closeup of that pinup. Hasn't aged a minute since the 1940s—lucky, inanimate girl. I love that the Indian Air Force didn't want to paint over her. Can you blame them?"

They worked around the aircraft, shooting footage that could be edited into the final package later. When they made the full round of the aircraft and returned to the nose of the plane, three officers approached the small crowd.

"Welcome, everyone. I'm Colonel Sanchez." The tall man positioned himself in the middle of the group of journalists. "Thank you for coming out today to join us for this unique opportunity to fly this World War Two plane. For those of us who have dedicated our life to flight, this is a dream come true, and we're grateful to the Indian Air Force, whose mechanics kept these beauties in function all these years," he gazed at the plane beside him. "I took this out on a test flight two days ago, and I can say you're in for a treat."

Lucilla felt excitement welling within. Admittedly, she'd been looking forward to a break today, but the last-minute call had been a blessing, in the end. She looked up and caught Jake's gaze on her. His green eyes appeared to sparkle with the same excitement she was feeling. He gave her an almost imperceptible wink, and she looked away quickly. It wouldn't do to have their peers gossiping.

The Colonel turned back to the officers standing behind him. "I would like to introduce Captains Miller and Goldstein."

The two men stepped forward and nodded to the crowd.

"These men are fine pilots and joined me for the test flight. I can guarantee you are in excellent hands today." He looked back again and smiled at an elderly gentleman dressed in khaki pants and a light blue shirt. Turning back to the crowd, he said, "It gives me even greater pleasure to announce one of your co-passengers, retired Colonel Gerald Scott. Colonel Scott was an extremely young pilot back in World War Two and he flew in the Flying Fortress in missions over Germany." He stepped back and placed a hand on his shoulder. "He will be up in the cockpit to observe, and it means the world to us to have him along on this flight. Jerry, would you like to say a few words?"

"Thank you, Colonel." He turned to the small crowd. "Frankly, I can't believe I'm standing here in 2010, about to board a bomber I used to pilot back in my twenties. You're all so young, but when you reach ninety like me, you're thankful for the small miracles. When I heard the old Flying Fortress would be flying again—and over Georgia—I reckoned I needed to get on that flight." His wrinkled face broke out in a wide grin. "Mind you, my wife's put up with me for the last seventy years and she is not one bit happy about today, so I know I'll need to make it up to her."

The journalists laughed, and Jake once more caught Lucilla's gaze.

"Thanks for coming up today and chronicling this flight for your readers and viewers. I'll stay around for any questions, if you have any for me. Reminding you all to buckle up. These aren't the cushy planes you're used to today." He looked down pointedly at one young man's hands. "Keep those vomit bags close at hand. You might be needing them."

Matt yelled out, "Lucilla more than anyone!"

The elderly man turned to Lucilla, easy to spot as the only woman in the crowd. "We'll see about that. Women obviously didn't fight alongside us, but the female nurses and support staff we had throughout the war always impressed us with their toughness. So we'll see, won't we?" He winked at her.

"Thank you, Colonel," said Colonel Sanchez. "Now I'll ask you to all climb onboard. Our flight will soon begin."

The journalists all formed a line and the Air Force personnel helped them through the hatch and into the main cabin. Lucilla looked around the open space, realizing exactly what they'd meant by no pressurization. The interior was painted olive green. It looked like some kind of corrugated tin gardening shed. Or a giant tuna fish can. Rivets all in plain view. Absolutely nothing between the interior metal and the exterior of the plane.

Two long benches ran the length of the interior and the Air Force assistants indicated they should take their places alongside one another. Zach took the seat next to Lucilla, who breathed a sigh of relief when Matt took a seat on the opposite side. Despite her false bravado, she was terrified of suffering motion sickness, and she needed a way to get those bags from her purse to her pocket without the macho journalists noticing.

Her heart beat faster. She saw Jake mounting up into the cabin and scanning the interior until his gaze caught hers and held it a moment too long, before his cameraman tugged at his sleeve and the two sat down on the opposite side, farthest from her.

Colonel Sanchez stood in the middle of the space. "In one moment, I will be getting off and we'll leave you in the expert hands of your captains. As you'll see, no frills here. We have belts connected to the benches. Again, we're flying low today, but you'll still notice the cold—just think about how much worse the soldiers had it flying so high over Europe. I'm not gonna lie to you. Takeoff and landing'll be pretty rough. And it's not gonna be smooth flying once you're at altitude either. Keep your belts on as we climb. If you need to move around once we're in the air, wait until my officers give you the green light." He pointed to the bags in Jake's hands. "It's not the moment to be heroes. You're not used to this kind of flight, so have these ready."

Lucilla didn't need more encouragement, she pulled her bags from her purse. Across the way, she ignored Matt's burst of laughter followed by a catcall. Lucilla shook her head.

"All there's left to do is wish you a good flight," said Colonel Sanchez. "It'll be bumpy, but a unique experience I promise you won't forget. We look forward to seeing you back here at the base on your landing. Enjoy!" He moved to the entrance and went out.

The hatch was closed, and Lucilla tried to ignore the sensation she could see through its edges, or the sensation that the air would simply rush through as it did with a drafty door. *Get ahold of yourself. Where did this fear of flying come from?*

Although, to be fair, she'd never been in a World War II-era plane that was older than her grandfather. One that resembled a cheap tin can. She closed her eyes and breathed slowly.

The engine hummed slowly, the intensity growing with each passing second. The cabin began to shake, and Lucilla felt the butterflies in her stomach raring to break free. As she gazed at all the confident male journalists she did battle with each day for scoops, she gave herself a little pep talk. If they could do it, so could she.

The hornet sound grew ever louder and the aircraft began to move, hurtling ever faster down the runway. She tried to ignore the clanging and the general sounds of an aircraft that may have outlived its lifespan—by a few decades, at least. Although she longed to close her eyes, she feared her journalist rivals would see it as a sign of weakness—something she would never allow.

She kept her eyes firmly open and willed herself to be at one with the bomber. How many stories could this plane tell? How many young men had flown in its hull, eager for a life of adventure, only to have their dreams shattered by the brutality and inhumanity of war? She thought of countless young men who had sat in her seat decades ago. Maybe many who never returned home to their families. Who was she to feel scared of a simple flight? She could do this ...

The plane hurtled down the runway, ever faster. Instead of feeling fear, she experienced elation. When she felt the front wheels tip off the runway, a smile broke out across her face. The bomber tilted up and the rattling grew louder, the hold shaking side to side. The Colonel had been right—it was nothing like Lucilla had ever experienced in the pressurized cabins she flew in frequently. But neither did the rattling and shaking jar her. Conversely, the elation grew as she thought about all the poor eighteen-year-old farm boys from Iowa or

Nebraska who had flown on this very aircraft, carrying them towards probable death on the battlefields of Europe. A 2010 demonstration flight was nothing in comparison.

The more she focused on this, the braver she felt. Soon, the constant rattling did not bother her at all. She managed to relegate it to annoying background noise on this great adventure she'd been asked to join. There was an unfamiliar churning in her stomach, but as she slid to the edge of her bench and watched the hold rattling as the plane nosed up ever higher, she realized it was a creeping excitement, not fear.

Seventy years ago, young soldiers flew in this very same plane on missions over Germany, Italy and North Africa. And all these years later, she was doing the same. This was miraculous, a story she had to tell to her viewers.

She nudged Zach beside her and screamed over the deafening roar of the plane. "Zach, shouldn't you be filming our takeoff?" She turned and saw Zach's freckles even more prominent in his face, a face that had turned ashen white in the time they'd been airborne. "Zach?" she said gently. "Are you okay?"

The look he flashed her announced that he was, in fact, very far from okay. He lifted the vomit bag up to cover his mouth and began breathing slowly in and out.

"There you go," she patted his hand. Isn't this how people used to calm themselves if they were having a panic attack? "That'll make you feel better."

With an intense heaving, he vomited into the bag. Lucilla shifted slightly away from him, but nevertheless managed to slip him another bag, since it appeared he had not yet emptied the contents of his stomach. Indeed, soon enough Zach was filling the second bag, too, and Lucilla was desperately trying to shift her gaze anywhere else.

She met Matt's watery eyes across the hold. He, too, looked worse for wear. He held the vomit bag up to his mouth and followed Zach's example. She looked on in horror as all the male journalists who, such a short time earlier, had been teasing her on the airstrip, emptied their own breakfasts into their bags.

The plane seemed to have levelled now, but that did nothing to dampen the thunderous clanging or the shaking of the hold. But as she looked at her fellow journalists—yes, even Jake—emptying out their stomachs, she felt only scorn for their weakness. Why should she be relegated to the patients' warden, when she could be experiencing this flight for herself?

She turned once more to her cameraman. "Zach, you stay here until you're feeling better. I'm gonna go and see what things look like from the cockpit."

He looked at her with a pitiful gaze and she smiled encouragingly. "Take your time," she shouted as gently as she could, while still allowing him to hear her in the cacophony.

She undid her seatbelt, stood and took long, confident strides across the width of the hold. Towering before Valdosta's most arrogant scribe, she looked down upon him, his miserable, sweaty face, the mouth in which he was fighting so hard to keep the bile contained. "Hey, Matty," she yelled down at him. "What's wrong? Not feeling too well, huh?" She handed him her last bag. "Looks like you need this more than I do!"

She could see he had no desire to take it, but necessity won out in the end. He snatched the bag from her grasp and vomited noisily into it as she moved hastily away, making her way to the front of the plane. Her gaze crossed with Jake's as she passed him by. He appeared miserable and impressed in equal measures, and she flashed him a quick smile before striding to the cockpit.

The cockpit was open. The glass divided into four windows below and two above. It provided maximum visibility, but nothing like the view the gunners would have had in their glass pod below. Two half-wheels reminded her of the type of steering wheel her grandfather used to have on his ancient speedboat. There were a dizzying array of buttons and levers and odometer-type instruments. The two pilots sat on tiny captain seats, built before so many individuals had been supersized in recent decades. Although, she imagined, not in the air force. Still, these clearly came from another era.

The pilots had not yet noticed her presence. She observed the look of sheer joy on their faces. These officers must spend their time flying multimillion-dollar state-of-the-art fighter jets, but having the chance to fly these historic bombers sparked their imagination. She thought of her Italian grandfather taking her to the Ferrari Museum, where he and fellow aficionados lovingly examined the old Ferraris and the early days of racing.

"Knock knock," she yelled loudly. One of the pilots looked back and smiled. "Ha! Are you the last woman standing? We were taking bets it would be you."

She couldn't help but smile. "Thank goodness. My fellow journalists were all betting in the opposite direction."

"Seems they'll owe you beers," he hollered. "Take that jump seat. It was the Colonel who tipped us over to betting on you."

She looked down and saw the elderly Colonel on a narrow jump seat, and noted the open seat beside him. She stepped over his long legs and sat down, strapping herself in.

She turned to him and yelled. The deafening roar wasn't any better in the cockpit. "Thanks for the confidence."

He winked. "Men don't change much, even over decades. Back in my day, the soldiers were full of bravado, but the nurses who flew with us sometimes if we weren't on a bombing mission always showed them up."

They sat for a few minutes in comfortable silence. From her position she could see the land down not so far below, the cerulean blue sky dotted by few clouds on this perfect day.

She leaned in closer to the old Colonel, still yelling, but more gently into his ear. "How is it for you being back in the Flying Fortress? Is it how you remember it?"

He shook his head and she saw the glimmer of tears in his blue eyes. "I never thought I wanted to get back up in one of these flying tin cans, but ever since I saw this voyage planned, I knew it was time." He patted the shoulder of the pilot before him. "No way would I still be able to operate this thing anymore, so I'm glad we have these young guns, with their perfect eyesight and reflexes, taking care of us today. But it's emotional to be back."

She smiled at him. They remained mostly in silence. Every once in a while, someone shouted a comment or a joke, but the rattling made sustained conversation impossible.

Toward the end of the flight, Zach made his way to the cockpit, still looking a bit weak, but certainly better than before, and got footage of the young Air Force pilots, the controls, and the old Colonel and Lucilla chattering away. She smiled into the camera for good measure.

It seemed in no time they were preparing for landing. Zach returned to the hold, but the officers joked that Lucilla had earned her wings and could stay up in the cockpit jump seat for landing.

Landing was just as bumpy as takeoff, but again, Lucilla managed just fine. Before starting their descent, the officers winked and handed her a pack of vomit bags to distribute to her hapless fellow journalists. Their bravado had long ago faded, but most refused to even look her in the eye as they mumbled thank you.

When they landed and the engines cut off, she marveled at the silence once again. As soon as she emerged from the plane, she asked the old Colonel for an interview. Zach set up the tripod. Colonel Scott turned behind him and laughed at the backdrop.

"You're shooting me in front of the old pinup? Any idea the kinda trouble I'll get in with my wife over that?" he chuckled. "For the record and on camera in case I need the evidence. My wife was much prettier than this model."

Zach and Lucilla both laughed. Zach walked over and clipped the lavalier mic more firmly onto the Colonel's shirt and Lucilla held her own mic.

"For me, that was quite an experience. I wasn't expecting so much noise. So much bouncing around. What was it like for you soldiers headed into battle?" she asked.

"I know. It's a feeling I'll never forget—even seventy years later. People accustomed to today's pressurized cabins have no idea what it used to be like." He looked up. "Keep in mind, today is warm and we were flying low. Try to picture what it was like for us. At night. In Germany in winter. Flying altitude. They gave us these electric long-john kinda things we were supposed to wear under our flight suits. They never worked. So many of the men lost fingers and toes to frostbite on these flights."

"Oh, I didn't realize ..."

"Plus, as you saw with many of your fellow journalists today ..." He winked. "Lots of people got motion sickness from the shaking and the tough takeoffs and landings, especially when we were transporting other soldiers not used to flying. Today was a reminder of how things were. I'm glad we're speaking about it now. And that these young pilots could take these old birds out for a flight. Everyone studies WWII in the history books, but this helps bring it to life."

"That's true," said Lucilla. "Today was an incredible opportunity for those of us who've only seen photos of these planes in books. What about changing perspectives? You told me you flew these planes for bombing missions over Germany in the war. Have you been back to Germany since then?"

"That's the thing they don't teach you about war. Life marches on. The world changes. And you have to adapt and change with it. My son went to study in Germany after college. He met a German girl. We went over to Hamburg for the wedding." He smiled. "It took forever for me to process that my son was marrying in a country we were fighting twenty years earlier. It was harder for me …"

He trailed off and looked down for a moment. Lucilla waited to allow him to continue, in his own time.

"But she's a lovely girl. My grandchildren and great-grandchildren are German-Americans, and my wife and I have travelled there so many times. But it's still strange. At the wedding, I was the American airman and the wounds were still raw. The father of the bride had been an airman, too. For the Boche … the Germans. When we first met, he took me aside from the others. We sat in the shade of an old oak tree in his garden. He loved to garden and he pointed with pride to all his trees and flowers and vegetables. Here he had this passion for cultivating plants and appreciating beauty. And just a few years earlier we were killing one another. So many of my friends never came home …"

He turned around and examined the busty pinup, and turned with a smile, although his eyes glistened. "There was a bench under that oak. He made me sit there and returned with two beers. We toasted, and he said the important thing was the happiness of our children. That we'd both made it out alive, when so many of our loved ones hadn't. That it was time to forgive. To forget. He toasted me again, and in his heavily accented English said, 'All's fair in love and war.'"

Following the interview, they got a few soundbites from the pilots and Colonel Sanchez and Lucilla did one last stand-up. They were done while the others were still finding their land legs, and they returned to the studio to edit the package.

"IT LOOKS GREAT, Lucilla," said Zach as they finalized the last edits. The producer had stepped into the editing suite earlier and approved of the report.

They both leaned back in their chairs. "So, eh," said Zach. "You okay with keeping that shot of the journalists … uh … not feeling well?"

"Yeah, that might have been the one I kept out, but what can we do if Scott insisted we put it in. Anyway, it's from far away and you only see distant profiles. And it's only a couple of seconds when the Colonel speaks about how bumpy the flight was. The viewers almost won't know what they're seeing."

Zach nodded. "True. But your hotshot rival will. Not sure he'll forgive us for that—even if he's slightly blurred and in the distance." His eyes examined her.

She paused. Looked up at the clock. "The news is starting now, and this needs to be ready to go. He's a big boy. He'll survive." She stood. "Now, if I'm no longer needed, I'm gonna enjoy the rest of my day off."

Zach snorted. "You do that."

She walked across the room and scooped up her car keys.

"And Lucilla?"

She turned.

"You did good today."

She smiled, waved and walked out into the sultry air, a chorus of crickets accompanying the crunch of gravel as she approached her car.

SHE SAT AT HOME with a chilled glass of wine before the television. The anchor had stumbled over a few lines. She'd heard whispers that management might be finding a graceful exit for him. Special features now and then, an occasional opinion segment befitting a station elder. Someone younger would be needed to fill that position, and her star was rising. Why not?

Her Flying Fortress package had looked great. Despite his motion sickness, Zach had captured a lot of the action on board, including her chatting with the crew in the cockpit. Yeah, it may have been overkill to have her fellow journalists in the hold clearly not handling the flight as well. But Scott, the producer and her boss, had insisted they keep it in. She felt slightly guilty Jake's hunter green shirt and chiseled profile could be easily discerned by those who knew. And honestly, in Valdosta, who didn't know?

Her phone buzzed and she plucked it up and read the message.

"What the hell, Lucilla? I saw your piece. Did you really need to rub it in?"

She placed down her wine glass and looked up at the window, at the perfectly framed Spanish moss gliding gracefully in the trees. She breathed in, out. In again.

She started tapping her phone. "Sorry, *amore*. But all's fair in love and war ..."

She clicked her phone off and placed it face down on the table. She picked up her wine glass again and took a fortifying sip.

Either he would come, bearing dinner, as promised. Or he wouldn't.

She took another long sip and stretched her long legs out on the couch, smiling as she watched the dancing Spanish moss.

MODERN ART

Rome

ELEONORA RETRIEVED HER HAT from the hallway table and placed it gently on her head, tucking in a rogue tendril of wispy hair. She squinted to examine her features in the hall mirror, with its flattering light, and was surprised by the old woman's face peering back at her.

She'd once been a lovely young thing, the toast of Rome ever so many years ago. Even Visconti had offered up a *brindisi* to her beauty at a distant soirée. And, although acting in films wasn't quite *proper* for a girl of her upbringing, she had to admit the idea thrilled her for a short time.

She leaned in closer and traced the deep wrinkles lining her eyes. When had this old woman's face and body supplanted her own elegant features? Years ago, this same mirror reflected glowing, supple skin, shiny dark hair piled intricately on her head in the latest styles, curves that could stop male conversation dead on the streets of Rome as she passed by in the latest designer fashions.

Now only an old lady stared back at her in her expensive, yet dowdy, threads, and a hat that had gone out of fashion sometime in the last century.

Eleonora sighed deeply. Livia would be waiting for her at the gallery, and she did not approve of tardiness.

"Maria, I'm going out to the museum. I shall be back in time for dinner!"

She heard a muffled reply from the kitchen. Wrapping her coat around frail shoulders, she slipped out the door.

LIVIA GLANCED AT HER WATCH. Eleonora was late. Again. She sighed and brushed her unruly, grey curls from her forehead.

A young couple stopped just before her, the woman in tight jeans and a clinging, low-cut sweater that left absolutely nothing to the imagination. There was a name for such women back in her day. Livia gasped as the young man pressed the scarcely clad woman against the glass wall and stroked her body, looking to all the world as if he might throw the woman to the ground at any moment and have his way with her at the museum entrance. Was nothing sacred anymore?

Even her own grandchildren behaved without shame, with their short skirts and low-cut tops. They reminded her of the fallen women who used to darken the doors of the Monti neighborhood when she was their age—the ones young men might visit for their first experience. Her daughters simply laughed at her and called her old-fashioned.

She probably was. But surely, there was no shame in preserving one's dignity.

And did old-fashioned women even know about MAXXI and the exhibition by the famous Burundian artist? Most certainly not! For she, Livia Bortoni, was a woman of the world, not some simple old lady past her prime.

Today, she would introduce her childhood friend to contemporary art. No one could accuse Livia of not changing with the times.

ELEONORA RACED to the museum entrance, as fast as her sturdy shoes and frail bones could carry her. She panted deeply, out of breath from the exertion. Although she spotted Livia from the corner of her eye, it was the young couple groping one another against the glass entrance that attracted her attention.

"Don't stare, Eleonora," said the familiar, scolding voice beside her.

"What's going on?" She turned her head and indicated the couple with a tilt of her head before kissing her friend on each cheek.

Livia shook her head dismissively. "Performance art, perhaps." She opened the door. "Frankly, when I see scenes like this, all I feel is an overwhelming sense of relief once I've verified it's not my own grandchildren. Shall we get our tickets?"

Eleonora slipped her arm through that of her old friend. The women made their way to the ticket counter.

"Two senior citizen tickets, please," said Eleonora to the young woman with the kohl-darkened eyes and what looked like a hat pin jammed through her lip. Why do the young women today work so hard to be unattractive, Eleonora wondered, not for the first time.

"No, I will be paying for the tickets," said Livia, pulling out her wallet.

"Absolutely not, Livia. It's on me this time." Eleonora fumbled as she reached for her purse. The trendy clasps were too complicated for her these days.

"I insist. It was *my* idea after all." Livia placed a fifty-euro note on the counter.

The bored young woman of the scarred lip placed two tickets on the counter alongside the change. She called out

"Next!"—most likely anxious to be rid of the bickering old ladies. For that is how Eleonora often felt others viewed them.

When they were younger, small arguments between them could elicit curious glances from young men and doting smiles from older women.

But as she grew older, she noticed how people expected you to be less vocal, to sit quietly and politely, to observe life, rather than participating. It seemed, at a certain point, one outlived one's usefulness. She often sensed it in the pitying looks cast in her direction with greater frequency each year. The young people most likely wondered why she ventured out at all in her ancient state. But then again, hadn't she felt the same about her elders when she was young?

Her grandchildren hardly paid her any notice at all, mesmerized by their iPhones and iPads. They messaged as she asked questions about school, only to elicit grunts and monosyllabic responses. They only bothered to look up and thank her when she gave them money.

"Eleonora," Livia's scolding tone broke the silence. "You're worlds away. The exhibition is this way."

"Sorry, *cara*. I was just remembering a doctor's appointment next week."

"Oh, doctors." Livia swooshed a dismissive hand before her. "Not today, dear. We have avant-garde art to admire." She marched up to the distracted young man who seemed much more engrossed in his cellphone than ensuring people didn't stand too close to the artwork. "Young man, where is the exhibition by the young Burundian Michelangelo?" She smiled.

He met her gaze blankly. "Huh?"

"But surely you've heard of him. The African sensation. Niyonzima." Livia dragged out each syllable, as if speaking to a slow child.

"Ah yeah, the African porn," he snickered, before returning his attention to his messaging. "Upstairs, galleries to the left."

LIVIA SHOOK HER HEAD and stormed toward the stairs. "What a cheeky young man! Pornography indeed. How provincial can one be? And someone who *works* in the museum, no less!" She heard Eleonora panting beside her.

"Livia, slow down. It is not a race to the top."

Livia stopped and saw her friend's flushed face, suddenly remembered how her friend had been hospitalized with heart palpitations less than a year ago. "How silly of me, my dear. I was angry with that young man. *La Repubblica*'s culture page said it was 'a not-to-be-missed exhibition.'"

Eleonora sighed. "And *La Repubblica* is as infallible as the Pope."

"We won't start on this again. No political arguments."

Eleonora's conservative politics had always rankled Livia. Although, one would expect as much from someone of her class. Even as young girls, Eleonora had firmly marched to the same beat as her father, and grandfather, and all the titled forbearers before her, never questioning the status quo. After all, it only favored her and her kind. Change was anathema to that type. Livia had always been revolutionary. So had Arturo. It was a wonder she and Eleonora had managed to stay friends over a lifetime, when you considered it.

"Here, take my arm. Let's go slowly. We should have taken the elevator."

"No, it's my fault. I raced over here and one should never race at my age." She hooked her arm under Livia's. "Grandmamma always said a woman should never be in a hurry to go anywhere. Always keep them waiting, she said."

Livia clicked her tongue silently. What a blue-blooded battle ax that woman had been. Sitting on her proverbial throne and casting judgment on those she deemed unworthy of her notice. Like young Livia. How she'd despised speaking with Eleonora's grandmother when she was invited to family events. How the old bat had raised her nose in the air whenever Eleonora approached with her friend. 'You remember my friend, Livia, Grandmamma.' The intimidating old woman would ignore young Livia's terrified smile, turning her gaze from her and offering her aquiline nose in profile. 'No, I am not acquainted with the family of your friend, and therefore, I would be unlikely to remember her.' Livia would long to flee from the grand *palazzo* where Eleonora lived, but would proudly stand her ground, fighting the blush she felt burning her cheeks. Eleonora would whisper in her ear, 'Don't worry, *cara*. You know how Grandmamma is. Now let's find you some lemonade, shall we?'

Livia attended that woman's funeral a few years later. Eleonora had just met Lapo, who stood proudly at her side, but she'd insisted Livia attend, too. 'Grandmamma would have wanted you here,' she'd urged. 'I spoke about you all the time. I know you became like a second granddaughter to her.' *I'm certain she viewed me more like the hired help.* But her friend sniffled, and Livia hadn't the heart to refuse. Lapo, working so hard to insert himself in Eleonora's life, was solicitous to Livia, complimenting her earrings and ignoring her threadbare dress. Standing beside him, she smelled his expensive cologne, felt the brush of the high-quality wool of his suit against her skin. Lapo's family history extended even farther back than Eleonora's, and Livia couldn't help but worry their relationship and the circle of privileged friends it would attract would distance Eleonora even more from her unconnected, childhood friend.

As Livia anticipated the rift that would likely develop between them, fat tears began to flow down her cheeks. How clearly she remembered Lapo turning to her, his face filled with concern. He'd already given his handkerchief to Eleonora, who was sobbing uncontrollably to his right. He'd reached into his pocket and extracted another handkerchief and handed it to Livia, a sympathetic smile on his lips. She could still remember the luxurious feel of the soft cotton as she dabbed her eyes, ashamed of the tears flowing that were for herself, not the woman whose coffin lay before the congregation. Livia felt nothing for the dead woman, who'd never considered her worthy to be Eleonora's friend. But now that her influence was removed, Livia was no safer. Perhaps the old woman had been correct. Fresh tears bathed Lapo's elegant handkerchief, and Livia was helpless to stop them.

They'd reached the top of the staircase now, Eleonora leaning heavily on Livia's arm.

"Ah," said Eleonora. "I see the ladies' room. Would you wait for me for one moment, my dear?"

"Of course. There's a comfortable chair here. The climb winded me, too. On the way down, we'll take the elevator."

Eleonora offered a smile. "At our age, that might be wise." She disappeared through the door.

Livia sank slowly into the leather seat, resting her head against the wall. She closed her eyes, thinking back to the reception following the church funeral. In the end, she never had to worry about Lapo coming between her and Eleonora. As they stood in the salon, with its grand windows looking out on Piazza Navona, a young man approached Lapo and greeted him. He kissed Eleonora on each cheek and expressed his sympathies. Eleonora addressed him as Arturo. She'd later learn that his father was the accountant for Lapo's family, and the two boys had grown up playing soccer together, studying together at the university. "Ah, so you're the famous Livia," he'd smiled as Lapo introduced her. "Eleonora speaks so much about you. I'm sorry a sad occasion like this had to bring us together."

She'd fallen in love with Arturo at first sight. As Eleonora, her parents, and Lapo accepted condolences from their elite circle of family and friends, she and Arturo sat in a corner of the library and spoke until the last of the guests took their leave.

Arturo walked her home that evening. She remembered how her heart beat nervously when he took her elbow to ferry her across the street. She remembered as if it were yesterday, how the evening sun set the buildings aglow, the orange tinge to the Tiber as they crossed over it on their way to Trastevere. Back then, Trastevere wasn't the picturesque, sought-after neighborhood it would later become. She remembered cringing as she saw the poor neighborhood through Arturo's eyes: the narrow, twisting streets, the dirty children playing soccer on the *piazza*, the harried mothers screaming down at them from windows above, the laundry crisscrossing the streets above their heads, waiting to dry in the first morning sunlight. So very different from the world Eleonora and Lapo inhabited.

But when she gained the courage to look up, his eyes did not reflect his distaste. He walked her to her door and asked if he could see her again, hope evident in those eager eyes. Livia still clung to that image of young Arturo, whose face lit up when he stood before her. She closed her eyes and saw that boyish face before hers.

"LIVIA, ARE YOU ALRIGHT? Have you fallen asleep?" Eleonora struggled to keep her voice calm as she clutched Livia's shoulders with her bony fingers. Panic rose in her chest.

Livia always insisted she was in perfect health, but Eleonora had been at her bedside after too many operations to believe Livia when she insisted she was still as spry as a teenager.

Familiar hazel eyes opened. Confusion registered on her friend's face.

"Whe- where am I?"

"Oh, my dear. Are you quite well? We're at MAXXI. I went to the ladies' room and you waited for me out here. Should I ask if there's a doctor present?"

Livia shook her head furiously, looking pained at the thought. "No. I'm fine. Really. I must have drifted off. I was thinking of your grandmother's funeral. When I met Arturo." She shook her head. "When I closed my eyes, his face was just before me. So young and handsome."

"Ah," sighed Eleonora, sitting beside her. "Can you believe we were all once so young? Remember that summer when we all drove up to Porto Ercole?" She laughed. "Do you remember Lapo's Maserati Berlinetta?"

Livia smiled. "Only you two fit in that car. Remember we followed you up in Arturo's old Fiat Cinquecento? I was convinced it would break down."

"How could so much time have passed?" Eleonora whispered, a sadness settling in her body. "Sometimes I feel like my grandchildren look at me wondering how I'm still breathing."

Livia shook her head. "We're ancient to them. My youngest grandson asked if I was around when they built the Colosseum."

Eleonora laughed.

Livia patted Eleonora's hand. "Too much reminiscing at our age is never a good thing. Let's go see this exhibition." Slowly, the two women pulled themselves up.

LIVIA FELT THE THROBBING in her toe. Her arthritis was acting up. Again. She fought the grimace attempting to break out across her face. There was nothing more tiresome than an old woman complaining about her ailments. She'd vowed never to become one of those. She stepped gingerly with her right foot, praying the throbbing would cease.

Over the gallery door, a large map of Africa was splattered with blood red paint. Large, ominous black letters painted across spelled out 'NIYONZIMA.' Livia reached to Eleonora's arm, and squeezed it with excitement. She pointed to the sign. "Look!"

"My dear," tsked Eleonora. "Don't act so reverential. You've never even heard about this artist before the *Repubblica* article informed you it was not to be missed. Frankly, I would have preferred the Botticelli exhibition over at the Scuderie."

Livia's frustration mounted. "You have always been so ... so ... conventional."

A flash of anger contorted Eleonora's face. "Conventional is not such a bad thing. Do you see any lines in front of this exhibition? The line will be snaking all the way to the Quirinale over at the Botticelli exhibition. All those *conventional* people, lining up to see *conventional* art. Art that been enjoyed across *conventional* centuries."

Livia bit her lip. She hated how Eleonora's blue-blooded tone was accentuated even more when she ridiculed original thinking. Arturo had been so different from Lapo and Eleonora. They both came from simple backgrounds, never had things handed to them on silver platters. How had they put up with such snobby attitudes all those years? Even the Porto Ercole trip, to Lapo's ridiculously lavish villa. The Maserati raced around the roads, and Lapo spent days laughing at Arturo about how his broken-down Cinquecento was left in the dust. Why had Arturo tolerated it? Why had she?

Livia stared into those blue eyes, the edges lined with wrinkles now. But they hadn't softened or sweetened with age. They were still superior, judgmental, utterly incapable of understanding others' circumstances.

"Left without words, Livia? That's out of character for you."

Livia breathed in deeply. "My mother always taught me if you don't have anything nice to say, it's better to say nothing at all." She turned to the exhibition banner. Her excitement at seeing the artist's work significantly deflated. "Shall we, Eleonora?" Without waiting for a response, she stepped into the gallery.

ELEONORA PULLED HER SHOULDERS back and followed Livia into the gallery. Why Livia always got so huffy about things, she'd never understand. So what if Eleonora appreciated classic European art, rather than some exhibition by an artist from Burundi no one even knew existed, except for the artist's own mother and some stupid staff writer at *La Repubblica*? A writer who was more likely than not a dead ringer for the nose-pin ticket seller downstairs.

She'd almost bowed out today. Whenever Livia read some cultural review in *La Repubblica* or *Il Manifesto*, it never ended well. Eleonora had been dragged along to a transvestite musical, a mock trial on the racist Italian state carried out by an immigrant group, followed by an endless question-and-answer session in an airless room filled with earnest, young participants who seemed to share an aversion to bathing, and a four-hour long, yawn-inducing Afghan documentary on the injustices of lives of women filmed with a handheld camera hidden under a burka.

Maybe it made Livia feel younger, sitting beside rumpled, radical Italian students, fighting for causes she pretended to care about. But Eleonora would prefer to see her friend at a mainstream film or theatre performance, or to simply chat over a cup of tea.

At her age, there were so few friends left. One couldn't open the newspaper anymore without seeing another old acquaintances in the obituary section.

Her thoughts were distracted as her eye caught the bright spots of color above her head. She looked up to see flashes of reds, pinks, blues and greens, all hovering in the air on invisible strings, high above their heads. Eleonora caught her breath, a smile spreading across her face. She touched Livia's arm. "Look, how pretty those balloons are! So high up in the air. I should have brought the grandchildren."

Livia groaned. "Were you always this naive, or have you worsened with age?" Her eyes were cold.

Eleonora stepped back, sorry she'd caved in and joined her friend. Why was Livia becoming so mean? She'd always been, well, *unpolished*. But what could one expect from someone from her station in life, raised by parents who were barely literate themselves and always ready to chase Livia out of their cramped housing?

That's what brought them together as children. Livia was always running around Villa Borghese when Eleonora's nanny brought her. The little girl looked half-starved. One day, Eleonora shared her snack with the skinny little girl with the dirty, torn dress and scraped knees, ignoring her nanny's protests to stay away from the urchin. They'd been friends ever since.

Eleonora met Livia's gaze. "Were you always so rude, or have you worsened with age?"

Livia sighed and took Eleonora's elbow, leading her to a series of black-and-white photographs. They were horrendous. Skeletal bodies of African men, women, and children, lying on cots in dirty huts, pain etched on their faces, sweat trickling down their faces.

"Those are not balloons." Livia pointed up at the ceiling. "They're prophylactics."

"Pardon?"

Livia shook her head. "Condoms!"

Her voice was too loud in the cavernous space. Heads swiveled in their direction.

"Shhh, Livia." Eleonora felt her cheeks warm up. She spoke in a low voice. "You don't have to speak like a sailor."

"I'm not saying anything untoward. It's simply the truth. The plight of the Africans in our modern world. Ravaged by diseases like AIDS, while all the preventative methods are literally a world away." Her voice became increasingly shrill. She swept her hands up dramatically to indicate the condoms floating high in the air. "And here they are on display for the colonial visitors in the indifferent West. They might as well be on Mars for all the good they do the suffering populations."

Heads swiveled once again. It was more than Eleonora could bear. She wished she could vanish. She moved away. Livia followed her.

"You can't escape unpleasant realities, Eleonora, simply because you were born privileged."

They stood before a wall of images of African prostitutes standing along Italian streets. Their wide hips were encased in short skirts. Their breasts were mostly bare and they walked in towering heels. Eleonora pivoted, but Livia's arms hindered her.

"Don't turn away from them! Internalize their anguish! Feel their pain! Haven't we all been turning our eyes from them for long enough?"

Livia's face appeared so smug that Eleonora wished she'd had the upbringing that would allow her to slap her friend. But her mother had always warned about making scenes.

"Livia, you are giving me a headache. This exhibition is simply an excuse to espouse your radical views. I am not responsible for the plight of these women."

"Ah, but you are, Eleonora! We all are. We are complicit. An injustice to one in our cruel, cruel world is an injustice to all." Livia, increasingly agitated, paced before the photographs. She placed a hand to her breast and, for a moment, looked as if she might cry. "I *know* these women. They are my *sisters*. I have lived in Africa and felt their suffering—their burdens—as if it were my own."

Eleonora looked her friend squarely in the eye and burst out laughing. Heads turned again, but she didn't care. When she'd recovered, she shook her head. "Oh, give it a rest, Livia. You and Arturo lived in an exclusive, gated villa, *in the Seychelles.* A consular position in Victoria hardly makes you an expert on the plight of suffering Africans."

Livia reeled as if she'd been slapped. "You were *never* supportive. Only jealous that we had such an opportunity to open our eyes to the injustices around the world."

Eleonora felt the anger surge inside her. "Jealous? Me? How did Arturo get that job, did you ever ask yourself? From overlooked junior paper-pusher at the Foreign Ministry to a management position at the Consulate overnight, and you never suspected anything?"

Livia clutched her chest. "You?"

"I could have managed quite as well, of course." She clucked her tongue. "But it was Lapo. He wished to help his old friend, but he never wanted Arturo to know." She shook her head. "I am certain he suspected, however. Arturo knew how things worked, knew someone must have been helping pull strings.

You were the one who preferred to believe his genius was discovered and he was plucked from bureaucratic obscurity and elevated to greatness. You were always so naïve, Livia."

The two women glared at one another in silence.

"I'm tired," said Eleonora, her voice subdued. "This exhibition was not a good idea. I will go rest my feet over there on that bench." She pulled herself up to her full height. "Under what I choose to believe are colorful party balloons." She strode to the bench, with decisiveness and speed surprising for a woman of her age.

COULD IT BE TRUE? Lapo responsible for Arturo's appointment? Livia's heart had nearly burst with pride and joy when Arturo returned home with the news. They'd packed up their house and moved to the Indian Ocean island archipelago with great optimism. Arturo had never been happier. They'd never been happier as a family than those years living in tropical paradise.

They'd eventually returned to Rome, and Arturo moved into higher-ranking desk positions after his time in the Seychelles, but he'd never been sent abroad again. There'd been talk, of course, but then his heart condition worsened. Had their time in the Indian Ocean been a one-off favor?

Livia sighed. Perhaps Arturo suspected, but she preferred to think he hadn't known. He'd been so good at his posting, so professional. It cheapened it somehow, diminished his achievement. And it *was* an achievement, no matter what Eleonora implied.

The whole afternoon had been a disaster. She suddenly longed to be home, reading in her quiet study, finally content with the silence that reigned in her home. But as Livia observed Eleonora on the bench, her still fine features raised to the ceiling, the bile rose in her throat. Eleonora had heard often enough how proud Livia was that Arturo had secured that position. What was the use of sullying that memory at their age? To gloat? To bask in her superiority? No, Livia was tired of always being the poor urchin girl, even decades later. Eleonora was no longer the denizen of the golden, sophisticated Rome as she'd once been.

Her heart beat dangerously fast as she strode to the bench and sat beside Eleonora.

"I suppose you'll want to apologize," said Eleonora.

"I most certainly do not." The anger welled up inside as Livia clutched her fists.

"I would think you would be grateful."

"Grateful to you?" Livia's voice rose. "You always fought to be in the limelight, no matter where we were. Always fancying that all the men were in love with you, that the universe revolved around you."

Eleonora tsked and shook her head prettily. "Center of the universe. Of course not. I was never so presumptuous."

She looked around her coyly, a look Livia remembered from their younger days.

"But," Eleonora paused. "Others may have been admiring way back when. I remember an evening at dinner ..." She looked out to an invisible point in the distance, her voice filled with a gentle longing. "When the film director Visconti toasted my beauty, and said he could have made me a star."

Livia snorted. "What a load of bull. As time passes, you can hope all the witnesses die out and no one will be around to challenge you. He said you looked a vision in your dress. Not surprising, considering what you spent on your wardrobe ..."

Eleonora's face turned red. Her eyes filled with tears. "And to think I considered you a *friend* all these years." Her voice shook with emotion. She sniffled. "I do not wish to see you again, Livia. Do not try to contact me. I leave you to your enlightening exhibition and take my leave of you. *Addio.*" With difficulty, she pushed herself from the bench and shuffled slowly, but with determination, to the exit.

Livia ignored the people around her. She sat very still on the bench, ignoring the throbbing pain in her toes. She breathed in deeply through her nose to stem the tears risking to flow over.

Looking up, she saw the colorful orbs overhead, swinging in the gentle breeze. They did indeed look very much like decorative party balloons.

THE BATH HAD NOT HELPED. The quiet reading only made her anxious. Livia sat alone in the study, annoyed by the resounding tick of the mantelpiece clock.

She reached for the remote control and flicked on the television, switching from channel to channel. There was never anything on. She sighed and turned it off again.

Picking up her cellphone, she scrolled through to Anna's number and dialed.

"Darling, how are you? How are the children?"

"They're fine, *mamma*. How are you? When are you coming to see us?"

"Oh, dear. You know how it is at my age. Can't you come to Rome? I'd love to see the children."

"You know we'll be down at Christmas. What's wrong? Why are you crying?"

Livia dabbed her eyes with her handkerchief. "Oh, it's nothing." She breathed in deeply. "It's only ... Eleonora and I had a nasty falling out today. Such a shame, since I'd organized the afternoon so perfectly at an exhibition I knew she'd love. But it was quite ..." she sniffled "... quite unpleasant. It's left me feeling lonely."

There was a pause on the other end. "Oh, *mamma*. It'll be fine. Just call her tomorrow."

The tears flowed down harder and Livia shook her head.

"I need to go. The children are wrestling one another. I'll check in with you tomorrow and see if it hasn't already been forgotten. You two never remain angry for long. *Buona notte!*"

The connection clicked off before Livia could even respond.

ELEONORA WAS SO ABSORBED in the old photo album that she didn't even hear the door open. When the shadow fell across the pages, she looked up to see Maria looming over her.

"You gave me a shock. You can't sneak up on someone my age. Please knock first."

"Yes, ma'am. I'm ready to serve dinner, but I see you've been moping around here all evening after the museum. I worked hard preparing dinner. I certainly hope you won't insult me by telling me you can't eat."

Eleonora sighed. "Oh, Maria. Where does the time go? Look at us so long ago. This is Livia and me. It must be '52, before we met Lapo and Arturo." Her voice grew soft. "How young we were."

Maria examined the photo. "You sure were. You must be the same age as my Marta now. You were a real beauty, *Signora* Eleonora."

Eleonora looked into Maria's eyes. "The director, Visconti, once toasted my beauty. Said I could have had a career in film."

Maria smiled and patted Eleonora's hand. "I'm sure he did. You were a knockout."

The tears, pent up all afternoon, rolled down Eleonora's cheeks.

"Oh, what is it?" asked Maria. "Are you in pain? Can I get you something?"

"Oh no," choked out Eleonora. "It's not that. It's ..." She blew her nose. "Livia and I fought today. We said terrible things. I don't think we'll ever see one another again." She dissolved into tears.

Maria slid strong arms around her and held her close. "There, there. No crying. It ruins the digestion, and that is unacceptable when I've been slaving away for hours in that kitchen."

The sobs grew louder.

"*Signora* Eleonora." Maria leaned back and raised Eleonora's chin. "You and *Signora* Livia are like an old married couple. You fight. It's what you do."

"No," protested Eleonora. "This is it. The end."

Maria shook her head and grimaced. "That's what you say every time. You always patch things up. You're worse than children, you two." She stood up. "You call her tomorrow and invite her around for tea. I'll make my special chocolate hazelnut cake she loves so much. You'll see. It'll be fine." She glanced at her watch. "Now, I should be getting home. Your dinner will be on the table in five minutes, and you will be in the dining room to eat." Her voice grew gentler. "You'll feel better tomorrow. Just wait and see."

Eleonora dabbed at her eyes with her handkerchief. She looked down at the photo of her young self beside Livia. Their arms were around one another's thin waists, their ball gowns shimmered in the lights of her grandparent's *palazzo* ballroom. Their hair was piled up intricately on top of their heads and their fresh skin glowed in the lights of the camera. What sprightly things they'd been, with their radiant beauty and youth.

Eleonora smiled weakly. Her friend for over seven decades. She looked down once more at the girls beaming out at her.

Gently, she lowered one wrinkled finger and caressed the image, tracing the contours of her youthful face, then Livia's. Inseparable friends, that's what people called them.

She sighed. Tomorrow she'd call Livia. She'd invite her for tea and Maria's famous chocolate hazelnut cake. They had weathered much worse. They'd weather this, too.

Friends always did.

EARLY MORNING JOGS

Guayaquil

THE SCREECHING OF THE ALARM violently ripped Beatrice from the lingering sensations. With a groan, she reached over to shut off the grating sound, while squeezing her eyes tighter, desperate to recreate a mental image of those sharp cheekbones, those soulful eyes.

That feeling she'd been experiencing mere seconds earlier, before the hateful clock radio buzz had intruded on her bliss. The harder she tried to reconstruct the face, the warm feeling it sparked in her, the further away it retreated.

Warm lips nuzzled her neck. A familiar body pressed against hers, strong arms pinning her in place. She fought the urge to elbow away the unwanted embrace. The embrace that utterly dissipated any relics of the dreamlike images trapped in the ether.

"Beatrice, *amore,*" voiced the mouth nuzzling against her neck as she allowed her unresponsive body to grow rigid. "We have time before your flight. A quick one before you desert me."

She lay perfectly still, counting slowly to five before responding in an artfully regretful tone. "Claudio, I'd love to, but you know how I am with long flights. I need to go for a jog before I'm crammed into a plane for so many hours." She turned to face him, tried to ignore the hurt reflected in his hazel eyes, framed by those impossibly thick lashes.

Years ago, he could cast a simple gaze at her across a crowded room, and her insides would melt. For the rest of the evening, she'd be counting down the minutes until they could reasonably make their retreat, hurrying back home and into their bed. Those eyes centimeters from her own were equally beautiful, but they'd long ago lost the ability to set off the butterflies raging within.

He sighed and pulled back, releasing his hand from her waist. "Lord knows we wouldn't want you to miss a morning of jogging. A real shame to break routine and all." He turned back over, his back to her, burrowing deep into his pillow.

She opened her mouth to say she was sorry, to ask him to come with her for a run, but they hadn't been running together these past years. Hadn't done much of anything together these past years. Instead, she pursed her lips and slid out of bed, clasping the jogging gear and sneakers she'd placed at her bedside late last night, before slipping into the bathroom.

Beatrice changed, brushed her teeth and combed her long, black hair into a high ponytail. Forty had hit her like a ton of bricks earlier that year, but everyone assured her she didn't look a day over thirty. She traced a decidedly not-thirty-year-old thin line appearing at the edge of her right eye, stubbornly setting down roots in her otherwise taut skin. How had it snuck through her defenses to claim its hateful marked territory, despite the expensive potions she massaged onto her face twice daily?

With a sigh, she flicked off the unforgiving bathroom mirror lights, wondering if she could replace them with bulbs that generated a softer glow, and retreated to the living room. She laced up her sneakers and gently stretched. She unbolted the door, clicking the lock and slipping the key into her shorts' pocket. She scurried down the condominium stairs, waving a silent hello to the doorman who was sweeping up the courtyard before the heavy rush-hour foot traffic began. Emerging from the main door, Beatrice gazed at the dusky pink fingers of light streaked across Rome's early morning sky. The city was always at its best at dawn, despite the fact that so few were out to admire its dramatic performance. Beatrice took a deep breath of the still-fresh air and set off on her familiar path.

She cut through Celio's streets, where the fruit and vegetable sellers had already set up their daily stands, awaiting the first early morning customers. She hit her stride as she passed the military hospital and crossed the eerily quiet Via Claudia, which, on her return, would already be clogged with early commuters. Passing under the Dolabella arch, she recalled how she and Claudio had always loved this little corner of Rome best.

She pounded down on the ancient cobblestones, making her way to the San Giovanni and Paolo Basilica, with its tiny square and picturesque medieval tower that would serve as a backdrop to Roman weddings later that day. Had served as a backdrop to her own wedding to Claudio almost two decades ago, back when they'd aspired to live in the neighborhood they now inhabited. Back then, they could only afford a tiny place in the outer reaches of Rome.

The flying buttresses of the church soared above her on her descent down the cobblestoned hill. She remembered reading Henry James' account of this perfect medieval corner of Rome, back in college, when she was sure she would be teaching literature. Sometimes it hurt to compare her youthful, hopeful self with the present-day version. How much did you have to lose to gain what you wanted? Or thought you wanted ...

Her footfalls took her past the austere San Gregorio church, with its stark white façade, before emerging down at the edge of the *biscotto*. The Romans called this one-kilometer dirt track on the opposite side of the street from the Ancient Roman baths of Caracalla "The cookie." Somehow, learning this expression made her feel more Roman. More like a local, less like a small-town girl from Rieti.

She wound her way onto the trail and began her morning routine. Her ideas flowed better out here on the jogging path. Back when she and Claudio first moved into a rental in the neighborhood, before placing the down payment on their current flat, most days had started here together. They'd jog and chat, planning out their days, their weeks, their hopes for the future. A university career for her. Consulting partner for Claudio. Two kids. An enviable apartment in Rome's center.

The apartment had panned out, at least. Claudio made partner last year and spent most of his time traveling to far-flung projects. Back when money was tight, she'd given up her dream of an academic career for a government job supporting international development projects around the world. Following her promotion three years ago, she rivalled her husband in racking up frequent flyer miles. Often they passed one another in their lobby—Beatrice returning from travel just as Claudio was racing to the taxi to embark on his. Their bank account was healthy, but most days their marriage didn't feel that way.

Beatrice missed how much they used to laugh together, back in their cramped, old basement apartment. She missed having friends over to dinner, chatting late into the night over bottles of cheap wine. Back then, they'd had so much more fun on a daytrip to Ostia than the weeklong vacations at some exclusive Sardinian hotel Claudio now favored—too often involving dinners with one of Claudio's clients. The weekends in Rieti visiting her friends and family had ceased long ago. Claudio no longer considered small-town life in her hometown quaint, instead complaining about being too far away if work issues cropped up. When Beatrice's mother passed away last year, Beatrice had been guilt-ridden, realizing how few times she'd been home to visit her in recent years, how her siblings viewed her as a snob who considered herself too good for them.

As her troubled thoughts tumbled through her mind, she glanced down at her watch, realizing she had jogged far longer than she'd meant to. After all, she had a plane to catch. With a last glimpse of the hulking dome of the Vatican in the distance, she headed towards the hill that would lead her home.

Back in the apartment, she removed her running shoes and padded silently over the cool marble floors. She eased the bedroom door open. Claudio was still asleep. Sunday was the only day he allowed himself the luxury of sleeping in. She tiptoed into the closet to retrieve the clothes she had prepared a day earlier and made her way to the shower. As she washed away the sweat under the strong jet, she shifted her mind from the past to the upcoming trip and what would be expected of her on the hectic week away.

Showered and dressed, she slipped her running sneakers into her suitcase and cautiously cast a look back to the bedroom, where Claudio remained unmoving on the pillow. She took a step towards him to plant a kiss on his cheek, but catching a glimpse of the clock on the bedside table, she thought better of it, and hurried to the exit.

The taxi would be downstairs. She'd text him from the airport.

THE FLIGHT TO ECUADOR SEEMED ENDLESS, and the brief stop-off in Quito where all passengers were forced to deplane seemed a cruel joke. Beatrice wandered aimlessly through the tiny airport, awaiting the return to the flight for the short descent into Guayaquil. The morning jog had helped, and she'd slept fairly well on the flight, but her exhaustion was bone-deep. One long flight could not remedy the emptiness that had long been settling within.

Bleary-eyed, she browsed the dizzying array of colorful weavings, bags of Ecuadorian coffees and tablets of dark, local chocolate until she heard the call for the flight to Guayaquil. With weary feet, she made her way back to the plane for the final descent down the Andes.

BEATRICE CAREFULLY UNPACKED her items as the bright sun streamed through the windows. Carefully ferrying between the suitcase sprawled over her bed, and her closet and dresser, she neatly tucked everything away. A place for everything, and everything in its place.

When they traveled together, Claudio was always grabbing her hand to pull her out to explore. "Who cares about the damn bags? We can do it later. Or just live out of our suitcase for a few days if we want to. Let's not waste any time."

More often than not, he'd succeeded in loosening her collar. Hand in hand, they would cast fresh eyes on ancient cities or stunning nature—eager to become one with their new destination. Claudio's familiar, strong hand in hers always gave her the confidence to confront each new reality with the spirit of adventure.

But in recent years, their adventures were entirely separate.

Claudio traveled extensively for his work, and she for hers. They often departed in opposite directions on the globe. In their infrequent leisure time, the promise of a long journey together no longer beckoned. It was a time to catch up with household tasks, doctor's appointments, paperwork, home repairs. The mundane. Their days of joint adventure were long behind them. At least, that's how it felt to Beatrice most of the time.

Now that she traveled alone, no one was there to nag Beatrice as she careful organized her hired room, trying to make it home. No one urged her to get out and explore, to ignite her spirit of adventure. But earlier today, she'd shifted slightly from routine. Beatrice stepped over to the plate glass, looking down at the square of green, the horseback statue of Simon Bolivar. The palm trees shading benches. After checking in to the hotel, Beatrice deposited her suitcase atop her bed, surprising herself as her feet led her out the door, clutching her key in hand.

She retraced her steps to the lobby, with its retro eighties' elegance. She stepped out of the cool air conditioning and into the sultry heat. It hit her face at once, but she took decided steps across the busy street and to the Seminario Park, where groups of tourists were gathering.

She made her way to the Bolivar statue, glistening in the strong sunlight. The gleaming white of the cathedral beckoned beyond, its rose window and dramatic, pointed twin towers beckoning visitors, but her eyes were drawn to the stars of the show—utterly indifferent to their celebrity status. The sun shone down on them as they pointedly ignored the fuss. Eyes lazy, munching lunch as cellphones clicked and filmed their every slow, deliberate move.

Fame and admiration apparently did not trump lettuce. The iguanas presided regally over their kingdom. Eyes open a mere crack, ignoring their admiring fans as they chewed on their lettuce deliveries in the shade of leafy trees. And why should they bother with the throngs? They had a whole park dedicated to them. For Seminario Park was more commonly known as Iguana Park.

She stood before a group of iguanas, all munching on their snacks, oblivious to the phones snapping their images. Beatrice removed her own phone to record the likeness of these modern-day dinosaurs. The dinosaur-obsessed seven-year-old son of Rosa, her officemate back in Rome, would be thrilled. She'd WhatsApp the photos to Rosa to share with Lorenzo. A family vacated a bench and Beatrice took their place, still staring at the unusual local fauna.

She looked down at her phone and saw two missed calls from Claudio. She sighed and looked out into the distance. Her dinner tonight had been cancelled to give her time to rest. She'd be meeting the Ecuadorian team tomorrow in the morning for a full day of planning before their coastal visit. She needed to be at the top of her game for those meetings. Despite all the sleep she did manage on the plane, the jet lag was still hitting her. She'd have a light dinner in the hotel restaurant and get to bed for an early night. Fresh for tomorrow.

She glanced at her watch. Technically it wasn't too late to call Claudio, but he'd never know. She'd tell him she got in later than expected.

She saw a flash of yellow beneath her and jolted on her bench. Yellow, reptilian skin. A prominent crest. A long tail patterned with yellow and green-black stripes. A flap under the chin that swayed gently with the slow movements. The iguana pushed up on his front legs, his beady eyes seemingly examined her from within his wizened age-old face. They remained still like that for a moment, woman and iguana, before the iguana lost interest and wandered away, attracted by the piece of mango a young boy lay out for him.

Figured. Even the iguana could recognize what a fraud she was, utterly insignificant. Slowly she stood, dusted off her jeans, and walked with careful steps—on the lookout not to step on iguana tails—in the direction of her hotel room. There she was determined to finish unpacking her clothes and put some order to her life.

NO ALARM CLOCK was necessary. It was still dark when Beatrice woke at 5:30 a.m. A hopeless thirty minutes ensued, as she tried to coax her body back to sleep. Better positioned pillows, above the sheets, below the sheets, diagonally across the bed, conjuring up an entire army of steeple-chasing sheep—nothing did the trick.

Finally, defeated, Beatrice rose from her bed. The sun, recently busy shining its warmth down on Rome, was now making its rounds further west; the clear night sky would soon give way to a dramatic sunrise, still just a promising glimmer on the horizon. Beatrice yawned and stretched, looking down at the deserted iguana park beneath her window. Those ancient creatures were far more sensible, sleeping as they bided their time before another action-packed day of soaking in the sun, posing for the paparazzi and an all-day-long, all-you-can-eat buffet of lettuce and mango.

Walking to her dresser, she opened a drawer and extricated her carefully folded jogging clothes. Exchanging her nightgown for shorts, jog bra and tank top, she began combing her long hair into a ponytail, before lacing up her running sneakers and warming up with a jog down the stairs before reaching the lobby.

"Buenos días," she said to the young man at the desk, handing him her key.

"Buenos días," he responded, with a smile. He looked her up and down carefully, a lock of his thick, black hair falling over his wide, young forehead. "I see from your clothes you plan to jog. There are guards out at this hour, but you must be careful. You will stay on the Malecón, *sí*?"

She smiled at this young boy—at least compared to her—gently lecturing her as if she were the child and he the wise elder. "*Sí*, yes of course I will."

"Good," he said, accompanied by a relieved smile. "Be safe."

She smiled again and walked out the door; the darkness and silence cloaked her. The streets that had been so filled with traffic yesterday were silent now, but the horizon was streaked with pink fingers. Soon enough the sun would rise and Guayaquil's day would begin, with its rush of people and traffic. She felt fortunate to enjoy it now in its pre-dawn silence. She began to jog slowly, her sneakers pounding down on the pavement, leaving behind the park and the slumbering iguanas, the colonial-era church.

Long strides led her to the Malecón, where a guard was opening the gate, greeting her with a cheerful, "*Hola*." She smiled and returned the greeting, admiring the colonial-era tower, intricate white carved features against the yellow. This would serve as a prominent landmark for her return. In too many foreign cities she'd wandered aimlessly, trying to retrace early morning steps to her hotel.

She ran to the edge of the river, with its wide boardwalk hugging its bank. The Guayas River was immense—more a sea than a river. How the Ecuadorians would laugh to view the tiny Tiber River that meandered lazily through Rome, or the rapidly moving, but narrow Velino that bisected her own hometown. This Guaya was altogether different: immense, ceaseless, powerful. She observed an early morning fisherman, returning to shore with his catch.

She jogged on, skirting the Guaya. She smiled as she passed large white and blue letters, joyfully announcing GUAYAQUIL to locals and tourists alike who passed by, perhaps pausing for a selfie. And why not? At this hour, the restaurants and bars were boarded up, but, last night, while she was slumbering through her jetlag, the crowds were certainly out in this same spot, eating and imbibing until the early hours. Maybe she'd manage to stay awake long enough to dine out here this evening and become one with the crowds.

The broad riverwalk continued, and Beatrice clipped along it at a comfortable pace. To her left, large numbers of young men wearing shirts emblazoned with "*Ejército*" were sweating through drills of push-ups and sit-ups. A little beyond them, a group of Navy personnel were doing the same. So much for being unsafe on early morning jogs. With seemingly the entire nation's armed services out training at the same time, she was bound to be safe.

The jogging guides she'd consulted online, the guides she always consulted before she travelled to a new city, had warned about insecurity in Ecuador's largest city, but it seemed to be well frequented. It should do nicely for early morning jogs during her stay here.

She continued onwards, trying to channel the relentless flow of the Guaya to the rhythm of her own pace. After her long flight and attempt to sleep off the jetlag, the burning in her calf muscles made her feel alive, grounding her to the here and now. She neared a hulking, slumbering Ferris wheel, with views it would afford over the city and the river to visitors who would buy a ticket to ride it later in the day.

As the red brick walkway of the Malecón ended, she paused momentarily. To her left stood a hill with a haphazard jumble of houses rising on the edge a distinctive lighthouse with the white and sky-blue stripes of the city flag. The road to her right seemed to lead her to that lighthouse, but, unlike the Malecón, it appeared completely dark and silent, not a soul in sight.

Hands on hips, she turned around, but no fellow joggers or walkers were out. Should she listen to the hotel clerk? Stay on the Malecón? She glanced down at her Swatch. She still had some time before she had to be back for a shower and breakfast before the work team would come to pick her up. She gazed up at the lighthouse once again, its colorful stripes beckoning. The views over the town and the river must be spectacular from that vantage point, especially in the early morning light. With a decided nod, she veered to the right and set off through the silent streets. Her pounding sneakers broke the hushed atmosphere as she jogged and gazed at the pretty colonial architecture, clearly recently renovated.

Pastel-colored two- and three-story buildings curved around cobblestoned streets, most of them with colorful shutters firmly closed against dawn's first light. Beatrice noticed the ground-floor bars and restaurants that would open later in the day, an upscale shop selling the popular Panama hats, bearing the name of that Central American country, while produced only in Ecuador.

A cat darted before her and she smiled as it leapt down a narrow alley. The colorful houses and the sense of peace permeated the deepest recesses of Beatrice's mind. *Claudio would love it here*, she thought, before chasing the thought away and picking up her speed.

Further along the road with its colorful homes, Beatrice saw a stone staircase to her left. She slowed to run in place, examining it. The position seemed correct. Did it lead up to the lighthouse? From the shadows emerged a short, stocky man in a blue uniform, a walkie-talkie in hand. Her momentary concern was quickly replaced with relief, as she realized he was a security guard. They exchanged greetings before Beatrice tilted her head in the direction of the stairs and pointed. "*El faro?*"

"*Sí*," the man indicated upwards with his arm.

"*Gracias*," she replied before turning and running up the stairs. Behind her, she heard the man speaking into his walkie-talkie, seemingly warning a colleague at the top that a tourist-jogger was coming his way. She smiled. Between the military troops and the private security guards, she started to feel she was safer jogging here than in Rome. As she worked her way up the stairs, the homes grew less stately and more haphazard, but their colors were bright and cheery.

The lighthouse still appeared far away. As she looked down, she saw the stairs had changed. They were now wider, and each had a ceramic number on its edge: 14, 15,16. Oh goodness, she could follow her progress with the numbers. But how many were there? And why did she already feel exhausted? She jogged much more than this at home. But then again, this was only her first day, and she still had traces of jet lag. She was no longer a twenty-year-old, after all.

She concentrated all her energy into keeping a pace on the stairs as the numbers grew higher—86, 87, 88 ... But she couldn't deny her breathing was growing increasingly labored with the effort. A persistent trickle of sweat slid down her back. True, here along the equator, it was much more humid than in Rome. She'd have to take that into account and not push herself as much. But this morning, she needed to see the view from the top. Beatrice continued with single-minded devotion to her self-imposed task.

243, 244, 245 ... The numbers on the stairs continued to increase, but the lighthouse didn't seem any nearer. What was wrong with her? Would she even manage to reach the top? Or should she eventually throw in the towel and walk? No. She could do this. Running was one of the few aspects of her life over which Beatrice felt she exerted some control. If she lost this, too ...

She slowed her pace, but ensured her legs continued on their steady, upward trajectory. Thank goodness there was no one around to see her struggling. In the 300s now. How many stairs could there be? Even Rocky didn't have to contend with this many. Up, up, the blue and white stripes of the lighthouse loomed ever closer, flanked by two giant flags fluttering gently in the breeze. To the left, the yellow, blue and red stripes signaling the national flag of Ecuador. To the right, Guayaquil city's sky blue and white stripes matching the lighthouse's colors. Training her eyes on those flags, Beatrice kept going.

At 432, she gasped in relief. A flat landing welcomed her, two benches beckoning beneath the cheery bougainvillea. She walked past them, wary of resting and not having the strength to rouse herself again. Turning the corner, she gasped when she took in more steps. On second glance, only twelve more, and still numbered. With a last burst of energy, she made it up the final twelve, raising her arms, Rocky-style, when she reached number 444.

Beatrice bent over, catching her breath. That had taken far more out of her than she'd imagined. She straightened up and looked around, the suffering soon forgotten as she neared the lighthouse. A female guard holding a walkie-talkie was observing her, looking relieved. Perhaps she'd received the warning of her colleague below. Beatrice proffered a smile and a friendly wave. The lighthouse was open and presented yet more steps, even if it was quite short for a lighthouse. After all, it had the hill to do all its work for it.

She slowly climbed the stairs, emerging onto the wraparound balcony with stunning views beyond. Before her was a tiny chapel, beyond it the jumbled homes of the neighborhood. The cacophony of bright blues, reds, yellows and oranges should have appeared gaudy, but somehow worked. Beyond them loomed high telecommunications towers and sprawling inland suburbs. She walked around the perimeter, the enormous Guaya River coming into view. To her left, shiny new buildings caught her eye. Along the river, these appeared to be luxurious, high-rise apartments. She took in the sleek rooftop terraces, with their lounge chairs and sparkling swimming pools—an interesting juxtaposition with the jumble of simple, decidedly nonluxurious homes on the neighboring hill.

Slowly, she made her way down the steps, recharged and ready to jog down the stairs and back to the hotel. She emerged from the lighthouse, waved to the guard, and walked down the twelve steps to initiate her jog. She startled to see a man, gasping for air, collapsed on one of the benches.

She raced over, asking in Italian if the man was okay, before realizing he would not understand.

He pushed himself upright, clutching his heart but smiling. "*Va bene, sì. Soltanto pigro.*" He tilted his head to observe her, his dark eyes dancing, his cocoa-colored skin glowing in the early morning light. Rippling muscles emerged from beneath his T-shirt, the word "*Ejército*" emblazoned across his chest.

She instinctively moved back. "*Parli italiano?*" thinking she may have misheard.

"*Sì,*" he nodded. "Five years working at hotels in Rimini. I only returned home last year."

"Oh," she said. He spoke excellent Italian, with a Spanish cadence. "But are you okay? I was afraid you were having a heart attack. Should I fetch the guard up there?"

"Oh, no," he said, sitting up straighter. "I'd die of shame. I was late this morning and had to run after the group morning run. The guys'll never let it go if they knew I had to be rescued on the Lighthouse Run. No way."

Beatrice smiled. "Okay, I get it. If you feel better, I was just like you fifteen minutes ago. I spent some time admiring the view from the lighthouse, caught my breath, and feel better now." She sat down beside him. "Not quite ready to run a marathon, but definitely prepared to run *down* those stairs."

He laughed. Sticking out his hand, he said, "I'm Javier."

She met his hand with her own. "Beatrice. Nice to meet you."

"Where are you from, Beatrice?"

"Rome, but I moved there in college. I'm from a little town north of there—Rieti."

"I've never been to Rieti, but I've been a few times to Rome. Love it. Love Italy. I miss it."

"Well, it's a nice surprise for me to be speaking Italian in the middle of Guayaquil, when I'll be struggling to work all day in my limited Spanish."

He laughed that addictive laugh once more and stood straight. "Well, if you want to chat some more in Italian, join me. I need to get back down, loop through Santa Ana and then through Las Peñas before I get back to the Malecón and the rest of the troops. *Che ne dici?*"

"*Va bene. Muy bien.*" She stood, too, surprised at how he towered over her. Even in her short time here, she'd become accustomed to being statuesque among the locals.

He winked and nodded. "I know what you're thinking. Too tall to be a local."

She blushed.

"No, I can't read minds. I'm just used to it. My mom's Ecuadorian, my dad Jamaican. From all accounts, super tall. He left when I was two, so I wouldn't know."

"Oh, I'm sorry," she said, before kicking herself. It wasn't as if he'd died. How did one express regret for an absent father?

"Yeah, well. I've had a good thirty years to get over it. Can't miss what you don't even remember, right?" He pointed to the steps. "Shall we go?"

They began to jog down. So much easier than the reverse direction, Beatrice couldn't help noticing.

Javier gestured to the right. "My mom's from Las Peñas, this neighborhood here. It's Guayaquil's oldest. And it's where I grew up."

"Oh, wow. I think I jogged through the lower streets," said Beatrice. "The colonial architecture is so pretty. It was weird having it to myself early this morning."

"Yeah, but only a few years ago, it was still pretty dangerous. They cleaned it up a lot, restored a lot of the old buildings in the early 2000s. It was a lot grittier when I was growing up, even more so for my mom." They were nearing the guard Beatrice had seen earlier and he waved. "*Hola*, Juan."

Juan waved a hand in greeting, cocking one eyebrow in a knowing look when he saw the two of them together.

"The guards are new, trying to gentrify the area. Keep it safe for tourists." He jogged on. "I'm not complaining, it's just different from what I experienced growing up."

They veered to the left, toward the rows of modern, sleek buildings Beatrice had observed from up on high.

"And this is all new, too. Santa Ana," he said. "Lots of luxury apartments, chic restaurants and bars. A tourist magnet—and all only a few steps from the bustling Malecón." They jogged along the river and he looked up at the sleek glass. "Not really within reach on an army officer's salary."

"Ah, too bad. I thought you'd invite me up for a rooftop swim. Saw all those pools when I was up on the lighthouse."

His booming laugh broke the morning silence. "Afraid not, but if I ever manage to gather together the cash, you'll be the first one I invite. Deal?"

"Deal," she chuckled.

They looped around, pace steady, breathing in the morning air. Beatrice felt a second wind returning. After struggling so desperately on the stairs, she now felt she could run for hours alongside Javier. The sun was rising higher now and more people were emerging from their homes. As they emerged into Las Peñas, Beatrice felt she had been transported into another city. Shops were opening, schoolkids walked along with heavy backpacks, mothers effortlessly maneuvered the steep hills with baby carriages. Javier called out greetings to old women and young boys alike.

"Yeah, I moved back here when Italy didn't work out. They kind of embraced the prodigal son into the fold again."

They veered out of the neighborhood and back onto the broad boardwalk of the Malecón.

"Why did you leave Italy? Did you miss home after being away so long?"

He shook his head. "Nah. I would've stayed. Girlfriend problems. A local girl and I were going to marry, and I would have had the resident's permit then. About a month before the wedding, she took off with my best friend." He turned and smiled. "That threw me for a loop, as you might imagine. And I came home. *Arrivederci, Italia.*"

Beatrice grimaced. "Oh, I'm sorry to hear that."

"Not your fault. Let's just say, my mom was thrilled. And I got in as an officer in the army, so it's all good." He smiled. "Speaking of the army, *conosco i miei polli.* We're getting closer, and these guys are going to pile on if they see us together. Are you here for work? Up for a jog tomorrow, Beatrice?"

She smiled inwardly. And here she'd been worried about the dangers of early-morning jogs alone. "Yeah, that would be great."

"Where are you staying?"

"The big hotel across from Iguana Park. Do you know it?"

"Yeah, of course. How's 5:45 tomorrow morning? I'll meet you in the lobby, and I can jog with you instead of my troop and get here earlier for exercises."

"Sounds great, Javier. *Hasta mañana.*"

"*A domani,* Beatrice."

He winked at her as they neared the soldiers, who began whooping and calling out to him. He shook his head slightly at her and smiled.

She jogged on, oblivious to the chatter she knew their being seen together would garner among the soldiers. With confident strides she jogged on, until reaching the colonial tower and taking a practiced right to her hotel. Almost like a local.

WHEN THE ALARM RANG AT 5:30, there were no pink fingers to offset the inky black sky. Beatrice dressed, brushed her teeth and pulled her hair into a high ponytail. She ran down to the lobby, half-fearing Javier wouldn't turn up.

But when she rounded the steps to the lobby, there he was chatting with the young man at the counter, who laughed. "I told you to be careful, and you went and found yourself an army guard as your bodyguard. Now I do not have to worry."

She laughed and headed out into the cool air with Javier.

"Ready?" he asked.

"Absolutely," she said. "In my dreams I flew up the lighthouse stairs like a pro. Today's my day, I can tell."

He chuckled, "Mine, too, I hope."

They ran down to the Malecón just in time for the guard who was opening the gates. They entered and hit their stride on the wide boardwalk. "So, Beatrice, you didn't tell me anything about your work. Why are you gracing us with your presence here in Guayaquil?"

She explained to him about the Italian development agency she worked for, the overseas development aid they were investing in small-scale fisheries production and certified coffee and cocoa production. How these rural projects would result in environmentally and socially sustainable products to be imported to Italy. How tomorrow she would go to Santa Rosa to meet the small-scale fishing community firsthand, and how she would meet separately with cocoa and coffee cooperatives.

"It sounds like rewarding work."

"It is." She bit her lip. "But my dream was something entirely different. I wanted to be a literature professor, and I veered off course."

"Yeah, well," he looked out across the broad Guayas. "My dream was to be a soccer star. I was in the competitive clubs here as a kid, and there was talk of going to one of the farm teams in Spain, eventually reaching the pros." He looked straight ahead as they veered into the streets of Las Peñas. "Blew out my knee with a brutal tackle. My dream died a pretty sudden and violent death. And I was only sixteen."

"Oh, that must have been rough."

He nodded. "Yeah, it was. Especially because, with a Spanish football club salary, one of those swish apartments over there," he pointed his thumb in the direction of Santa Ana, "would have been child's play."

Beatrice chewed her lip.

"On the positive side, I learned dreams don't always come true. Sometimes we have to learn to readjust those dreams and make the best of what we've got. Whether we like it or not."

She sighed. "I guess you're right there."

He slowed. "On another positive note, even with my knee injury, I can still tackle these stairs."

They had arrived to the dreaded 444 steps, and Beatrice looked up.

"What do you say?"

"I'm in," she said.

Side by side, they pushed each other to the top, content to reach stair 444 and the views that greeted them far below.

THE NEXT MORNING, she watched the colorful fishing boats glide through the water. The colors mirrored those of the homes of Las Peñas, with their bright-blue bottoms and white, red and yellow stripes. They bobbed joyfully in the crowded bay as fishermen headed to shore to offload their catch. Men in high yellow boots offloaded the glistening *el dorado,* its yellow-green scales shimmering in the bright sunlight. Gluttonous frigate birds circled greedily, attuned to the rhythms of mahi-mahi fishing season and on the lookout for untended fish.

Indoors, in the surprisingly hygienic facilities, the fish were weighed and recorded. Fisheries inspectors explained to Beatrice their catch documentation schemes, the shift from paper to electronic tracing of the catch. The fish were quickly placed in ice and made their way to the processors, who skillfully carried out their expert knifework with impressive speed.

All was exactly as it should be, and Beatrice filled her notebook with copious notes that would inform her reports—but the whole time, her mind was back on the Malecón and her early morning jog with Javier, their easy banter and compatibility. To the feeling of being seen once again.

THE DAYS PASSED QUICKLY, with the Ecuadorian team ferrying her about, speaking about products, business plans and investment strategies. She and Claudio never managed to speak, but they sent messages to check in. Each morning began with an early morning jog with Javier. After a week together, the guard opening the gate to the Malecón, recognized them and offered them a hearty good morning, some of Javier's neighbors in Las Peñas began greeting her by name, and even many of Javier's army colleagues, whom she was sure sniggered behind their backs, offered her a warm smile each day. The four hundred forty-four stairs became slightly less daunting with each ascent. Today, her last morning, she ran them with an energetic spring in her step, while Javier jokingly begged for mercy.

Earlier in the night, she had enjoyed a closing dinner with the Ecuadorian team, laughing over beers and pots of *cangrejos rojos* (harvested by the very mangrove communities Italy would be supporting!) at a popular restaurant on the bustling Malecón. The atmosphere with the crowds, and music, and laughing was so different from the jogs she and Javier took together in this same spot as the city slumbered. Just the two of them chatting and laughing together as the sky shifted from black to blue to pink to a warm, burnished orange, and the Guaya River rushed along in all its strength and glory.

Tomorrow morning before dawn, she would be in a taxi ferrying her to the Guayaquil airport to embark on the long journey home.

And so, after the jolly dinner, when she saw the delegation watchful with that hopeful glint in their eyes, she explained to them it was not she who would make the final decision, but that she could assure them her report would be glowing, and that she very much hoped a decision for a new strategic partnership between Italy and Ecuador would soon be announced. The relief in their expressions was palpable, and when they offered to walk her back to her hotel, it was easy to decline, saying she was meeting a friend for a drink in Las Peñas.

Now she and Javier sat at a small table, a second round of mojitos in hand, heads pressed close to continue laughing and talking over the blaring music. The crowd was young and trendy, but Beatrice felt as if she were in a snug cocoon of two. Javier's crisp white shirt glowed against his dark skin. His firm pectorals strained against the fabric. His eyes crinkled when he laughed, and they'd been laughing since they first sat down together—but not before Beatrice had given him an appraising once-over and commented on seeing him for the first time out of his army kit. "Looking good, soldier."

His sparkling eyes took in the curves of her clingy dress, the flouncy above-the-knee skirt, and the heels that brought her closer to his towering height. "Not bad yourself when you're out of your jogging gear, *Signora.*"

Beatrice waved away the third mojito, expressing concerns she'd never wake up for her flight. Javier tucked her arm in his as he accompanied her on the long walk along the Malecón and back to her hotel. They passed the same route they had run religiously each morning at dawn, and Beatrice wondered at how someone whose existence had been unknown to her only seven days earlier could now occupy such a large portion of real estate in her brain this entire week. She breathed in the scent of his cologne and committed to memory the feeling of his muscular body against hers, his infectious laugh and Spanish-tinged Italian. Tomorrow, he would jog the Malecón in the company of his army buddies, while her flight took off from the Guayaquil runway, hurtling her far away across the ocean.

They stopped before her hotel, on the edge of the Iguana Park, where the creatures with roots back to prehistoric times slumbered silently in the trees, preparing for another lazy day spent under the warming sun as their adoring fans snapped souvenir photos.

Javier turned and pressed his body against hers. He tilted her face up to meet his and stroked her cheekbone. Beatrice strained to stop the shiver of anticipation she could feel working her way through her body. Javier's strong hand moved down from her cheek, stroking the length of her neck, skimming across her shoulder and down the edge of her body, pausing gently under the swell of her breast, where she was certain Javier could detect the wild galloping of her unfaithful heart. He let go and enveloped her hand in his, stroking her wedding band.

He gazed into her eyes again. "It seems I'm destined to always be left by Italian women."

The silence was absolute. Beatrice struggled to breathe.

"I don't want to put pressure on you. I've so enjoyed our week together, and I'm going to miss you. I know you're already taken, but I sense you're looking for something more than what you have at home." He lowered his head and placed his forehead against hers. "If you invited me up tonight," he whispered, "I wouldn't refuse."

Beatrice closed her eyes and took a deep breath. She stepped back, but kept her hands in his own. "Javier, you're right that I'm searching for something. This week has been so special for me, too. Definitely something I never expected. Certainly, wasn't looking for. I've loved our connection, loved how much space you've taken up in my mind this week. I think I'll always be changed by our time together." She looked out onto the darkness of the park, to the illuminated cathedral standing guard at its edge. "But I've been married for over fifteen years. Together with my husband for almost twenty. I've never even considered being unfaithful to him." She looked him directly in his glittering eyes. "Until now ... But I can't. I've made a promise, and I can't break that." She whispered. "Even if I want to." Standing on her tiptoes she leaned in and brushed his lips, wrapped her arms around his broad shoulders, feeling a warmth rising within her. Just as suddenly, she broke away. "*Addio*, Javier," she whispered, turning away with firm steps, not strong enough to glance back.

Striding to the elevator, she wiped away a tear escaping from her eye.

THE SUN STREAMED THROUGH THE WINDOW she'd forgotten to close last night. She watched his muscular form rise and fall with his breaths, and she smiled.

Beatrice crept out of bed as silently as she could. In the bathroom, she brushed her teeth, changed into her jogging gear and combed her hair into a tight ponytail. She gazed into the mirror with eagle eyes, seeking out the stubborn wrinkle. Still there. Still worrisome. But perhaps not as tragic as she thought only one week earlier.

She made her way back and shook him, laughing. "Hey, sleepyhead. I know it's Sunday, but I want to go for an early morning jog? Together?"

He cracked open one eye and groaned.

"C'mon. I'm running downstairs, where I'll wait for you. Don't let me down." Her ponytail swung gently from side to side as she pocketed her key and ran down the stairs.

THE RUN HAD BEEN EXHILARATING. The morning air was fresh, the city still sleepy. They laughed. They talked. They planned for the future.

Her muscles burned, but she continued with a steady pace, pushing her body to its limit. As soon as they returned, she ran through his grasp and beelined for the shower, turning on the spray. Peeling off her sweat-soaked jogging gear, she stepped into the hot water blast, allowing the warmth to envelop her. She scrubbed herself with soap, shampooed her long hair. "*Amore*, don't leave me here alone!" she yelled.

He came in, stripping off his clothes and joining her under the spray.

"Will you wash my back?" she asked, handing him the soap. He massaged it in circles, the heat rising from her body, nothing to do with the steam surrounding them.

He nipped her ear. She groaned.

He spun her around and kissed her firmly, pushing her hard against the shower wall.

Pinned to the wall as the spray pounded down, Beatrice felt his firm body pressed against hers. Felt how he was as ready for her as she was for him. She wrapped her legs around his as they moved in rhythm, the water cascading down.

He stopped moving for a minute, kissed her wet eyelids. "Where have you been, Beatrice?"

"I've been far away for too long, I know that. But I'm back now." She felt a warmth rising within, a return of the fluttering butterflies. She groaned and kissed his familiar lips once again. "I'm back to stay, Claudio. I promise."

ROMAN SNOW

Rome

"SNOW IN ROME! How on earth did that happen?" Geraldine struggled to keep her voice light as she spoke on her cellphone, standing amidst the chaos of Rome's Fiumicino airport, but she was no world traveler.

She'd been prepared for a flight back to New York this morning, followed by a connection to Buffalo. Geraldine was thrilled at the prospect of sleeping in her own bed that very same evening. Now all flights were cancelled, and she would have an extra night in Italy, at an airport hotel.

Taking a deep breath, she willed her voice to sound more confident than she felt. "I'll be just fine, Martha. Don't you worry about me. You have enough to handle after the funeral. You know you always have a room waiting for you in Lackawanna … Okay, dear. They have me on a shuttle bus to the hotel—don't want to miss it. Bye!"

Geraldine ended the call to her cousin and reached behind her for the blue trolley bag. She was intimidated by all the stylish people who walked past her with a sense of purpose her hesitant steps could never imitate.

One more night in Italy, then you'll be back in your own house and your own bed. Just one more night. You can do this.

"*CIAO*, NICOLA. Just wanted to let you know not to expect me. We're snowed in here in Rome and they've put me up in some dreadful airport hotel."

Kate left the voicemail message as Italian announcements blared throughout the airport. The cancellation of one bloody flight after another. A disaster. One didn't expect snowstorms in Rome, after all.

"I hope to be back tomorrow and we'll talk then. But it looks like we may be flat-hunting soon. Things didn't go as I'd hoped. I'll explain when I'm back." She sighed. "Bye."

Kate reached behind her for the blue trolley suitcase and walked purposefully to the hotel shuttle bus, her Prada heels clicking throughout the Fiumicino departures hall with each confident step.

GERALDINE FINGERED THE COMPLIMENTARY SOAP and shampoos, delighting in their luxury. She cast a longing glance at the bathtub. Although it was only a brief flight from Brindisi to Rome, her day had begun early, and the stress from the change of plans exhausted her. For Geraldine preferred certainty and schedules to chaos. And Italy was nothing if not chaotic, and so utterly devoid of rational schedules.

She unzipped her carry-on suitcase, eager to settle into her thick, terrycloth robe. Good thing she'd packed it in her carry-on, in case of emergencies. As she opened the lid, she caught her breath. Whose clothes and toiletries were these?

Black silk and lace greeted her. Gingerly, she lifted up an item of racy lingerie. Beneath it lay a slinky black dress and a pair of impossibly high black heels. She examined the outside of the suitcase. Same color, same model. But the nametag read "Kate Tucker."

Just what I needed—a final disaster to this day. Why couldn't I just be on my way to Buffalo?

A SPOT OF DINNER was all Kate needed. That, and some hard alcohol.

Salvatore had altered her plans when he dropped the bomb. Now she and her sister would have to move out of the Holland Park flat, when she'd been certain she'd have it made for years with this one. He claimed the wife suspected something, but Kate knew he'd found someone else to take her place. Someone younger.

They always were.

She unzipped her trolley case. Her silky little Bottega Veneta dress would cheer her up. The snow was too blinding to go out, and the hotel lobby bar was below her usual standards, but there were sure to be some well-heeled businessmen stranded in the storm as well.

A little male attention was exactly what the doctor ordered to heal a bruised ego. And at least Salvatore hadn't left her completely empty-handed. The expensive diamond necklace he'd given her as a parting gift was nestled in her suitcase. Kate knew enough not to pack it in checked baggage, where so many items went missing in Italian baggage control. She longed to feel the weight of the cool rocks against her bare neck.

She anticipated the sparkle of the diamonds boosting her shattered confidence as she unzipped the suitcase. Clearly, they would have to be sold before long. But tonight, they would ensure that every male eye was focused on her.

An ear-splitting scream ricocheted through the hallways of the Rome Airport Marriott.

"MS. TUCKER, I'M VERY SORRY for the mix-up. It must have happened while I was on the phone. It's what I get for being distracted. I reached for my bag without looking."

Kate rolled her eyes, at the earnest, frumpy voice on the other end of the line. How she hated the American twang.

She cut the speaker off in her clipped London English, with its plausible public-school accent, acquired after years of careful practice and precious hours of expensive diction lessons.

"Yes, Ms. Waters, so you already told me. Now, where did you say you're staying?"

"The airport Sheraton," said Geraldine. "I've already asked, and there are no shuttles or taxis in this snow. Perhaps we can meet at the airport tomorrow and exchange bags."

Anger boiled up inside Kate, but there was nothing to be done. After arranging a meeting point at the airport, she slammed the phone down. *Goddamned snowstorm in Rome!*

KATE, AMORE, IT'S BEEN A WONDERFUL THREE YEARS that have changed me forever. But my wife knows about us, and I'll need you out of the London flat by April, at the latest. Accept this small gift as a token of my affection. Il tuo, Salvatore.

Geraldine placed down the note and held the sparkling diamonds under the glaring hotel lights. An expensive parting gift from a lover.

Geraldine knew about these things, of course. From soap operas and naughty romance books she and Irma exchanged back home. But she'd never been in proximity to such unbridled lust off of the written page, and it sent a shiver of excitement up her spine.

Gathering her courage, she slipped out of her sensible slacks and flannel sweatshirt, and hooked the lacy bustier around her slim frame. She observed her reflection in the mirror. The transformation was miraculous. Curves she hadn't known existed were prodded into place.

Eugene had never seen her like this, even as a young bride. Despite three children, they'd only ever clumsily made love in the dark, quick grappling sessions that were over almost as soon as they'd begun—on the rare nights he returned with energy from his late-night shifts. It was hardly worth the effort to wake from her slumber, nothing even remotely resembling the steamy scenes she loved to read in the romance novels hidden safely under her bedside Bible.

She slipped the luxurious silk over her head, taking care not to damage the expensive dress. Her shoe size was the same as the woman's, though Geraldine was not adept in towering heels. She paraded back and forth before the mirror, trying to get the hang of it.

Her courage flagged and she poured another swig of minibar gin into her glass. As she allowed its warmth to seep through her body, her gaze fell back to the suitcase.

Surely, Ms. Tucker wouldn't mind, she thought, as she looked longingly at the cosmetics case filled with luxury items.

Despite her clumsiness in applying cosmetics, her hazel eyes glowed as she examined her handiwork. An attractive stranger peered back at her from the mirror. Geraldine's hands shook as she slipped the diamond necklace out of its velvet case and delicately caressed the stones. A shiver of anticipation ran up her spine as she clasped the shimmering necklace around her bare neck.

Teetering only slightly, Geraldine made her way to the door, locking it firmly behind her.

DEAREST EUGENE,

I can hardly believe it's time for my annual letter. I am sorry not to be at your grave for our anniversary— thirty-five years!—but Martha needed me in Lecce. You know how you and I always meant to come to Italy together. I never thought my first visit abroad would be alone, and for her husband's funeral. But you know how like sisters Martha and I were. It broke my heart when she moved to Italy to marry Giuseppe. At least I felt I could be helpful. She told me how much it meant for her to have me here.

The children are all well. At least they tell me they are the few times they think to call their old mom.

I miss you, my darling. I will visit you when I'm back home.

All my love,
Geraldine

Kate slipped the letter back into its envelope, careful not to wrinkle the creamy paper.

Letters to one's dead husband? She could never imagine loving anyone so much. Then again, the men she chose were mere business transactions, not life partners.

She lifted out a frumpy woolen dress, carefully unrolling it over her bed. A framed photo fell from its folds to the mattress, and Kate picked it up to examine it. Three handsome faces beamed out at her—a boy and two girls. She guessed they were in their mid- to late-twenties. The kids from the letter, she supposed.

Kate always claimed she never wanted children, but as the age in which she no longer had a choice loomed near, she began to question her earlier certainty.

How long could she latch onto wealthy protectors? Salvatore must have been plotting for some time to cut her loose, but he wanted one last weekend from her in his Sicilian villa. The farewell note and present were waiting on her pillow this morning, once Salvatore was long gone to his Palermo office. The coward.

The rent-free flat that had been part of the deal would now have to be vacated. And she'd have to start again.

It had been easier in her twenties and early thirties, certainly easier than working a nine-to-five job, and far more lucrative. But now that she was pushing forty, she no longer had it in her.

Kate slipped her designer clothes off and slipped on the shapeless grey dress that smelled of fabric softener. Its forgiving, well-worn fabric felt soft against her skin. She slipped a terrycloth robe over the dress and pulled out the fuzzy pink slippers—did women really own such things?—kicking off her uncomfortable heels to slip her feet into their beckoning comfort.

With her feet propped up onto the bed, Kate stared at the three grown children in the photo. The desire to seek out well-heeled businessmen in the airport lobby bar subsided. Maybe things should change when she returned to London.

GERALDINE FELT AS IF SHE WERE ON DISPLAY. Her breasts were pushed up in an unnatural way, her cleavage spilled out from the shockingly low cut of her dress. Had her own daughters worn clothes like this in front of her, they would have received a stern scolding. Yet here she was, her flesh on display for every man to see. In an airport hotel, no less. Nervously, she fingered the expensive diamonds between her thumb and forefinger.

And yet, as she sat at the bar sipping her *prosecco*, she felt a frisson of excitement tingle throughout her body. For the first time in her fifty-five years, she felt desirable. Sexy, even. Like a heroine in the racy stories she could read without embarrassment now that she lived alone. She saw it reflected in the eyes of the men who passed her, even if she was too shy to meet their gazes directly.

She'd been modest, even as a young girl. As a teenager, the world changed around her, but she clung stubbornly to values that had faded decades earlier. Following her husband's death, her rapid slide into old-matron status simply accelerated. Geraldine had grown accustomed to invisibility as she walked along the street. She'd never garnered much attention, not even in her youth, but now she felt acutely her expire-by date. Did she really have to feel she already had one foot in the grave in her mid-fifties?

Slipping Kate Tucker's clothes over her body, feeling their sensuous caresses against her curves, sparked something in Geraldine she hadn't even known existed. Not even as a timid teenage girl.

An unfamiliar, sly smile played at her lips; she sipped from her glass. A man loomed before her, indicating the seat across from her.

"*Posso? È libero?*"

"I'm sorry," Geraldine apologized. "I don't speak Italian."

"Ah, you're American," he said, in a lilting accent. He sat down. "Dressed like that, I would never have known."

Geraldine noted the appreciation in his eyes, and she fought the urge to blush as she remembered the drab slacks, sweatshirt, and sensible walking shoes she had shed upstairs.

"I am Giorgio," said the man, offering his hand.

"Kate," she replied. "Kate Tucker." Pronouncing the name gave her courage, caused her to sit up straighter and pout her lips in the seductive way she'd observed other women do.

"Stranded here, too, I imagine. Where were you headed, Kate?"

"Back to New York, where I live. The storm took me by surprise."

"Yes, very unusual for Rome. I'm hoping the flights can get out tomorrow. I've been on a long business trip and I need to get back home to Milan."

"How lovely. I've never been to Milan." The breathy quality of her voice surprised her. She tilted her head slightly, wondering if the table's candlelight set off her diamonds fetchingly.

Giorgio didn't have to know that Geraldine never travelled much beyond metropolitan Buffalo. After all, tonight she was Kate.

"Ah, so you should definitely come. Surprising that a woman like you," his eyes slipped over her dress and her necklace, "doesn't get up for the shopping." He signaled the waitress over and ordered a whiskey. "Would you like another *prosecco*?"

"Yes, *grazie.*" It was the only word she'd learned during her week in Lecce. She'd stood beside Martha and said it to all the mourners over Martha's thunderous sobs. "I'd love to, of course, but I always seem to be passing through Rome and visiting dear family friends down in Puglia, in Lecce. The dreadful tourists never seem to make it all the way down there."

Giorgio didn't need to know the closest she'd ever been to Rome was the airport hotel where they were chatting, or that she'd be first in line to travel the well-trodden tourist path, had she only been offered the chance. Kate would probably find it vulgar. Judging from the way Giorgio's eyes lit up in amusement, so did he.

"Ah, I should have known you were a woman of taste."

Her *prosecco* arrived and the waitress cleared away her empty glass. Geraldine sipped deeply, inhaling the bubbles, feeling how they floated up into her head and bolstered her new persona. A warmness, a sense of comfort enveloped her. Like her cozy slippers and worn terrycloth robe, only more exciting. Did Kate feel like this all the time?

"I'm just back from Japan, and I picked up some lovely woodcuts." Giorgio leaned across the table, his face close to her own. "Would you like to come up and see them?"

Ah, she smiled. *Here's where the real Kate and the imposter part ways.*

Geraldine took a last sip of her *prosecco*, her head dancing. "It's so kind of you, Giorgio, but I'm afraid I've had rather a long day. I need to call it a night."

"Of course," he said, recovering quickly, but not quickly enough to hide the flash of disappointment Geraldine observed on his face. Disappointment *she* had caused. She fought the urge to smile.

"If you do make it to Milan, here's my card. Call me."

"It would be my pleasure."

She stood and so did he. He kissed her on both cheeks and she felt a spark of electricity.

"Good night, Giorgio, and I wish you a pleasant trip tomorrow."

"You, too, Kate. *Buona notte.*"

Geraldine walked carefully in her vertiginous heels, hoping the swaying of her hips looked more natural than it felt. For Kate would know how to do these things correctly.

KATE CLOSED HER SUITCASE and stood before the woman. A sense of calm washed over her. Her necklace was safe. "Thank you for taking care of my bag. I had a valuable present inside and its return means a great deal to me."

"Don't give it another thought, my dear," said Geraldine. "The important thing is that we were able to get our luggage back, and that our flights are departing today."

She examined Kate's face closely. Yes, she was lovely, but the lines around her eyes were beginning to show, and her skin lacked a certain glow Geraldine felt sure she must have possessed in her younger years. Yes, one day even this beautiful woman might find herself invisible as she walked along the streets of London. *It happens to us all, Kate, the swans as well as the ugly ducklings.*

"Thank you again, Ms. Winthrop. I truly do appreciate it. Have a pleasant journey."

"You, too, Ms. Tucker." Geraldine gave a brief wave as she disappeared amongst the crowds.

KATE MADE HER WAY to the check-in desk for London. A large line had already formed, two days' worth of passengers hoping to get on board.

A tall man in an expensive Italian suit stood before her. He kept turning around to face her, his eyes gliding up and down her form before he spoke. "It's not looking too good. We might wind up spending another night in a Roman airport hotel."

He offered a broad smile and Kate noticed that his teeth were uneven and tobacco-stained.

"I hope not. I have a husband and three kids waiting for me back in London, and they won't be at all happy about my extended Roman holiday." She smiled warmly at him, but noticed the tight set of his jaw as he turned back to his phone and busied himself tapping. Glancing down at her blouse, she buttoned it up one higher.

No use having men getting the wrong impression of her. She stood quietly in line, unperturbed by the crowds, a small smile playing at her lips.

GERALDINE PASSED THROUGH PASSPORT CONTROL and made her way to her departure gate with plenty of time to spare.

Stopping before a shop window, she looked down once again at her watch. Yes, she definitely had time. She looked up at the window with its displays of sexy lingerie that appeared to nip and shape in all the right places.

Trolley firmly in hand, Geraldine entered into the shop and smiled confidently at the salesgirl.

ACKNOWLEDGEMENTS

I have always adored reading and writing short stories. Sadly, I quickly learned publishing short story collections today is an uphill struggle.

When I first thought about publishing, I would meet with agents and publishers at writing conferences, and I would always ask their views on publishing short story collections in the current market. The look of good-natured displeasure or outright groans that tended to meet my query became a rather easy tell. When I decided to indie publish my work, I was excited to think that, like E.M. Forster's unprepared English travelers who set out into the unknown in Italy, my short story collection could also venture out into the world. I am very proud it finally begins its journey and hope it attracts enthusiastic fellow travelers along the way.

Gratitude, as well, to the fabulously talented novelist Camille Pagán. I was taking her excellent author coaching seminar, Author Mastermind, and attended a coaching session where I discussed my desire to indie publish my stories. Her encouragement to be willing to take risks for projects you believe in – especially as an indie author – solidified my resolve to finally publish my collection. Thanks, Camille, for the needed push to follow my dream!

The short stories in *Drink Wine and Be Beautiful* have spooled out over a decade, thereby making it even harder to remember all the individuals who were instrumental in reviewing my stories over the years. Many of these stories won contests or were in anthologies, and benefitted from numerous individuals providing editorial suggestions and advice.

First and foremost, thanks go to the wonderful women of "The Best Writing Group in Rome": Terianne Falcone, Rebekah Junkermeier, Amber Paulsen and Amanda Ruggeri. You reviewed so many of these short stories and provided me with valuable feedback that helped to improve many of these tales before I would submit some of them to contests or anthologies.

I workshopped many of these stories through Critique Circle am so grateful for the input of so many fellow writers, but especially Grace Tierney, Ashlinn Craven, NJ Layouni, Linda Collins and Chantelle Rhondeau.

I am so pleased to belong to the wonderful Women's Fiction Writers Association, and am appreciative of the fantastic ladies of my WFWA critique group, fellow writers who kindly reviewed some of the latest stories and provided helpful suggestions and readers' notes to improve them. Deep gratitude to Patty Warren, Jarmila Sawicka and Lori for their much appreciated review.

This is the fourth publication I work on with Valerie Valentine as my editor. What a wonderful surprise to learn that she, too, loves short stories. Thank you, Valerie, for your strong editorial support and your personal appreciation for this project. It is always such a pleasure working with you. Special thanks, too, to Roxana Coumans for her professional proofreading support.

This is also the fourth time I work with my amazing Italian design team of Joanne Morgante and Roberto Magini of Maxtudio. You know I keep the stories coming, in large part, because I want to discover the beautiful covers you create for me. Thanks for the gorgeous art, and also for making our joint work so much fun.

As always, I am grateful for the support of my family that allows me to moonlight as an author. Thank you to my husband, Francesco, and our sons, Alessandro and Nicolò. And thanks to my Mom for so enthusiastically reading all my work.

The biggest appreciation I reserve for my wonderful readers. Thank you so much for reading my novels and stories. I do read your reviews, and appreciate all feedback. As an indie writer still at the start of her writing journey, I am especially appreciative when those who read and enjoy my work leave a short review on Goodreads, Amazon and other sales sites. It doesn't have to be long, even a line or two helps other readers to discover my work. I'm deeply grateful for your support.

If you would like to stay updated on my writing, please follow me on social media or sign up to my newsletter through my author website.

Thank you for reading!
Kimberly

Kimberlysullivanauthor.com
Instagram: kimberlyinrome
Twitter: @kimberlyinrome

A NOTE ON SHORT STORIES PREVIOUSLY PUBLISHED

Caves was selected as the first place winner in the SnoValley, Washington writing contest and first appeared in the SnoValley Writes! anthology (April 2012)

Holiday Bliss first appeared in *Terrine de mots* anthology, France (September 2012)

Missed Connections was first published in the *Foreign Encounters* anthology (October 2012)

Bitter Harvest was selected as the second-place winner in the Hartlepool, UK short story competition and published online (December 2012)

Amica del cuore first appeared in the *Far Flung and Foreign* anthology (October 2013)

Stari most was first published in the *Milk Sugar* literary journal (October-November 2013)

Balinese Traditions first appeared in *Anak Sastra* magazine (October 2013)

Abandoned Towers and *Gender Equality* were both published in the *Digital Papercut* literary journal (October 2014)

ABOUT THE AUTHOR

KIMBERLY SULLIVAN grew up in the suburbs of Boston and in Saratoga Springs, New York, although she now calls the Harlem neighborhood of New York City home when she's back in the US. She studied political science and history at Cornell University and earned her MBA, with a concentration in strategy and marketing, from Bocconi University in Milan.

Afflicted with a severe case of Wanderlust, she worked in journalism and government in the US, Czech Republic and Austria, before settling down in Rome, where she works in international development, and writes fiction any chance she gets.

She is a member of the Women's Fiction Writers Association and The Historical Novel Society. She has published three novels: *Three Coins, Dark Blue Waves* and In *The Shadows of The Apennines* and one short story collection, *Drink Wine and Be Beautiful.*

After years spent living in Italy with her Italian husband and sons, she's fluent in speaking with her hands, and she loves setting her stories in her beautiful, adoptive country.

kimberlysullivanauthor.com
Instagram: kimberlyinrome
Twitter: @kimberlyinrome
BookBub: kimberly-sullivan